The Young & Luxurious

LOVE AND FIRE

THE YOUNG & LUXURIOUS
BOOK ONE

LULA WHITE

The Young & Luxurious: Love & Fire

THE PLAYLIST

Hey Loves, here are the songs I listened to while writing this story:

The Young & Luxurious: Love & Fire on Spotify.

If you're reading the print version, you'll have to go look up this playlist.

It's for those of us who want a 90s vibe, with deep and emotional ballads (Mariah Carey and Celine Dion). At the top of some of these chapters, I specify which songs I had on repeat while writing the scene.

On Spotify it's free to set up an account.

🤍

Chapter One

THE COGNAC OF US

KORIENNE

The sealed envelope trembles in the sweaty palms of my hands. On a sun-kissed terrace filled with some three hundred professionals, I work this charitable event with one goal—escaping.

"Tell me when she arrives, will you?" I whisper to former law school classmate and close friend, Mackenzie.

"All right, but calm down. You look as scared as a runaway slave in the forest."

"That's not what I am?" I joke, despite my heart thudding so hard it beats on my eardrums.

"Kori Haughton! You have outdone yourself again," another judge gushes at the tables, from the peach and violet snapdragons I had delivered, to the eggshell-colored tablecloths, and peach-cobbler-flavored cupcakes, down to the designer plates. "Is all of this you?"

My air sacs fill up with the breath of what I was born to do.

"Thank you so much, Your Honor. Yes, the decor and style are all me, but the hard work of raising the money for these scholarships are

Teneil and her committee." I'm careful to shift the attention back to my board member so she gets the credit she deserves.

I designed today's event at Shutters on the Beach Hotel to mimic the fields of flowers blossoming outside in the lagoon for California's "super bloom" season.

The judge leans toward me like we're sharing a secret. "This is all very lovely, but you *are* still becoming a judge like your father, right?"

"I'm grateful I get to be a prosecutor, and I'm not really thinking about other career paths at the moment," I lie to the judge.

From one side of the hotel terrace to another, I make the rounds and accept hugs and congratulations from people I've known my whole life. Throwing their arms around me, they pepper me with questions.

"So, Kori, what are you doing once your presidency is over? What's your next move?" one official after the other inquires.

"To dip my toes in the Caribbean and sleep until noon for a change!" I always answer questions about my future with a joke and a hearty laugh that's good and convincing, so that I'm careful to preserve my facade I've spent a lifetime building.

Meanwhile, on the other side of the portico, a whole other spectator event occurs. Where the sun rises and sets on the most scenic man in the west.

Though I'm a ball of nerves over one of the biggest decisions I've ever made, I can still walk and chew gum well enough to notice how he electrically charges up Shutters all by himself.

He and I network in different circles, but in the rare moments we're near each other, his electric sparks take control of every nerve I own.

It starts with his vocal cords, which distract from how terrified I am.

"Oh, for sure. For sure," he says in a different group behind me. His voice must flow from the land of milk and honey. "I'll be drilling down deeper into those corners of our membership that need our attention most. If our prized sections are not satisfied, I'll be courting them personally. And trust me, as I spend time with them, they won't be dissatisfied. I won't miss."

My womanly muscles strain to hold in my cervix.

And speaking of reproductive parts, another longtime friend of my family's leans toward me.

"Girl, you need to slow down. These social events will always be around. But at some point, you'll have to slow down and pop out some babies."

"Kori!" another voice calls out to me.

Thank God. I'm tired of standing here telling bald-faced lies.

But, no, the person coming toward me is not a good look.

Larry is already undressing me with his eyes before he takes me in for a hug. Seven years post-graduation from law school, ten years after our last bang, and he's still shooting his shot. "Damn, girl, come here. Let me get one in."

I'm praying he'll keep it moving.

"How are you doing? We hardly ever see each other anymore."

"And that's all your fault since you don't ever return my texts. It's been too long, girl. When are you letting me take you out so I can spoil you?"

I barely manage to hear the words coming out of Larry's mouth.

"There's a lot going on for me."

Larry winks and licks his lips that flap on and on. "You've always got a lot going. Slow your roll, have fun, and breathe some. As a matter of fact, I can help you breathe a lot."

Yet the current owner of my breaths navigates today's charitable fundraiser and works his way to the other side of the terrace. He stakes out a spot near the bar and orders a drink.

One admirer after another—one *woman* after the other—approaches him for a photo, a handshake, a hug or a few words. Hooting breaks out around him. Laughter and applause are so loud the noise drowns out the crashing waves of the ocean a few paces out.

Yet still, through this soiree of suits, dresses, and hats, his eyes make a toast with mine. Once I tumble into the rabbit hole of his attention, he snatches it away.

"Worthen! Worthen! Worthen!"

The decibels of them screaming his name reverberate through me.

Resentfully, jealously, I pry my focus from the biggest personality at the event, and continue threading my way through a growing sea of professionals and corporate sponsors from across Los Angeles, gathered here to support our two-hundred-and-fifty-dollar-a-plate luncheon.

Time for Larry to catch my fake smile. "When I slow down, I'll give you a call. Until then, take care. I should hug a few more people before the bell rings for lunch. Good seeing you!"

Before Larry can get another word in, I haul off. I've got too much on my mind as it is.

"Kori! Madam President, come on over for pictures," one of my board members calls out to me. "We've been looking for you."

The luxurious Shutters on the Beach Hotel stretches along the sands of Santa Monica, to crest an ocean line the color of cerulean that reflects a flawless sky soaked in paint.

"Korienne," Teneil says to me, "your boss is here."

The letter. I'm reminded. These last precious few minutes, I've been so mesmerized, the weight of my decision was overpowered by the magnetism of Easton Worthen.

As if the Batman signal just flashed in the sky, my girls scope me out from various points across the terrace. Mackenzie flicks her head in the direction of one of the most consequential people in the city.

On my way over, I pass by *him*.

We don't have to talk. Our eyes hold the conversation. His clenched jaw punctuates his message, and the flare of his nostrils seals and delivers it to my head.

Forcing my attention away, I enter the arms of the Los Angeles

District Attorney, Gloria Gray. "I'm so glad you could make it, Ms. Gray."

Beyond her shoulder stands Easton, hands in his pockets, the portrait of elegance.

"Thank you so much for honoring me," D.A. Gray gushes.

Onlookers around us must snap a million shots on their phones and cameras for the photo op that's an infomercial for black prosecutors—an older protector of justice guiding the next generation, two black women fighting to protect the communities of LA.

"No one deserves it more than you do," I reassure her. "Our board agreed to select you unanimously for the award."

"You're the one who should be rewarded for all you do, young lady." The afternoon reflects clearly on her face. "You're at the height of your journey, but your real shine is coming. I'm so excited for the road ahead of you."

Gripping the envelope that contains my declaration of independence, I take a big breath. "Actually, I do need to speak with you privately, if we might."

Her face brightens. "You don't say? How funny! I want to talk to you, too, Korienne."

"You do?" Stunned at how she just caught me off guard, I lock my knees so they don't buckle.

With a side smirk, she guides me from other professionals waiting to speak to one of us. My friends help out by coming in and filling the attention vacuum.

"So a huge situation has come up over in the West Adams district," she says, her eyes beaming. "A murder."

"Oh, well, I'm sorry to hear that."

D.A. Gray shakes her head. "It was a police officer. Shot by a black woman."

We certainly don't hear that every day. "Wow."

"Happened just a few hours ago, Kori, and that's not all either. This could be a big whopping deal of a case." She places her hand on my wrist. "It happened on one of the properties of Carol Worthen. Do you know who that is?"

My kneecaps almost give out, and I'm pretty sure my lungs do, too. "Y-yes. I know who that is."

All too well.

Her eyes shine with excitement, their pupils quickly darting from side to side in their sockets, apparently to ensure nobody lingers around us. Where we stand in a side cove, I do the same. A few paces away, my friends check on me with curious expressions.

The D.A. continues, "The biggest black real estate developer in the country. And residents are saying he may have some sort of involvement."

Again, I strain to push up my game face and not let my professional facade crack. "That does sound pretty colossal. Every deputy D.A. in the city will be breaking their necks for that assignment."

Now, her gaze on me narrows. "What if that deputy D.A. was you?"

I'm definitely not breathing now. "Excuse me?"

"Kori, with your reputation, training, and your background, I'd like you to be the one to prosecute it. You've definitely earned your stripes, and this has all the makings of a high-profile conviction—lots of television airtime, news media, press conferences. But more important than that, because of your connections around town, your work in the community, you have a certain grace and thoughtfulness that will be required with these sensitive issues of race and class. This will make you a star. You can go anywhere you want, and when you hit ten years as an attorney, your judgeship is practically guaranteed."

Shit.

My heart must plummet because I no longer feel movement in my chest.

Quickly, I scan the room in search of him. Where did he go?

Instead, over Gloria's shoulder stands my father, and *his* expectations.

"Kori! Over here!" another person calls out for me to come and join a group photo.

Through throngs of people, I search for only one now. But the terrace is packed, and I'm surrounded by too many smiling faces, too many big hats, tall bodies, and full glasses of liquor.

"Go on to handle your presidential duties." The D.A. grins, proud as a peacock. "I know you have a lot to do. Let's finish this conversation later. Come to my office next week?"

But my letter.

"Sure," I answer, just as I'm guided to a group photo of all the biggest organization leaders on the West Coast.

"Kori, why don't you stand next to Easton?" A determined Judge Sharpe guides me toward him with a scheme in her eyes.

Teneil, the chairwoman of our luncheon today, slightly scowls from her position a few bodies down the row, visibly upset *she's* not standing next to the most picturesque of California's natural wonders.

"Madam President." The warm Cognac of Easton's voice drizzles over me.

He must not know yet.

"Mr. Worthen." In my off-shoulder dress that is strategically feminine and playful, I wiggle into position between him and another organization president. And insert my shoulder inside the crook of his arm, where I and the curve of my breast fit snugly. My hand rests in the valley between his back muscles, defined and insistent as they roll under my fingers. "Maybe here pretty soon, I'll be calling *you* Mr. President."

Atop the rich clay of his physique sits smooth lips that tilt up into a confident grin. "Among other things you can call me."

It was so low I barely caught it, but my sixth sense is extra sharp for this man. His effect on me twitches in my right eye. And along my panties, in my right womanly lip.

We both stare ahead for the shot, and then Easton's body heat disconnects from me, but the solar flares burning off him remain on my flesh. We disengage, and I tear away longingly.

For the slimmest moment, his eyes sip me up.

Maybe I should ask...

The bell rings to signal the end of the reception and that we should begin finding our tables for the luncheon.

"Kori." Teneil lays a hand on my arm to get me away from him. "We're getting started, and it's time for you to take the stage for the welcome, girl."

On my way into the dining room, my friends rush to my side. Mackenzie's focus flies to the envelope I still hold.

"Woman, what is going on? Why were you and the D.A. over there talking so long but you still have this?" she demands.

Still stuck in the fog of what I just heard, I'm unable to answer.

Shallon pushes me onward. "Can't worry about it now, chile. That'll have to wait. You need to get up there."

Instinctively, picking up my brick feet, I head for the lectern where I set down my palms and face the entire ballroom for one of my final speeches.

"Good afternoon, everyone, thank you so much for coming to be with us at the African American Women Professionals' Annual Scholarship Luncheon. We are humbled and grateful to give back and nurture the dreams of our youth, our community, and our neighbors who could use our help, as part of this year's theme, *Back to Our Future*."

My heart pounds. No, not because I'm giving yet another speech.

But situated directly across from the District Attorney sits *my* future.

Chapter Two

"COUNTRY CLUB KORI"

KORIENNE

"You should have told her," Mackenzie admonishes me a few minutes later once we're seated at our table.

"Not right now," I fuss back.

The server comes toward me with the bottle of Louis XV, and I politely stop him.

"I'm good, thanks. But please take care of my friends."

"Madam President, why aren't you drinking?" one of my board members asks.

"My boss is here. This is an after-hours event, but I still prefer to keep a clear head, in case she wants to discuss anything else."

"She's holding a drink, though," my board member's nosy ass counters.

Polite as I can, I reply, "And if I'm ever the D.A., I'll have my drink then, too." It's none of her business how I'd never want that job.

For the server's flawless service and easy smile, I slide him a twenty.

The young brother grins and shoots out his hand in a rejection. "I'm not allowed to take that."

I quickly roll it up as he starts to fill the flute next to mine, and I shove the roll in his pocket. "Oops, how did that get in there?" I tease.

Surrounding me, my colleagues also pad the waiter who makes his way around our table, until he's got at least a hundred dollars in his pocket.

My longtime friend, Shallon, winks at him. "Sir, you keep these glasses full and we'll keep accidentally dropping these bills."

Humble gratitude spreads over the young buck's face that seems to light up his hotel uniform. "Thank you, ladies."

Shallon adds, "And if you want a little bonus, I can help you with that, too." In a move so subtle it can't be challenged by sexual harassment lawyers, she leans over the table in her peach-colored, spring wrap dress so the flaps fall open just enough to show off her size DDs.

"Oh, my God, Shal." My other friend, McKenzie, rolls her eyes over her champagne.

The guy's got enough sense to get in his eyeful and quickly avert his gaze. "You ladies, excuse me. Let me know if you need anything else."

But I don't miss the tiny upturn at the corner of his lips.

Shal wastes no time and drains her champagne flute, holding it in the air, catching the server's attention at another table. With a pristinely manicured nail, she taps the glass, and her smiling bottom lip disappears under her tongue. "I need... something else."

"Your whorish ass," McKenzie mutters. "A damn waiter, Shal? How old is he? Twenty-five? *Maybe?*"

Shal's lips glisten. "Do you see him in those cheap polyester pants? The way they scrunch up around his basketball booty? It's a sign. I bet you that boy can pump," Shal retorts. "Look at him over there acting all shy and shit. And he don't give off gay vibes either."

Mac scowls. "Of all the men here today, you go for the help."

"*What* men?" Shal shoots back. "Half the men here are community dick. And the other half are too pretty and can't fuck."

"How would *you* know?" Mac hikes up an eyebrow.

Shal hides behind her liquor. "That's for me to know. But young buck over there might work for his dinner. I've got damn good eating down here, too."

With a hard eye-roll, Mac chuckles. "The problem is you've *had* half the men at this event, and that's why you're salty toward them today."

Shal's full attitude cocks back with her neck. "And you would be *correct.*"

I crack up laughing with a few of my other board members. The humor at our table distracts from how my heart cracks in two.

More laughter bounces over our table settings. It feels good to relax after a year of us damn near breaking our backs to run this organization. I wouldn't have gotten through it without this bunch, especially not my longtime friends—Shal and Mac, the parliamentarian and vice-president.

In just a few hours, my life was supposed to be my own again, to wake up in the morning and not have to rush off to a meeting or an event, answer emails, assuage somebody's panic, or scramble to put out a controversy. I was only to be Korienne, a woman pursuing *her own* dream.

But instead of relaxing at the end of my successful presidency, I'm frozen.

Two tables away, the D.A. finishes receiving her award and delivering her acceptance speech. She rises with her entourage to leave. But with her eyes, she finds me for a final and subtle meeting of the minds. Or at least, an invitation for *my* mind. Then, she slips off.

Carol Worthen stands from his table and heads toward the foyer after her. His handsome two sons remain.

Not surprisingly, his younger son, Easton, is flanked on both sides by two admiring female doctors. The temperature of my body *would* rise, but over the rim of his glass, he finds me. After a jiggle of his drink, he sucks up an ice cube, holds it between his lips, and then it disappears.

I want to be the ice on that tongue...

Clearly, he doesn't know yet. Or if he does, he probably doesn't care.

"Kori, will you get your friend and tell her to behave?" Mac chastises Shal. "Let that boy do his job."

My friends rip me out of my fantasy.

"I've got a job for him all right." Shal snickers. "And I'm not in grade school. I don't need to behave."

Mac fusses at her. "Girl, how will you explain yourself to the man who finally decides to marry you?"

Unashamed, Shal throws out big-girl energy. "First off, you can keep that marriage-and-a-ring BS." She peeks over both her shoulders, apparently making sure nobody important is close enough to hear. "Second of all, if I'm feeling maternal and want to play house, a man will have to demonstrate his bank load *and* his payload are enough to meet my criteria. He should consider himself blessed if I approve. Because I can get the treatment from *several* dicks. Why would I be stuck with only one?"

The girls at our table fall apart with hushed giggles, and guests at the surrounding tables stare at us.

But now it's my turn to read her and tighten her up. "So what you're saying is your pussy is community pussy?"

Mac almost spits out her drink. "Oop!"

"No, heffa." Shal flips her sew-in and points her fingernail. "My pussy is VIP access. Like the Delta Sky lounge at the airport. Only high-net-worth individuals get in here."

Our table breaks into another round of raucous cackling all over again.

Over my white seabass and the champagne bottles, sure enough, several tables away, *he* stares at me and sips his drink. Up and down, in repeat motions, his Adam's apple is triggering.

Teneil comes to the table and plops into an empty seat, doubling over. "All right, subject change." She interrupts my thoughts. "Do you all see what Vashti's got on?"

Across the room sits one of our board members, Vashti Burns, the current treasurer whom Mackenzie is not too fond of. And that's putting it nicely.

The war between them has already begun, in a tussle over who'll take my place. Who'll reign as the next goddess of the Los Angeles professional scene? Elections are in a few days.

"Dayum," Mac adds, "why didn't somebody get her? Who told her it was okay to put that on?"

"Do you see that, though?" Shal ruminates. "Is it just me, or can you see some nipple through that cheap material?"

There's no telling who around us might be ear-hustling.

"Ladies, did you all hear about that big fallout at Singleton Hospital? Dr. Graves has been put on leave?" I deflect. I'm still in president mode, and we don't need the scandal.

Mac is onto me. "We will *definitely* return to our previous subject later."

Finally, the event winds down, and I am most definitely ready to go.

A little too eager, I rise. "Come on, ladies, let's get up and work the room. Thank folks one last time. Especially you, Mac," I suggest since she's running to be AAWPA's next president and needs every powerful connection in her corner.

"You all can work the room," Shallon says and takes another sip from her glass. "I'll stay here and hold down this bottle."

Tapping her shoulder until she grunts, I'm not having it. "Get up, woman. BEN or not, you've got a rep to protect, just like the rest of us."

Shal is in-house associate counsel at Black Entertainment Network.

As an alumni of UCLA School of Law, Shal won big when she snagged that position two years ago. The job would be great for her future as an entertainment lawyer. That is, if Shal actually wanted to work.

"Shal!" Her mother, Mrs. Jacobs, waves her to a group of people a few tables away.

"Ugh," she whines. "Before you stood up, she couldn't see me."

"Girl, bye. Get over there. Our year isn't up yet. You're almost finished." I turn to Mackenzie. "Make sure you hit the Goldberg table, plus City Union Bank, and the past presidents table. They write our biggest checks."

"Already on it."

"Hey, Kori, girl!" A familiar voice approaches. "Mac, Shal, how y'all doing?"

We turn, and in uniform fashion, our gazes all drop.

Damn.

Vashti's nipples *are* protruding through that flimsy material.

"Hey, Vashti!" Teneil speaks first to smooth over the awkwardness. "Girl, you are *wearing* that dress."

It gives the rest of us a moment to recollect ourselves.

"What's up, Vash? Good to see you," Shal says and scatters off to find her parents.

"Yeah, hey, Vash. See you later." Mac starts toward the tables I identified to her.

Vashti attempts to flag her down. "Oh, Mac, don't go anywhere. You and me, we need to rap for a minute."

"Let's do it another time."

Before Vash can manage a reply, Mac jets off, leaving Teneil and me.

Vash plops a hand down on her hip, and in a sense, brings her proverbial attitude. "For the officer elections at the board meeting next week, have you decided who you're supporting yet?"

"Um." I don't have the mental bandwidth. After five long years of being the "capable" leader who can solve everybody's problems and situations, I'm at a ten for today. "I'm still thinking it over, Vash."

Those AAWPA elections are in the farthest corners of my mind. As I said earlier, today is the first day that nothing else truly matters. And my own life, joy, and potential outweigh *all* else.

"What's for you to think about?"

She snaps me back to her priority.

"What AAWPA needs, and that's my responsibility as the president. You know what, Vash? Why don't we talk about this tomorrow?"

Just over her shoulder, yet another woman rubs her hands all over my destiny. With fake laughter, she throws her head back, angling her hips in such a way that they happen to connect with his.

"That man is so damn fine," Teneil gushes as she ogles Easton and makes her way to stand in the line of women chatting him up.

Vash steps into my view. "So you're blowing me off after you just had an entire two hours with your girls?"

I met Vashti in undergrad at Howard, in the birth of the Black Lives Matter movement. She was one of those activist types raising all kinds of Cain in her social justice clubs. Once more of us started volunteering and marching, she and I crossed paths. Back then, it surprised me to learn she was from California, too. Before college, I'd never met or heard of her, and she and I grew up within a few miles of each other.

"We just had a chill event. But go ahead. Get it off your chest."

Distracted with my own dilemma, my stomach upset with feelings and not food, I labor to give Vashti my attention.

"You should have a clear choice on AAWPA's next president. My friends on the defense side have been pushing me to go all the way to the top."

With my best unbothered face, I respond, "You would make a wonderful president, Vash." Carefully, *very* carefully, I form my words. "But you do realize Mackenzie is vice-president, and she brings a lot to the table where financials are concerned."

Vash is unmoved. "But I've been on the board longer than her. This is only her second year, and I've got five in, just like you, Kor. Now fair is fair."

This is true. Mackenzie was never concerned with organizational leadership or the drama that goes with it. But as I was becoming vice-president myself, and headed for the presidency, I asked her and Shal to come help me and guard my back against some of our big personalities. One of them being Vashti.

"I hear you, Vash, and I'll be straight with you, girl. Mac is probably what's best while AAWPA is growing our bank and our corporate brand."

Her lips curl in, as if she's entering her activist mode from college. "Kori, you've known me longer. I'm *from* LA. I would do a lot of good as president. You and me, we were at Howard together." Through her squinted eyelids, she delivers a sharp side-eye. "This is *my* city, these are *my* people, and you know what I'm about."

On the terrace yet again, Easton stands and poses for photos with his brother and father. And one woman or another who pushes herself on him.

He is indeed the most scenic man in the west, with his squared chin wrapped in coconut-brown skin that extends up his angular jaws.

"You remember how folks used to call you 'Country Club Kori' back at Howard? Would you be surprised if I told you some people still do?"

To bring up an insult that has followed me my entire life, she just crossed a red line.

"Vashti, you are out of pocket. Now you asked me my position, and I just told you."

Sucking her teeth, she backs up. "My bad. Didn't mean to upset the queen. You know, Kori, you really could stand to come down off your pedestal some. You might be used to looking down on everybody else from your place on a hill—"

"*Vashti.*" I keep my tone low so nobody notices and she doesn't command the reaction from me she wants.

"But your precious little life isn't what you think it is. One of these days, somebody just might knock you off your high horse." Her nostrils flare.

"Away from me. Now."

Once she's gone, I let that exchange roll off me. The people in my inner circle constantly remind me that I need to practice boundaries. What other people want isn't always my problem.

Shal and Mac return, and we say a few more goodbyes.

"Kori, you should have given it to her," Shal says. "How long have you wanted your own company?" she tells me once we're in a foyer and they're walking me to the elevators, away from all our colleagues.

"She offered me a murder case." I stare into the elevator as its doors open to elevate me, in what must be a sign. I'm just not sure of what. "It'll be a big deal."

But I don't tell her who it may involve. Not yet.

My lifelong friend releases a labored sigh that's really an ultimatum I already hear. "Shit."

Which is what must sit in my gut.

"Kor, I'm happy for you, homie. I realize that's a big deal... for lawyers who actually *want* to spend their lives as prosecutors. But let's be real, Kor. The only reason you keep doing these projects that don't fulfill you is you're scared. Cut the cord and *do* that shit."

"The press coverage and name recognition will open doors for me later."

"Woman, it might be a little harder without a big name-building case, but you've got enough doors open to you already. Besides that, you just got your confirmation today." My best friend lays into me with her eyes. "It's time."

Surprised, Mac asks Shal, "She's the one who's going upstairs, but where are *you* going?"

"Upstairs. I'm about to get busy, too." Shal winks over her shoulder.

My mouth drops. "You are not!"

A self-satisfied grin on her face and a switch in her walk, Shallon keeps moving. "The hell I'm not."

"You little nasty..." Mackenzie mutters without finishing the rest.

We leave behind a stunned Mac and enter the hotel elevator. All the other luncheon attendees are exiting toward the valet to leave the hotel and have their cars brought around.

I reserved a suite to stay overnight. With every major event, the hotel grants a discounted room block for people who want it, and a few of us took advantage even though we live here in town. It's a chance to kick back and let our hair down after all the months of hard work, before we return to real life.

But now I cross-examine Shallon. She didn't book a room in advance. "You were able to get a room on short notice?"

"I had a hookup." After a final hug, she nudges me off the elevator. "But stop worrying about me and my business. Time for you to take off that 'Madam President' hat and tend to *your* business, woman."

"Tell me how you like the waiter," I call out.

Just before the doors snap closed, she yells back, "Who said it's the waiter?"

Part of my chuckling is at this damn girl, but most of it is from me being so damn nervous. For many reasons.

First and foremost, what will I do?

This weekend is to be a beginning, a celebration, the first of many.

On my way down the hall, my heartbeat raps louder in my ears than my footsteps until I arrive at the Beach House Suite of Shutters. With quivering hands, I swipe the key card at the door that buzzes me into the next phase of my life.

On the other side lies the Garden of Eden, full of flowers emulating the vast fields of Carlsbad. Shades of persimmon, fuchsia, lavender, and canary wrap a rainbow around me. On the top floor of the hotel's Beach House, situated right on the sand, I'm only a few steps from the ocean line. Right outside the floor-to-ceiling windows stands a massive palm tree, swaying in the spring breeze.

Atop the table in the small dining area sits a gift. More boxes lie on the bed. Through the open bathroom, more boxes and bags sit on the edge of the full, heated Jacuzzi. I laugh at yet even more gift boxes spread out across all four balconies outside the living room, dining room, and the two that surround the bedroom.

A note is stuck to the windowpane that I pick up: *Open me first.*

Unable to suppress all my grinning, I do as instructed and tear through the wrapping paper. In the box is a bottle of jojoba oil. Cracking up laughing and holding my gut, I jump.

The shuffle of bare feet approaches me.

My breaths caught in my throat, I wait.

And wait.

A blindfold drops over my eyes.

"Bend over."

Chapter Three

MY FOREVER GIFT

"Easton." Her voice is breathy and hesitant, as it is when her spirit catches on her internal snag. "We need to talk."

"We're about to."

Kori wiggles her toes when she's fully immersed in her joy. Her little booty dances in her seat, and she can hardly sit still. And just about *every*thing is funny. A monsoon could come and it wouldn't blow the smile out of her. If I don't ever get anything for another Christmas, Kori's fullness is my forever gift.

But she doesn't wiggle her toes on Sunday nights. The evening before Monday, they're buried underneath her butt, as if her dread for going to work the next day suffocates her. Even though today is Saturday, she's not wiggling them now.

Instead of my Kinetic Kori, she walked in here with tight, knobby ass muscles all distressed like that palm tree trunk outside the window, her emotions and state of mind flailing in the wind.

So her feet are where I begin.

Unlacing her strappy stilettos, I slide them off. Around her waist, I reach to unbutton her off-shoulder dress that displayed her delicate neck and graceful collarbone that had me jonesing over lunch. Soon as this fabric rolls off the peach-curves of her hips, I bite the dimple on her cheek to which she jumps and giggles.

"I told you to bend over."

The blindfold leaves her in the dark and her remaining senses hyperaware of every sensation. A captive of my next move, she's subject to my will, and the element of expectation transitions her state of mind from angsty to wonderment. On the chaise lounge, her cheek rests on the fabric, her toes balled. Kor's body arches, eager and expectant, but still somewhat loaded with whatever mental baggage she carried in here.

Placing a large pillow under her, I lay her all the way down with her ass to me. Warm, edible oil I spread over her foot, from its heel, up her arches to the balls, and along each toe.

A sharp gasp flies out of her at the hot sensation of the basalt stone I ease down the calf of her leg, and her exhilaration twitches at the entrance to her womanhood, oozing cream and beckoning me. An oyster that longs for me to taste, it glistens with her anticipation. But in a trail down her calf, I follow the heat of the stone with my mouth that holds ice.

Again, she jumps at the unexpected change in temperature, followed by my fingers that decompress her shin, calf, Achilles tendon, and the intertwining muscles and bones along the front of her foot and then the back. Each toe spends time in my mouth, while I suck, tug, nibble off the remnants of outside influence over her body, and measure her level of pleasure in the intensity of her breaths and the amount of cream drizzling from her pearly womanhood, until her final pinky toe pops out of my mouth.

More soothing, warm oil over her other calf, another hot basalt stone, followed up with tender pressure in my hands, slow and communicative, as I reconnect her to me. The stiffness drifts from her body, feet and toes and hanging limp, her relaxed state evident in her steady, calm exhalations.

From her pedicure and up her tendons, over her remaining light scar on her shin from the tumble off her sled at Lake Tahoe at age six, past the faded scrape on her knee from the fall on her rollerblades at age eleven, and along the bruise on her thigh from the jam into a broken tree log at age thirteen, I now lavish with warm oil, a smooth, hot stone, ice, then my fingers, and finally, my tongue.

Up the sloped hills and down the curvatures of her overthinking, hyper-organized, politically inclined, risk-averse womanliness, I listen to the breeze flowing from Kori, to the rhythms of her fear, reticence, and insecurity I've discovered over nine years, to the depth of her ecstasy at its heights and its shallowness in its restrained lows.

And arrive at her lustrous pussy that waits for me to sedate her.

The pressure of my thumbs tenderizes each inch of her thighs, methodical and intentional, and sculpts one hip and then the other, where she houses many of her anxieties. Lastly, starting from the outside, I mold her gluteus, in round circles deep in her flesh, to the maximum of her elevated breaths, until I massage the opening of her pussy.

Ice on my tongue meets the fire of her womanly lava spilling onto my taste buds.

Kori cries out, and I go in.

The arch of her back deepens, her latissimus dorsi flexing, which catapults her meaty, toned ass onto my voracious sucking. There I lock her in position, control her squirms, so she can only tremble. Her opening contracts and expands around my tongue, its fever rising with my caresses on her clit. With tender licks of her clit, alternating how I taste her, manipulating her pleasure, pulling back once I feel her climax, and returning to her with ice, she screams for mercy.

I show her there is none.

My fingers command her sweet spot along her pink, pearly walls, and with my tongue, I savor the jewel of her clit, relish the slits in her valley. Hot and flooding my mouth with her cream, Kori's pussy dances on my face and damn near break my neck.

And I finally give her permission to let that shit out. She whimpers, kicks and beats the hell out of the chaise on her way to glory.

Since this is a nice-sized chaise lounge, once I wipe her up, I reposition the pillow under her abdomen and climb over her.

Instinctively, her fingers spread and wait to link with mine, and she raises her head to offer me her lips.

"Is Larry spoiling you anytime soon?" I whisper.

She chuckles, and I laugh with her ass because that shit was funny as hell.

"You were not listening to that."

"The hell I wasn't. I could have slapped him for standing a too close, but I went ahead and let you handle it."

Now that she's good and relaxed, making her back and booty pliable as putty, I don't waste any time. Stunning her, I dive in suddenly. After wanting her all afternoon, I've waited long enough, and my need meets Kori at the intersection of my dick and the apex of her womanhood. Still, slick and juicing, she circles her ass cheeks on my meat.

Soft and fat and warm, Kori throws her sumptuous booty up and down, fucking me back and taking me on a luxury yacht around the world. Watching my dick plunge in and slide out wetter, I want to curl up and take a bath in Kori's pussy.

And until I figure out that part, I'm getting as close to luxuriating in her belly as I can. I throw her up and bury all of me *past* her cervix.

The music of her whimpers drives me harder.

Her walls are now perfectly tailored to me, but when she's about to climax, they burn hotter and contract so her kegels and crunch exercises hug the hell out of wood. She knows how to work and put me in *The Twilight Zone*.

"Fu…"

Remembering to swerve and hook left on her favorite spot, I press on her clit with one hand, amplify her ecstasy, and yank her on my dick.

"Shiiiyaaaat!"

Nasty and out of control, we nearly fall apart when the chaise lounge busts underneath us, and one of the legs sends us flailing to the side. But Kori's mid-climax, still bucking, and her volcano-hot bathtub is flooding a Negro's whole life squirting onto my legs and on the towel and the chaise.

My earthquake follows, and she rides me down its cracks and ruptures to the hottest, most glorious place on Earth.

Lopsided, our upper limbs on the carpet, lower extremities still jumbled on the chaise, we try to catch as much ocean air as we can and collapse.

"Why are you in here breaking shit?" I joke between heavy breaths.

She sputters and giggles. "I only get like that with you."

"I'd better be the only dude you're getting like that with. So what is it you don't want to tell me?"

With a slap on her butt, I help her up and get ready to throw her over my shoulder so we can go bathe.

I'm pretty certain I know. She was talking to the D.A. for a while today, and Ms. Gray's got an election coming up later this year. She's getting hammered over the rise in crime rates and needs Kori's connections for something.

But when I attempt to lift her, she stops me.

Kori takes a breath first and throws on a robe. Her eyes deepen, focused as they are when she is gearing up for trial.

Luscious and wet, she sucks my lips, caresses my jaw, and wraps me up with a fresh towel. Opening the French door, she guides me by my towel to the balcony where, a few yards away, the beach buzzes with a few couples lying out and children playing.

"Damn, this must be serious." I flick my nose and snicker some.

"What did your boss ask you to do? Get her a speaking gig? Endorse her for what? I know she doesn't think anybody's voting for her to be a judge or the mayor right now."

Now Kor wears an expression I'm not sure I've ever seen—not pensive, not nervous or fidgety, or upset or excited.

"Baby," I prod her.

"I'm pregnant, Easton."

I didn't hear that right.

"Preg..."

She nods and blinks, wiping away the tears creeping out of her. I'm not sure what this reaction is on her, from some ocean inside her. But it is not of panic or unease. Not this time.

"A baby?"

"Yeah."

Wagging her head up and down, she confirms I'm hearing straight. Her emotion doesn't match her angst and worry the first time she told me, seven years ago, in the middle of studying for the bar.

But I'm not even a lawyer yet! How will I build my career and reputation? What will I tell my parents? I don't know if they'll support me.

I'll *support you. You'll be my wife.*

You're not ready, E, and I'm not either.

I'm so overjoyed I want to run around this entire hotel. But my zeal is short-lived when I remember seven years ago.

"I'm not agreeing to another abortion, Kor." My chest is already twisting at the horror of it. "That shit hurt too much last time, and I'm damn sure not taking you to the clinic and waiting while you kill my..."

Her hands encircle my face. "I'm not asking you to."

"Then what are you...what are you telling me?" The last time we talked about a family, marriage, and when we would start, she was planning for the right chance to leave her job.

She no longer wanted to be at the county. We needed to figure out how to reveal our relationship and finally involve our fathers, bring our families together. All of our career activities and goal-chasing takes up our lives as it is, but especially, most of all...

"I'm ready, East." That's the expression on her I've never seen.

"You're kidding me. You're playing." I don't want to allow myself to revel in this, or let my heart swell, or get my hopes up. "Don't fucking play with me, Kor."

"I wouldn't play with you like this."

"We're having a..."

"You're going to be a daddy."

The ground is no longer under my feet. Or either my vital organs must already function inside Kori and I've lost them. All that brings me back to myself are her fingers brushing my cheeks.

"And you're ready for what?" Dare I ask. "Exactly."

"To do this with you. I'm ready for us."

My jaw drops.

It'll probably be a long time before those words truly take up residence in me so I'll believe they're real.

Our solar system's biggest star is surely illuminating our galaxy from inside Korienne the way she's beaming. "I saw the results last night, and the hardest part of my presidency is mostly over. That's not the best part. I've got my two weeks' notice in my purse. Already typed up."

In our last discussion over our future together—over when I would become more than her boyfriend on the sneak—we kind of argued.

"Are we deciding together, East, or are you calling the shots and choosing what's best for me while I'm supposed to jump to your beat? Just like your daddy expects everybody around him to do? That's the kind of marriage we'd have?"

"The only person around here who's been calling the shots, who controls every step we take, is you."

"You know I'm happy as hell and this is all I've wanted, but how are you ready now, but not a week ago? What changed?" Today—the suite, gifts, exquisite massage—are my way of putting us back on one accord. Or at least not letting us lose our accord again.

She goes to her purse, takes something out, and pads back to me. A pregnancy test, two pink lines so prominent in the tiny window, transports me back seven years.

Back then, she was twenty-five and I was twenty-six, and we were both fresh out of law school. She was still studying for the bar. When she told me about the unexpected pregnancy. I was thrilled for three weeks—started planning our lives around her and a baby, how I'd build a law practice, raise a kid, somehow chase the broad future ahead of us, and the kind of support network we'd need. But that anticipation died a quick death. Kori couldn't do it.

"Nothing has changed," she says to me now. "This here speeds up my timetable. Easton, for the thousandth time, us marrying was never a question of if, but when. I want to be your wife once I have my *own* accomplishments and my *own* value I bring to the table. That way, your father can't treat me like I'm beneath him, and his friends can't look through me as only some appendage who's attached to you. I was hoping we'd make this move later this year or early next year, once my presidency had ended."

She places my hand over her belly, and that must be some damn portal that transports me through the galaxies.

"But God is clearly confirming for me what you're saying. How I need to step out of fear. You're right, we're not kids anymore. I'm ready to start Kori Kouture. As your wife."

My drop to a knee isn't necessarily out of chivalry or tradition, but how I'm mind blown.

"So you really will marry me? If I asked you right now..."

Her tears fall on me, and onto my heart.

The world—our world—has clearly changed in the last seven years. Instead of anguish and heartache, her tears are spring rain falling out of nowhere on a clear day. Only no storm clouds darken her.

"Yes."

For the next several seconds, her staring at me, me staring back, I just sit in that.

"Seriously, if I go home and get the ring right now, Kor…"

"I'll put it on."

The Pacific Ocean might not be big enough, or hold enough water, or sustain enough life to compete with the massive astonishment in me.

She licks up my lips and deepens her affection, sliding in her tongue that I suck.

"And our families?" I ask.

The reason we broke up the first time. And why she wanted to keep us a secret this time. Why I went along with it.

Realization flutters over her, and I'm not sure what that means.

"Can this just be ours for a minute, E?"

The sky plummets. My head drops. "So you're not ready?"

"I am. I'm having *your* baby. I'm marrying *you*. *Not* your daddy. What will happen the moment he finds out, E?"

She's not wrong.

My father is a phenomenal man, of whom I'm damn proud.

"Answer me," she murmurs, her soft fingers gentle as they ease up my chin for me to face her. "I need to know you hear me and you understand."

"I do." Unfortunately. We've been down this road already. Twice.

"Let's elope."

She didn't just say that.

But the clarity in the pupils of her eyes is flawless-grade, and *they* say it.

"When?"

My heart soars, but it's also swinging and flapping in the wind, because I'm still trying to harness all this news at one time, let alone that she's actually talking the way she is. Until now, her objections have been her career, my father, and earning her respect.

"Whenever you want. I just don't want your father in this process. Let's do this ourselves first. We can make our own rules and not worry about anybody throwing bombs on our joy." She takes a seat on a lawn chair. "There's something else. The D.A. told me some shooting happened on one of your father's properties, and she's all excited because she's looking for a big fish to fry?"

"I don't know about any of it. Been grinding this week with my campaign and meeting clients around town." I shake my head and rise, because although I'm thirty-three, these knees aren't getting any younger. "But what's the deal? Why would she tell you?"

Kor wiggles her toes, signaling excitement.

I'm confused.

"Ms. Gray offered me the case."

My heart takes a couple of stumbles down my ribcage. "So she's shooting at my dad."

Business competitors, investors, other developers, politicians, there is no end to people who attack my father and our family's company. It's part of the hustle and is no surprise.

The cocked gun for me would be if Kori were to join them.

"She's shooting at whoever she can to score points before she's up for reelection next year." Kori grins. "Little did she know I came here today with other plans."

Again, the constant flap and crack of trees being beaten by wind, is me blown away in my amazement. Five years ago, this would never have been the move—her walking away from a major case.

"You gave her notice?"

"I will. Today, she started talking my ear off, and she left before the event was over. So I'm emailing her for an appointment to give her notice personally. I owe her that much." Her eyes are truly shining.

Hell, now I'm the one who's scared. Scared this is actually going down. Scared she might change her mind. Scared of the uncertain future. Just scared.

"Kor, you're sure about this? Regardless of Dad, and whatever D.A. Gray thinks she knows, you're giving up a case that's high profile? It could change things for you."

"E, who wants to be the black woman prosecuting another black woman in that scenario? It sounds like dynamite about to go off. There won't be any winners. I've had good cases, and now I'm leaving on top, as AAWPA president. The D.A. thinks she's doing me a favor, and she is. Here's where I exit."

Unable to contain myself, I pull her to me and tongue her down. "Then, baby, marry me as soon as possible."

"We'll need our lawyers to drop up paperwork, and that will take a few—"

"No prenup." My hands, my gaze, my heart on her abdomen that protects my seed, I make a decision of my own. "I trust you. We build this together. Without other people trying to manage it. Before you can change your mind. We can have a big wedding later. For now, this is ours only."

Toes wiggling, her butt dancing in my lap, she's effervescent. "I'm not changing my mind. We're about to be parents. We can do it Monday. That gives me a day to get cute and round up Shallon and Zak. He won't tell our dad," she says.

"But I know you want him there." As ecstatic as I am, my heart is a little heavy, as it always has been, that we need to hide it.

"E, our fathers don't even know we're back together. Now we're pregnant and getting married? The way we're doing it is safest for your life."

We get to chuckling at how it'll go down once our parents do find out.

"Agreed. I'll get Kevin, and the ring. Nothing or no one is stopping *us*."

Chapter Four

ALL GROWN UP

Nine Years Prior - After Kori's First Year of Law School & Easton's Second Year

"Yes, Mr. Knight, just follow me and we'll get set up."

"Aren't you the son of that one man who's building those high-rises I keep hearing about?" he asks, walking behind me.

"Hey, East," one of the female law clerks calls out in passing through the hallways of black-owned law firm, Jackson, Avery, Dinkins & Associates.

"I don't know about the man you keep hearing about," I reply to the firm's new client I've been assigned to interview, "but I am the son of one demanding, shrewd, and annoyingly hawk-eyed ball-buster of a businessman who will not accept anything substandard from me."

"Hey, East." Another honey checks in with her eyes, to which I throw her a nod.

"Well, damn, man. You are clearly somebody around here. It must certainly pay to be you. I'll have to take you to lunch one day so you can

pass me this magic sauce these ladies seem to appreciate in you," Mr. Knight says jealously.

With a dip of my head, I attempt to hide my devilish side.

On our way into the library, one of the women law partners is walking out. Her eyes glaze over a tiny bit, and she holds the door open for me. "Easton."

"Ms. Nichols. Thank you."

The client marvels. "To hell with lunch. Next time I head to Monaco, I'm bringing you with me."

The answer to the unasked question is "yes." Many times.

At the other end of the library stands a Coke-bottle-stacked, picturesque figure with her voluptuous apple bottom calling to me. It doesn't appear I've seen her around here these last few days. Or I would have noticed. She's swift and focused, frantically scanning a list in her hand and searching the bookshelves, tapping legal treatise books with her finger before unplugging it from the shelf.

"Give me a moment, Mr. Knight, so I can clear out space for us to meet."

"Sure, go ahead."

I approach her from behind. "Excuse me."

She jumps several inches at my voice disrupting her mental zone.

"My bad," I continue. "I didn't mean to startle you." But I recognize this face. "Oh, hey, I know you. I mean I-I've seen you before." Damn. I snap my fingers. "You're, uh..." I keep snapping. Shit. Goodness, I can't blank out on Keshia Knight Pulliam's twin sister. So precious.

No smile, all business. "Korienne Haughton. And you're Easton Worthen."

"Right. You...you used to be in..." Why am I drawing a blank?

"Jack and Jill."

"Right. And isn't your daddy that one judge...?"

"Mitchell Haughton. The one who ruled against your *father* in the—"

"Malibu Hills development case. Yeah, Dad won't stop talking about it," I murmur, my focus spiraling out of control as I check her out.

She clears her throat and steers my attention back to her eyes. "Good. That means my father did his job. So, now that you're finished staring at my breasts, do you need a book?"

Staring isn't all I want to do either. But she's clearly not the type who goes for that.

"I actually need to use this library for a client interview, if you don't mind coming back in a couple of hours. I'm sure the books will still be here. And then, maybe this afternoon, I can take you to lunch."

She hammers the nail of her glare straight into mine. "I have a memo due at two o'clock that requires these treatises. Since I'm already here, you can take your client somewhere else for your meeting."

"But my client is actually standing here."

When she steps back to reach for the sign-up clipboard, I enjoy how the silk blouse underneath her suit gapes open between buttons, offering a bird's-eye view of her perky titties that have definitely blossomed since the last time I saw her as a teenager...since she doesn't want me looking outright.

She flips back around, and I quickly flip my eyes back up.

"You see here?" Her short, straight-cut, perfectly manicured nail seems to reflect her personality as it taps the lines on the library sign-up sheet. "My name is here, because I reserved this room in advance. And, oh, look. Your name isn't on here at all. So, Mr. Worthen, it appears you can't have this law library because I've already got it. But maybe you can come back in thirty-eight minutes when I'm finished."

"You think you could do me a solid this one time? Help me out?"

Her eyes form a question of where I get the nerve. "No."

Without further conversation, her focus returns to her list of books.

I recognize her now. She was a smart teenager, a cute know-it-all with glasses and braces. The type who everybody tagged to do the grunt *work they didn't want to do, so they would vote for her to be the "leader" or the president of this and that.*

Damn. Wherever she went to undergrad, they must have put some shit in the water. She has definitely grown up and filled out. Think Rudy on The Cosby Show, *all innocent and adorable as a kid, who metamorphoses into a stunning chocolate drop. So fucking cute.*

She goes back to fingering the books along the shelf in search of the ones she needs.

I've got something hard she can finger.

"You didn't answer my question about lunch, though."

I know the client is standing at the door waiting, and I'll wrap this up soon, but he seems like the kind of man who understands.

Not bothering to look up again, Korienne Haughton asks, "Did you not hear me say I had a memo due at two o'clock?"

"Okay then. Lunch tomorrow."

"Mr. Worthen, I appreciate how you're on the hunt for somebody else to add to your roster, but if I wanted to entertain you for summer, I would have gotten a job at Disneyland. I'm here for a clerkship. That's all."

Any of her fellow female law clerks would have hauled ass immediately, in hopes I would "reward" them later. That's the kind of treatment I'm used to.

"Problem, Mr. Worthen?" Mr. Knight asks me on our way out.

"No, sir, no. I actually have a better office with a nice view of the city you can enjoy."

After my meeting, some of the law clerks hook up for a lunch outing, but Korienne still works away with the books.

"What's good, East?" Monica, another 2L, asks and gives me "that look."

I point over her shoulder toward the library. "Korienne Haughton in there. You know her? What's her story?"

Irritated, Monica crinkles her nose. "Oh, Country Club Kori?" She shrugs. "Grew up in Baldwin Hills, went to Harvard-Westlake.

Wannabe white girl. Nothing special. Her silly ass really did say in her high school salutatorian speech one day she'll be the president. Who does that? So anyway, tell me about that kickback you and Steven are having this weekend."

Hell, I'm trying to kick back and fuck all that edge out of Kori-enne's voice. Then, *she can go out and be the president.*

* * *

EASTON - PRESENT DAY

At the entrance to my folks' street, I'm more than a little stunned. A handful of reporters camp outside our front gate.

The day before I'm marrying Kori, I decided to swing by and spend a while assuaging Dad. Or more like clock some face time with him now so he's less inclined to unexpectedly pop up at my crib through the week as Kori is getting situated.

"Sir, are you related to the Worthen family?" one of the reporters asks me.

They shove their microphones and cameras at my Porsche, apparently thinking I'm some damn bug they can inspect.

Another asks, "Are you Mr. Easton Worthen, son of Carol Worthen?"

"Do you, in fact, represent your father as his attorney?" one of them asks.

Dammit. I left my remote to the gate in my Mercedes at home. So I have to call inside for the housekeeper to open it, and then sit here for photographers to snap photos of me during my wait. Somewhat uncomfortable for a dude who's been able to live his life under the radar.

With the news Kori gave me about this shooting situation, I expected light chatter on a couple of local news segments, but certainly not this.

Normally, reporters don't care about a real estate developer, not even one as wealthy as Dad. It's not like he's a pro athlete or a sexy A-list actor or some controversial politician everybody's interested in. As his son, I'm blessed to enjoy the perks and privileges of money, but none of the scrutiny that comes with fame.

So reporters don't bother driving up North Crescent Heights Boulevard, down our narrow streets that are perched at the edges of steep hills, elevated over eleven hundred feet. Strategically tucked in thickets of tall, overarching trees, and bushes that hide people with money from the rest of the world, my family's home since I was age six sits more than a hundred stories over the streets of Beverly Hills. Higher than the Wilshire Grand Center, the tallest building in Los Angeles, with a hundred-and-eighty-degree view of the city, our backyard scopes Wilshire Boulevard from downtown in the East to its outer reaches at the Pacific Ocean in the West.

"The bastard's been holding up my applications for a year now," Carol Worthen's larger-than-life voice booms from inside the house. "He's refused one meeting after another. Now he's going to use this shooting as an excuse to screw me."

"Carol!" My mother, Essence, chastises him and follows up with a side-eye.

He pauses from his diatribe with his most trusted longtime lawyer, city planning engineer, and media consultant. The two of them hold a quick exchange through the open doors that they clearly understand after thirty-seven years.

Dad speaks his next words in a more subdued tone. "Easton, it's about time you got here. I've been calling you since yesterday evening, and you haven't been picking up."

"Yeah, where the hell have you been?" My older brother, Charleston, rolls his eyes so Dad doesn't see.

"Hung out with the fellas last night. What's good, Dad? Why you got folks working on a Sunday like they don't have to be at their jobs first thing in the morning?"

"Because they like money as much as I do. Hell, you should be working, instead of 'hanging out with the fellas.'" He reaches for my neck and grabs it, studying the area under my jaw before I can dodge. "What's this? So you weren't with your boys. You were out getting ass while your family's in the middle of a problem?"

I check the living room mirror and find a love mark Kori left.

"Dad, I'm a grown man. I can have a life. Aside from that, since when are you not caught up in some fight? You like to brawl."

He points in the direction of the front driveway. "*You* should like to brawl. See all those wolves sitting outside that gate when you drove in here? Just waiting to devour me? If they eat me, they eat you. And the possibility that you can't ride around here in that pretty Porsche of yours ought to make you want to work on a Sunday."

"I do work on Sundays. For myself." And this is why I have my own law firm. I opened it up with some of my college and law school buddies. Only a portion of my client business consists of my father's real estate holdings and land deals across the country. Since I am not his direct employee, and my firm represents his company in a separate capacity, it's my way of working with Dad, without working *for* Dad.

Charles, however, an engineer and MBA, is vice-president of Worthen Development and carries the biggest, most direct load for Dad's every whim. My father would love for that to change, though.

"What's going on? Why are you so worked up?" I ask him.

"You hear about this shooting? The cop." It's got him nervous, as I figured.

"Yeah, I did. But what about it, Dad? You're here stressing like you pulled the trigger. Did you?"

He squints in that chastising way he uses to try and humble me or mold me into a son who'll care about his concerns as much as he does. "I'm glad *one* of us thinks this is funny. The Los Angeles City Council certainly doesn't. I'm getting calls that, since the officer was shot on one of my properties, the council wants to hold hearings on how Worthen handles our tenants. It's basically

Feldman's way of stopping me from breaking ground in a couple of months."

"*What?*" It takes a moment for me to make sense of what he's saying. "Hold up. City council is blaming you for one of your tenants killing a cop? Why? What does Worthen have to do with somebody's death?"

"Exactly!" he snaps. "Nothing."

Charles strolls over. "The bottom line is Councilman Feldman doesn't want us breaking ground on Angels Rise in two months. He's been working to hold this up for years. He plans to use this Paradise Gardens murder to shut Dad down. And the black activists around the city will beat on this drum, because they're mad at high rent prices in general and they'd love to use us as an example."

Spread across the table in the dining room is a miniature three-dimensional model of Angels Rise Towers. It will be historic, one of the largest real estate developments in the country, and the tallest that's all black-developed. What could become my family's legacy.

"We need you, son," Dad says, his eyes laying into me.

"That's right. We need our pretty boy to be out front," Charles echoes with a teasing smile and leans on a chair. He loves to instigate this cat-and-mouse game between Dad and me.

"Of course. I'm not letting anybody come for my family. Just say the word and it's done," I tell them.

Dad nods, and his squint becomes a proud gleam. "That's what I want to hear. Starting tomorrow. You can make the rounds over at the city for the next few weeks and include the board of supervisors. Plus, you should set appointments with state legislators. We'll need all the politicians in our corner we can find. Also..."

The longer he talks, the harder it is for me to breathe, as if he sucks all the air from the room and leaves me gasping harder than a goldfish who accidentally flopped out of the fishbowl where he keeps me. Part of this reaction in me is how his high expectations are burdensome. The other part is me being a son who appreciates him and doesn't want to let him down.

Tomorrow, I've got plans of my own.

It's tough filling my lungs with the oxygen to say it.

There's a reason he's not invited to mine and Kori's nuptials, and why for the past two and a half years that she and I have been back together, we've kept him in the dark.

"Dad, look…" I place my hands perpendicular to one another in a timeout symbol. "Slow your roll. I'll help and will have your back, but we should coordinate the outreach with my work schedule. I have a business, and you're not my only client. Plus, I'm running for president of NAABA, and this summer will be chaotic."

He nods. Today, his mood, his energy, is not sharp or quite so calculating. And it confuses me, because I'm always prepared to unsheathe my sword for an intellectual duel.

Yet now, a pained expression on him, like I just popped the man's balloon, he aimlessly waves his arm around at everybody else. "Gentlemen, can you give us a minute? Thanks."

From the backyard, where Mom talks on the phone with relatives back in D.C., she scopes me out with clear concern.

I face the man head-on. "Dad…"

"Son." His voice is definitely doing something different. He drags himself over to me, places both hands in front of him. "We're *this* close. Your granddaddy built his first house sixty-seven years ago—"

"I know, Dad." I grab his hands and shake them. "With just his two bare hands."

His eyes deepen. *Soften.* "But you don't act like it, Easton. Why do you punish me this way? What did I do so wrong that you won't hang it up with this rebellious streak you're on and come join your family?"

Today, he's not demanding, not yelling, or talking to me as if I owe him. He's asking.

"All right, you proved your point. You can successfully run your own shop without me. I'm damn proud of ya. Nothing makes me happier than hearing colleagues talk about the awesome deal you closed. But if there was ever a moment for us all to come together, now is it."

I enjoy my freedom. Need it. It's the only way he and I can coexist.

"Dad, I said 'yes.' My secretary will contact yours and hash out a schedule and the details. And I promise you, I will be by your side and we will get Angels Rise up together."

"And what about when I die? Hm, East?" Measured and calm, he continues, "You going to have your secretary call mine and arrange our family's legacy? You going to dictate to your administrative assistant how all this hard work will carry on? Do you ever think of anything outside of yourself?"

He and I stand at the same height of six feet and one inch.

"Do *you?*" I clap back.

He flinches like I struck him.

"Dad, I'm sorry." The man put me through Harvard and Stanford, sent me to camps and schools around the world, and gave me the best childhood that money can literally buy.

"So you'll allow your pride to slow us down. You've got skills your brother and I simply don't, Easton. Shaking hands, putting people at ease, negotiating and getting things from people they don't want to give up—all your mama's gifts, you got 'em honest. That 'people' dynamic has always been your strong suit. Well, we're in trouble."

"You have vice-presidents and public relations people."

He drives his next point with his index finger. "The company doesn't bear their name. It bears yours."

"I said I'd help. I'm right here."

"No, you're not." Plugging his hands in his pockets, my father gives me a once-over. "Your head is somewhere else. You only stopped through here on your way to another place. I can smell the restlessness all over you. What is it? A new girlfriend? Leaving town? Hooking up with Kevin on a new investment? What country you jetting off to this time? Who are you putting before your family while we're here tearing out our hair?"

The words, *Fine, I'll do it*, sit right at the tip of my tongue. That's how heavy my heart is at his worry that decades of labor are now at stake.

But if I give him what he wants and become his employee, I'd never catch a second of peace.

"I'll have Bev call Cynthia in the morning to coordinate the visits you want me to prioritize."

He's already rolling his eyes and heaving a disappointed sigh.

"Dad, I won't let you down, and I won't let anybody destroy you. I swear."

"Oh, where are they? Through here?" a woman asks in the front of the house, with a sound that's too familiar.

His eyes brighten, and he whips around. "Hey there, girl, come on in here. I've been waiting for ya."

"Good afternoon, Mr. Worthen. Sorry I'm late, but I actually had a brunch meeting before this one. I got here as soon as I could after receiving your call." Reed Lennox throws her bag on the table and comes toward my father with open arms, her loose Afro slicked back to a puff at the back of her head, bouncing back and forth between my father and me.

What the fuck?

"Reed, thank you for coming on such short notice, girl." He waves my brother and his colleagues back into the room. "Sit yourself on down. You want a drink? I need to hear more about this internet-scrubbing process you mentioned at the conference."

"Hey, East, long time no see." She slides her arms around my waist in a light hug, and for an instant, her fruity scent transports me to our playtime in exotic places like South America. Doing exotic things. With more people than just us.

"Reed, how've you been? Yeh, a while has passed, huh? Three years now? What brings you in here?"

Befuddled, first I shoot a glance through the patio doors at Mom, still out on the lawn, now shaking her head in a clear indication she's not in on whatever this is.

A playful smile on her fresh-made face, Reed stares at my father. "Mr. Worthen, are you being sneaky? You didn't tell your son I was on my way?"

He shrugs. "He was too busy acting obtuse on other matters I needed to address. I hadn't gotten around to telling him yet."

"Telling me what?"

"Mr. Worthen is hiring my firm leading up to the ground-breaking for Angels Rise. We'll help Worthen Development and Worthen Properties maneuver its good name through these thorny political battles coming up, and whatever goes down with this tragic shooting of a cop." She spins around in her wedges, in her strategi-cally deployed muscular legs that she sculpts at the gym several times a week, which now disappear under a casual, knee-length dress that's loose but still just tight enough for my imagination.

She owns a brand and reputation management firm. "By the way," she continues, "has anyone issued a statement expressing our sincerest condolences for this terrible incident that occurred? And how unfortunate this is for the police department, the officer's family, and the shooter—this Miss LaShauna Posey's— family? If we haven't done so, I'll have my people get on that right away."

Dad's already drooling all over himself, eyes lighting up at another formidable captain who'll go to war for him. Not to mention her being very easy on the eyes, as evidenced by the uniform way all these men adjust their nuts at the same time.

"Dad, can I talk to you for a minute?" I ask.

"Not now, son, this is important. I'll have my secretary call yours, as you requested."

"Oh, East, you're not staying for our little powwow? That's too bad. It would've been fun for us to put our heads together again. Just like the old days, back at Harvard." Reed struts over and plants a kiss on my cheek. "We'll have to touch base soon. You can tell me what you've been up to since we fell off, or rather, since *you* fell off."

With a wink, she pivots away from me again.

"So, like I had mentioned to you at South by Southwest a few weeks ago, Mr. Worthen, we can totally scrub all the negative articles about Worthen off the internet. Wipe it clean completely. Positive information on you only—the scholarships you sponsor, the jobs Angels Rise will create, construction projects and vendors this will employ..."

I march out of the house, fuming on my way into the backyard.

Reed doesn't do anything by chance, and neither does Dad. This is a clear ambush.

But still, my guilt has dropped anchor in the center of me for walking out, like I'm abandoning him as all the attack dogs close in on him.

"Mom, seriously?" I stare across one of the biggest cities on Earth that simply does not seem big enough for him and me.

"Rachel, cousin, give me a few minutes and I'll call you back," she says, hanging up from her weekly Sunday gossip sessions with our family back in D.C., where we're originally from. She stares up at me. "Hey, son, I had no idea he would go there. You know what this is."

"I know exactly what it is. And I would actually consider a spot at Worthen if he wasn't always pulling shit...excuse me, I mean mess, like calling up my ex, Mom," I mutter.

She pats the lawn chair where she sits. "Come here, sit down." She tugs me to where she is.

"Yeah?" In an attempt to let out some frustration, I pinch the bridge of my nose.

"Are you happy?"

I reflect on her question a moment.

This morning, I woke up to sunrise on the ocean and my sun rising in my arms.

My soon-to-be-wife.

And she didn't roll over with her normal, uptight angst before she has to rush to work at the D.A.'s office. The nerve in her neck wasn't thumping. This weekend, for the first time in a while, it didn't take her as long to relax and get into the lovemaking. Instead, her muscles melded with mine, and one hundred percent Kori fucked me with fervor. As if she truly is ready.

"Yes. Crazy happy, Mom." I cast a glance over my shoulder to ensure the others are still inside and whisper, "Kori's pregnant."

My mother knows everything, and she's never slipped up. Now her mouth plops open, eyes mushroom, and the beautiful thrill on her face matches the celebration in my chest.

"Oh, East..." Clasping my hands, and then her mouth, she almost jumps up.

But I rein that shit back in. "Shh..."

"Right, right." A quick glance back at the house, and she returns to beaming at me. "And I can see it all over you. Since you and Kor started up again, your growth has been phenomenal. You're not running the streets anymore, having me all worried with those hoe parties you go to, me sitting here wondering who you're around and when you'll get arrested."

She presses a hand to her chest and rubs, as if the mere memory causes her physical strain.

"I'm sorry about all that, Mom." With another kiss on her cheek, I follow up by squeezing her.

"You were just being a little runt, like boys do. But Kori got you together, and I love seeing it. Your daddy sees the change in you, too, and he wants to be part of it but he doesn't know how. If you don't tell him, he will eventually figure all this out. How do you and her plan to handle that?"

"We'll think it over, but we're exchanging vows tomorrow, and I'm moving her in over the next few weeks. Quietly."

She draws back. "Negro, your ass is about to—"

"Mom. Damn."

More discreetly, she continues, through clenched teeth and a mean stink-eye, "The hell? You *don't* think *my* child is getting married and I'm not going to be there."

But the fake anger immediately returns to what it really is, and she's back to glowing and squeezing my cheeks.

"Kori really said 'yes?'"

Mom's astonishment matches the disbelief I'm still wrestling.

"Yeah, and we're just going ahead and doing it. Later this year, in the fall, we'll have something bigger."

She stares into the house at Dad. "You sure you don't want to include him?"

"How do you think that will go?" I ask her.

The immediate answer materializes in her knowing frown.

God must have surely been on mine and Kori's side, because that has to be the only way neither of our fathers have found us out all this time. She and I have never stayed longer than twenty-four hours at either's house, and with our busy schedules—her trials and AAWPA activities, my depositions and out-of-town meetings and conferences, and us hanging out with our families separately—we don't see each other that often anyway. Which led to our argument a few days ago.

"I'm not the one who wants it like this!"

"And I'm not the one with an asshole for a daddy!"

A pang of guilt hits me, and again, I ruminate on whether to go back inside and tell him. This will be his grandchild, too, and he and Kori need to start burying the hatchet and making peace. Plus, I should be in there, by his side, helping him figure all this out. I'm not trying to live off his money while contributing little, the way he thinks.

"And you and Kori are sure you don't want to wait a while?" Mom prods me.

"I'm ready, East."

"And you're ready for what? Exactly."

"To do this with you. Ready for us."

Kori's peace with this was everything yesterday. Gone was all the panic and upset from years ago.

I motion toward the house, where Dad still meets with the others. "Do you see what he just did? Calling in Reed to bring up old stuff without discussing it with me? The longer I wait, the more likely Dad finds out and tries to put his hands in it. This way, we control how this goes down. When we tell our fathers, she and I will be a united front and not you all's children to be dictated to."

She nods her understanding, her features calm but a little worried. "I'm proud of you."

Kissing Mom's cheek, I rise. "I'll text you which courthouse in the morning once you leave here." This way, there's no chance of Dad incidentally seeing my text.

I've still got to ready up for tomorrow and what will be a crazy week, blending our homes and juggling our meetings and jobs.

My marriage to Kori is the pinnacle of a mountain we've been climbing for years. The air up here needs to remain clear. Eventually, she and I will have to go back down to earth, but not today.

These issues with Dad will have to wait.

* * *

Nine Years Prior - Last day of Kori's & Easton's Summer Law Clerkship, Law Firm Barbecue

"East the Beast, you and your boys throwing another kickback before you head up to Stanford?" Monica asks at the food table. "You all taking out the yacht? We know you're doing something to close out the summer." With her little nudge on my side, the bodice of her dress

pushes open for a better view of her cleavage. "Or are you trying to get down in another private session?"

Across the lawn of the country club stands Korienne with some square-ass dude who's been trying to creep up on her these last few days. But he wears high waters.

"Actually, I'll be headed back to school to get a jump start on law review. It was dope seeing you again, Monica. Best of luck with your last year at UCLA."

"I go to USC," she retorts.

"My bad. Excuse me. I need to..." Clearing my throat and unable to think of a lie, I just walk away.

Approaching the little huddle where Isaiah is trying to do his thing with Kori, I place a hand on his shoulder. "Hey, Isaiah, how you doing, bruh? Did you know the law firm is out front handing out free Pink's Hot Dogs gift certificates and they're about to run out?"

Isaiah's eyebrows shoot up. "Really? My mom loves those things. Kori, you want me to get you one?"

"Do you mind?" she asks.

"Cool, I'll be right back. Thanks, East." He gives me a fist bump before taking off.

"Always here to help."

Trying to suppress her chuckles, Kori tilts her head aside, complete with twitching lips and squinted eyes.

I squint back at her.

Her fucking cuteness should be outlawed.

"I didn't hear anything about Pink's. That was so not cool."

"You know what else isn't cool?" Eying her, I sip from my wine glass.

"How the firm's not offering you free trips to Vegas, Mr. Worthen?"

I feign shock and disappointment. "How I keep checking my phone and your number's still not in it."

Her pretty, slender, glazed lips break out across her perfect teeth.

Thank you, Judge Haughton, for shelling out cash for those braces.

Kori rolls her eyes. "You don't have enough numbers in there already?"

"I don't have the right *number in there already, Ms. Haughton. So what's the deal? You got a secret man hiding somewhere? You've dissed my invites to come chill with my friends and me. After work, you never hang out with us summer associates for too long. You've always got somewhere else to be. You only talk to me in these work groups, never alone. I'm starting to take this personally."*

In my pocket, my cell phone buzzes with messages, but there's no way I'm letting this connection slip.

Laughter dances in Kori's eyes that light up, sparkling under the soft, golden string lights. "I think you're just shocked at not getting what you want."

"That's true," I murmur. I bite my tongue from uttering my next thought on how shocked she'd be once I do what I want. But I refrain. Not the time. "So I've waited all summer, like a good boy. Can I put your number in my phone?"

That pretty smile begs for me to kiss it, and she thinks behind those almond-shaped eyes. "You mean now that you've finally reached the end of the line?"

"I mean, now that I've reached the cream of the crop."

The penlights in her eyes flicker as my words land inside her.

And that's not game either. There are a lot of baddies at this firm, no doubt. But around that pretty, focused, disciplined head, Kori wears a halo.

"Thank you." Her gaze darts across the green at everyone else. "I won't give you my number, though. You have a reputation. I wouldn't want our colleagues to get the wrong impression if they see our phones out. They can't think I'm another notch on your belt."

"Then let me take you to dinner before you head back to Berkeley.

Tomorrow evening, I can pick you up. Spit your address, and I'll remember it."

Her eyes remain steady. "Spit the time and place, and I'll meet you there."

I can't help chuckling. In an odd way, that stubborn energy fills up my nut sack.

"Seven o'clock. The Hotel Bel-Air."

Her clipped gasp is a stop sign. "A hotel?"

"For the ambience. It's only dinner. And you are driving yourself, so if I try anything, you can easily go get your dad and sic him on me."

That gets me another heavenly smile.

"Seven it is."

"Easton." Isaiah comes back. "That was a good one. You got me, bruh. If you wanted to holler at Kori, all you had to do was say that."

I offer him a shrug. "Wouldn't have been as fun. No hard feelings. It's all shits and giggles, buddy."

After one last dose of Kori, I walk away, already planning out how I can work tomorrow night like my life depends on it.

I finally pull out my cell phone that was buzzing in my pocket with a string of text messages that whole time.

Reed: E, y hvnt I heard from u these last 2 weeks?

Reed: Our senior yr, u said once u got to law school, u wld settle down. U been bk n Cali 2 yrs. I get it. U still doin u. But u said at the start of summer we'd discuss the future.

Reed: Now ur startin ur 3L final year. B real wit me. Ur dad says ur still in town and haven't headed back to school yet. So we gonna talk or nah?

Chapter Five

CAN'T WAIT...

KORIENNE

Nine Years Prior - Kori's Home the Same Evening Easton Asks Her Out

Shal runs through my walk-in closet, pulling off dresses. "Girl, what are you wearing? You need to choose a bomb dress that doesn't say you're trying too hard."

Mac takes out my makeup and jewelry. "In that case, maybe you should wear shorts. Casual and summery, and you can show off those cute legs."

"What's all this noise in here?" Mom comes in and asks.

"Mrs. Haughton, your daughter is meeting the finest man in the city," Shal answers. "I don't know why she didn't let him pick her up when women are out here throwing themselves in the street for a ride in his Aston Martin convertible..."

We all bust up laughing at that one news report of some chick in Vegas who really did try to throw herself on his car as he was taking off from a club.

"My girl doesn't need a ride. She's got her own convertible." Mom comes over to the bed, kisses my forehead, and sits next to me.

"I know that's right, Mrs. Haughton," Mac replies but adds a shrewd grin. "But she can still get in his and enjoy the ride, though."

"Right! Right!" Shal adds, coming out with dresses she hangs on the three-way mirror.

"Now which one is this?" Mom asks. "The one whose mother is a Google exec? The one whose father played in the NBA?"

My friends and I all stare at each other with hidden smiles.

"Uh-oh," Mom mutters. "I'm not going to like him, am I?"

"Dad ruled against his father a few years ago. Easton Worthen," I tell her.

She thinks for a moment. "You mean Carol Worthen? He started out in apartments and is now getting into these fancy luxury condos. I remember that case. Your daddy hates that man for buying up all these LA properties and selling them at nosebleed prices. You're going out with his son?"

My brother, Zak, comes and stands in my doorway, leans against it. "Worse than that, Ma, he's a hoe. Dude turns up, throws some wild parties, I won't lie."

Mom spins toward me on the bed. "Korienne, why are you going out with somebody like that?"

Mac and Shal offer me condolence stares.

But I recall how my heart transforms to a hummingbird about to flap out of my chest whenever I'm caught in the thickets of his eyes.

I mean, now that I've reached the cream of the crop.

"Mom, he's actually been a gentleman, very sweet and considerate these last two months. And thoughtful, bringing me back lunch when I'm stuck on a brief and can't get out with the others. He tells good stories and makes me laugh. I'm curious on what other conversation he's got."

With dripping cynicism, my brother side-sniffs. "Yeah, I know what she's curious about. But I've been coaching Kor on how to deal with him all summer. I don't care how rich he is, he's not hitting. Why she's still entertaining this dude is a mystery to me, but not to worry, Ma." Brushing past Shallon, he wades into my closet.

"What are you doing?" Mac shrieks.

"I'm taking care of everything." He pulls out a long, summery, but fitted Reformation maxi dress with a halter top. "Here. You're not showcasing nothing. Not your legs, your boobs, your booty, nothing. Your arms. That's all of you he's going to see," Zak says. "And ay, you got a safety pin? Close up this little cutout right here in the middle."

"Ugh!" Shal claps her hands. "Boy, you need to go somewhere."

"Negative. I'm telling you. I'm a man. I know what's going on in this Negro's head." My older brother by three years taps an index finger to his temple. "The only reason he's taking Kori on this exquisite dinner, while all the other chicks get a blow job under his steering wheel —sorry, Ma—is she's not accessible. He likes the chase. And don't even think about kissing him. If you kiss him on the first date, he'll know you wanted him all summer and you were just playing games. Keep your same energy of you haven't made up your mind about him. Wait for date two."

Shal butts in. "Nah, bruh, that doesn't make sense to me. They're not kids. They're grown adults."

"Exactly!" Zak shoots back. "It's not like she's in junior high school and is falling all over herself because she's never been kissed. They are professionals who work at the same firm. Don't start doing backflips when he comes toward you. Stay measured and cool."

"But you know he'll try it. So what does she say?" Mac asks.

"'Hold up there, buddy, I thought this was just a fun outing among colleagues,'" my brother coaches me. "I got you this far, didn't I, Kor? While he's out racking up easy booty, your objective is to send him back to Stanford with something on his mind."

* * *

PRESENT DAY

"So you didn't turn in the letter? Instead, your boss offered you a case that could turn you into a household name?" Mac waits for my answer, almost tipping off the edge of her cot in our private spa treatment room at the Waldorf-Astoria Hotel in Beverly Hills.

The facial specialist massages caviar mask on my face in preparation for our secret nuptials. The woman's got magical fingers that rub out my stress from weeks of a heavy courtroom calendar, of speed-racing after work from one event across town to another, and of grappling with who I am once AAWPA is over and I marry into Easton's family. Especially if I'm no longer a deputy D.A.

Twenty hours before I marry East, the inside of my chest is a not-so-quiet storm.

"I didn't have a chance to give her the letter, so I'm doing it on Wednesday."

"Girl, maybe you ought to rethink this," Mac says underneath the hands of a massage therapist working her over.

"No, she shouldn't," Shal replies through her own twenty-four-carat-gold facial. "This damn girl has been tortured at that office that shall not be named for years. It's time for her to chase her real dream and live her best life."

"Let's enjoy our massages. I really need this relaxation." That's my way of cautioning her and Shal to stop talking in front of strangers.

I'm only a prosecutor and a local leader, not some famous celebrity, but I still guard my private business, particularly among ear-hustlers in LA who love to supplement their income by selling mundane info to tabloids, the *Los Angeles Times*, *TMZ*, or wherever they can hawk it.

This morning in a FaceTime, I told the girls about our vows tomorrow, since it's why we're here. On my hand sits the five-carat, flawless grade, pear-shaped Harry Winston that Easton first bought me seven years ago, the only other time I got pregnant.

But I waited to tell them the rest in person.

Once the facial and massage therapists are good and gone, Mac and Shal are hot on my tail.

"Spill, bitch." Mac gets up and checks to ensure no one hovers at the door, and still murmurs quietly but with hot sauce on her excitement. "That is the case everybody all over America is talking about now—how a black woman shot a *cop* who was in her house. Oh, you know that trial's going to be lit."

"I'm not taking the case." I'm sure to hush her and keep my voice low even now. "I'm pregnant."

Mouths dropping, they're on their feet and swarming me with love.

"We're about to be aunties! This kid is about to be the most ruined brat on Earth!" Shal beams. "None of us have any kids yet, and you all's parents don't have grandkids. We're going to be fighting over this damn child like it's Jesus or something."

"What did his daddy say?" Mac whispers.

"CW doesn't know." I use Mr. Worthen's initials, out of caution. And still, his name sticks in my airway and clogs my breathing. "We're not telling him for a while. We don't want any hurdles blocking this joy we've waited on for so long."

Mac squeezes me again.

"Now *that's* what I'm talking about. Boss up on his ass!" Shallon chuckles behind her champagne. "Show him he's not any of *your* daddy."

That might sound cute, but when Easton took the ring out of his safe and slid it on me again this morning, I was equal parts thrilled *and* mortified.

The last time I wore it was five years ago. That twenty-seven-year-old woman still had so much to prove. To the world, yes, but mostly, to herself.

Now, Mac and Shal settle in next to me.

"Heffa, last time I saw you, you were supposed to turn in two weeks' notice and plan your lifestyle brand. Now we're about to be a mother and somebody's whole wife?" Mac beams. "I *love* it. But how are you even pregnant?" She motions at my birth control injection. "I thought you had a Nexplanon implant in your arm."

"She does," Shallon answers. "Apparently, East's got that *power* plant in his dick, and ain' nothing shutting it down."

At that, we all bust up cackling.

I didn't tell my friends about mine and Easton's argument last weekend. It was over our timetable to marry, move in together, and start a family. Or the shocking positive pregnancy test I got the next morning.

"I'm going for it," I declare now, with my heart thumping loud enough that everybody in the hotel might hear it. "All of it.'"

That I'm pregnant at the end of my AAWPA presidency, right as I'm planning my next moves, seems to be God giving me the green light.

"Ma'am, you're about to be a mommy *and* a wifey *and* a business owner. You're my she-ro," Mac gushes.

"Damn straight," Shal adds. "You're my idol, Boo. One of these days, Imma start caring more about my future and fuck a dude so good he'll defy his whole family for me and take care of me the rest of my life."

"Shallon!" Mac throws a rolled-up washcloth at her.

"E is not taking care of me," I snap, maybe a little harder than I intended to. "I'll have my own business, my own identity..."

"Kori, chill," Shallon says. "Girl, this is me you're talking to, not CW. You don't have to be defensive. There is nothing wrong with you being a wife *and* a CEO."

"Yeah, but the rest of the world won't see it like that. They'll see our marriage as 'Country Club Kori' living off of E." I cringe at the notion of being a stay-at-home anything, and that's why I haven't left my career before now.

Mac beats the cot to get our attention. "But we're not talking about him today, Mama, give us the details on this business."

I almost jump out of my skin at the chance to talk about it. "Okay, so I've already started talking to Elaine Russell, from high school—"

"We went to Harvard-Westlake with her!" Shal points. "She manages social media and branding for—"

"Politicians, lawyers, White House staff, who want to switch to TV and entertainment. Like that one doctor who's got a talk show now, and the former prosecutors who appear on CNN," I add, super excited. "She's already given me a schedule to start recording videos. Five per day to start!"

"*Five* videos a day?" Mac whistles.

It sounds like a lot, but my pulse thumps at warp speed that I'll finally get to do what I love. "My co-workers will roast me."

I can hear them already, judging me for claiming to be a hard-nosed prosecutor while I put up "how-to" videos on pairing shoes with suits, and color-coding a closet.

Shallon scrolls through her phone. "Kori, you've always been too worried about what other folks think. Forget them. You have to put yourself out there. That's the *only* way you can go out and claim what's yours."

"What are you calling this?" Mac asks.

"Kori Kouture: Style Is Life."

Mac nods. "That's what's up. A lot of professional women would love to hear what you have to say, Kor. About a lot of issues, not just clothes and home interior. Everybody thinks our lives get easier with college degrees, but women are out here fighting for our lives. While we deal with bullshit from every direction."

"Speak on it," Shallon adds, scrolling through her phone. "We are definitely not represented on YouTube."

Mac sips champagne. "That's because professionals can't disclose what we go through."

"It'll be perceived as whining," Shal says. "What the hell?"

"You good?" Mac asks.

Shal stares at us and holds up her phone for us to see.

Other lawyers are sending around screenshots of protesters gathering at Paradise Gardens where LaShauna Posey lived.

"I don't get it," Mac says. "Why are people mad when *she's* the one who killed that officer?"

Shal shrugs. "I have no clue. That makes zero sense to me."

In the back of my mind, I recall the excitement lighting up the eyes of D.A. Gray.

"It happened on one of the properties of Carol Worthen. Do you know who that is? The biggest black real estate developer in the country. And residents are saying he may have some sort of involvement."

"I'm not sure," I lie. "Good question."

Out of respect for Easton, for the airplane crash on his face yesterday when I shared this with him, I still haven't told my friends that part.

My own cell phone vibrates now.

Teneil: *This LaShauna Posey situation is getting wild. As black women, AAWPA must address. You want me to draft a press statement and send it over?*

Me: *Start a draft, but my eyes only. No one else. Let's give this another couple of days, see where it goes. We don't want to jump the gun.*

Several more text messages roll in from concerned AAWPA members, and friends and former classmates in other states asking what's going on here in Cali. What should be a magical afternoon slowly starts evaporating into fairy dust.

This shouldn't matter to me. I'll only be a prosecutor for two more weeks.

Stunning the hell out of me, our door opens.

Large, loud footsteps crash somewhere behind me.

Shal jumps up and snatches her robe together. "Easton, what are you doing here? You can't be in here!"

"I just came to bring y'all some food and say—"

"No!" Mac hollers. "Negro, you are not allowed to see her now."

Outside our suite, the hotel staffers hold boxes of food from Post & Beam, one of my fave black-owned restaurants.

"Y'all got clothes on?" my man's voice asks.

I whip around to see a blinded East with one hand over his eyes so he doesn't see us, while his other hand swats at the cots, the sofa, and he crashes into the coffee table.

A broad smile on my face and in my soul, I chuckle at this Negro popping in unannounced.

"Babe, I'm over here," All giggly, I reach for him.

Mac cuts in and stops us from connecting, as we crack up. My friends are real serious. "No!"

"All right, all right! Just let me kiss her real quick! Damn!" East pleads.

Shal places her hands over his eyes so he can't see while he stumbles to stay on his feet.

Helping my poor baby out, I climb on the cot and grab his face. Pull him to me, feast on his sexy, slick lips I fell for nine years ago, that first day we met in the law firm library while I was serving up all that attitude.

With Shal's hands still covering his eyes, quickly, blindly, he catches my bottom lip and bites, clutches my ass through my robe, runs his hand down my thighs. "I love you."

"Love you, too, baby." I lick his tongue and taste the sweet whisky and cigars on his taste buds. His law firm partner, Steven, or one of his boys must've driven him here.

"Can't wait for you to be Mrs. Worthen."

"Can't wait to have your baby."

"That's enough!" Mac claps from the doorway. "Shal, bring that ass on out."

Our lips rip away, and they unplug him from me.

After he bumbles out the door, my friends turn to me, hands over their chests and gushing. The stars in their eyes match the galaxies where I float.

"You lucky bitch." Shal wipes her eyes. "You and him just might change my mind on this love shit."

He and I are finally doing this, and nobody is stopping us this time. My gaze drops to the ring on my finger. Now, Easton's had it sized to fit perfectly. It no longer spins around my finger as if wondering who it belongs to, as if it no longer waits for me to become *me*.

Chapter Six

PINKY SWEAR

KORIENNE - SONG: THE FIRST TIME EVER I SAW YOUR FACE BY ROBERTA FLACK

Nine Years Prior - Kori's and Easton's First Date

"A blindfold?" It's exhilarating, but, "Why?"

I haven't been blindfolded since my parents got me my first car at sixteen.

Waitstaff at the Hotel Bel-Air's front desk giggle, leaning against the counter, nudging each other, their hands covering their mouths as they ogle us.

"If I told you, it wouldn't be a surprise." Tall and handsome in jeans and a button-down, his sleeves rolled up, he makes his way around me. "Girl, we are at a public location. Turn around and let me put this on you."

The pulse in my neck and over my eye don't come close to the throb between my legs. His fingers brush along my face but may as well caress my clit. They sweep my hair where he ties the scarf, and my body reacts like he swiped my nipple. He takes my arm and hand to guide me

outside, into an August, Southern California night that's the right amount of velvet on my skin.

"You been to the Hotel Bel-Air before?" he asks.

Each time I take a step, my leg bumps into his muscular thighs. So he directs me at my hip, which does nothing to slow down the cellular collisions in my nerves.

"Yes, my cotillion was here when I was thirteen."

"I should have known you had a cotillion," he whispers.

Instantly, my guard goes up. "Country Club Kori" and the other slurs my cousins hurled at me as a kid, and some girls snicker behind my back, now bounce through my mind. Defensively, I ask, "What's that supposed to mean?"

"It explains why you're elegance in motion and don't take crap off anybody. You're used to being treated like royalty, and you've had practice."

Little does he know just how bad I want to drop this class act and take him under one of those trees. Now I brace myself for the icky pond I've seen a few times over the years when I've come here with my family or somebody's birthday or my grandparents' anniversary.

He removes the blindfold from my eyes and snatches every particle of air I own.

Glowing lights surround me, strung among the overarching clusters of palm trees, grand oaks, and tropical greenery, where I stand in an enchanted forest. Purple peony flowers add splashes of color where they're tucked in the trees and bushes.

In the small pond, between large water lilies floating along its surface, swim white swans for a recreation of Swan Lake.

A Midsummer Night's Dream *has come to life, or* The Great Gatsby, *or* The Princess and the Frog, *or any picturesque fantasy we've read in classic novels or admired on film.*

Along its edges, an all-black quartet serenades us with the first song, Roberta Flack's The First Time Ever I Saw Your Face.

"Have a seat," he murmurs and escorts me toward the table where five-star waitstaff stand ready, and a waiter holds out my chair.

Once we sit down, the waiter lays the napkins over our laps before pouring sample flutes of white wine for me to taste and choose our bottle for dinner.

"So how was your day?" Easton is mesmerizing over the candlelight.

You mean, when I wasn't getting my hair done, nails done, eyebrows threaded, face worked up, and armpits laser-shocked? *I think to myself.*

"It was relaxing. First day with no work was kind of weird. I missed everybody from the firm. But it was...boring."

"I can't believe you missed us. You hardly ever even kicked it. What do you do with yourself in the evenings anyway?"

The waiters set down catered Afro-French cuisine Tajine d'Agneau aux pruneaux. In the backdrop, the Marian Anderson String Quartet continues harmonizing softly.

"My parents, my brother, my friends and I are pretty close. Since I've been away at school these past few years—first at Howard, all the way in D.C., and now, up at Berkeley—we don't get to see each other as much, except for when I'm home for summer. So with me in town, it's always something going up. My parents' friends, my friends' families, somebody's always barbecuing, movie nights, golfing, boating, going out to eat, my sorority stuff, plus my side..."

I let my voice trail off, because my private hobby sounds crazy to people who don't know me well.

"Plus what?" He waggles his head, and his eyes grow with intrigue. "Do tell a brotha about this secret side of Kori nobody knows."

Giggling, I shake my head. "Nothing. I just spend time with my people."

"Nah, don't do that." He waves his hand in protest and motions for me to give up the intel. "Stop bogarting. What is it? I waited for this all summer. I think I earned it."

Biting my lip, I wonder whether to trust him with my business, because I really don't discuss myself with people at work. I learned the hard way in high school and college, not to let so-called associates and classmates have access to my dreams.

He apparently senses my doubt.

"It doesn't go beyond this table, beautiful. I pinky swear. I will only snitch on you if you tell people I'm out here using my damn pinky."

He holds it out, and I lock pinkies with Easton Worthen.

Lock eyes.

Lock attraction.

"Come on. Let's have it."

"I decorate people's houses, design their weddings, offices, and events. In my spare time, after work, I do it for my close childhood friends, and my parents' friends. Their rooms, organize their closets, restyle their wardrobes, help them bring out their inner selves, who they really want to be." There, I said it out loud. Now I wait for the silent judgment.

"What?" he gasps in exaggerated fashion. "Don't tell me our future president, Kori Haughton, is a little fashion icon."

I roll my eyes. "Stop it."

"No, but really, the way you just came alive right there. Eyes all big as cue balls. It's like you disappeared into another portal while you described it. So I don't get it. Why are we a lawyer, instead of some hot designer in Paris?"

This time, behind my eye-roll, I recall all the times people gave me a polite but blank stare when I told them I wanted to be in fashion. "My mom is an engineer, and my dad is a former prosecutor, now a judge. It's hard to go in a more artistic direction when you're coming behind professional giants and everyone expects you to step into their shoes."

As if he's been struck, East stops eating, still holding his fork and knife.

"You all right?" I ask.

Slowly, he nods, studies me over the lone candle. "I feel that. Most definitely. And for what it's worth, I never would have known you wanted to be anything other than the sharp-ass lawyer you are."

For the next three hours, during the whole time that we swap silly stories about camps, school, and humiliating activities our parents forced us into, I rack my brain over the big moment—the kiss. Will I or won't I? I still haven't decided. He is so *not this conceited, self-righteous girl magnet that he is at work.*

After dessert, he leads me onto the grass, under these romantic trees and the summer night stars, to dance.

Each time Easton lowers his head, I inhale and close my eyes, because fuck Zak.

But it doesn't happen.

He must think I'm nervous. So I try to loosen up, even stroke his arm during our dance, with him over me and his mouth in my hair, us swaying to the music. His fingers tap my hip, right at the top slope of my butt, without drifting too far, and he's a damn good dancer.

After coffee, he walks me out, has the valet deliver my car.

He leans forward, and I inhale for the last time.

And close my eyes.

He lifts my hand, and I'm astonished at the gentle kiss he lays on it.

My eyes flutter open to find his gaze serene and steady.

Like in a Looney Toon animation, my disappointment plops, bangs, thumps, and thuds down each ridge of my windpipe.

"Thank you for gracing me with your presence this evening, Ms. Haughton. Since I can't have your number, do you mind if I follow you on social?"

"Y-yeah..."

The valet holds open my car door, and by my hand, Easton guides me toward it.

Forcing up my lead feet, I get in.

"Until next time, Ms. Haughton," he says, peering at me over my door.

"Th-thank you for...the lovely evening."

Please, Lord, let this be a joke and he's going to swing inside and pull a sweet move like in the movies.

Easton closes my door shut.

Bitch, *why* were you so dumb?

Rolling down the driveway, my fingers touching my lips, my mind imagining the moment that evaded my tongue, I can only wonder if he'll ever ask me out again.

* * *

PRESENT DAY - EASTON

"Carol Worthen, come out here and face the people you overcharge!" a man tells the news reporter on my television screen.

From my office, I'm in damn shock at protestors yelling and circling outside my family's home now. Not many are out there, maybe a hundred. But early this morning, there were only around twenty. The crowd is growing.

"Those police should *not* have been in LaShauna's house! How did they get in there? Why?" one of the most recognizable activists in LA, Fannie Kilpatrick, declares to the reporter. "All we want are answers. We want Carol Worthen to come down from living large up in those Hollywood Hills and explain why the police are always at Paradise Gardens."

Two hours before my vows to Korienne, my cell phone buzzes off the hook. My friends and classmates want to know what's going on with my family's company.

Charles: *Dude, where the hell are you? Dad is asking. We need all hands on deck this week, and he wants you out front for some press conferences.*

Me: *He's got Les, his VP of Comms and PR. Technically, it's her job. Omw out of town, will check in on Thurs.*

Charles: *Thurs? Da fuk, E? U said u wld help out n pull ur weight. U been MIA for yrs but reaping all the benefits. This is an emergency.*

I pick up the phone to call my brother and tell him I'm on my way.

Before I activate the call, Steven, my law partner and former law school classmate, enters my office and turns off the TV.

"Why are you doing this to yourself, man? I thought your mind was made up."

"That's my *family*, Steve. Those people are right outside our damn house!"

My old classmate and frat brother steps aside in the doorway so I can see the exit. Since my boy, Kevin, isn't available and I can't tell my brother, Steve is standing up for me at the courthouse.

"And what about the family growing inside Kor?" he asks me. "You took off for the next three days. You've been waiting years."

I think back seven years, and then five years ago. The memory is a damn bullhorn screaming from my heart to my head.

Nodding, I stop myself from calling and send a text instead.

Me: *What part of I got my own bus & clients don't u get? It's not like you all don't have staff.*

Charles: *His staff ain' his sons.*

My brother and I are close, as are my father and me, for the most part, despite our disagreements. But Charles blurts shit out even when he's trying to keep a secret. On the other hand, my moms will go to war with Dad so she can keep our secrets. Hence the reason she is invited today and Charles is not the one standing beside me.

Steve grabs my luggage while I go for my laptop bag and personal effects.

"And just how does your dad think you'll help him solve a mess that's clearly of his making, whatever it is? You had nothing to do with it," he says on our way to the courthouse in Beverly Hills.

"He's like any man with money. It's not about what he wants, but *how* he wants things. Me actually helping him isn't as important as him securing his legacy."

"And what of this business with you leaving behind what *we* built to go join your pops?" Steve asks, checking in for my next decision.

Eight years ago, when I graduated law school and passed the bar, I wanted to prove a point to Dad. I was tired of him funding my life, and I was no longer his "boy." My friends and I talked about it during our final law school 3L year, and once we had our bar results, we struck out on our own.

Dad was livid, and he called it a phase. We fell out for a while, and unfortunately, Kori got caught in the crossfire.

I rub at my chest, where the scars of that devastation still mark me.

"I'm not there, but if I'm ever headed in that direction, I'm never leaving you high and dry, dude." I'm well aware that, of all my four law firm partners, I'm the most well-connected and well-financed. Most of our top-dollar clients come through me because of my family name. So I can understand why my boy is uneasy. "You'll know before anybody else, and I'll always shoot you top clientele."

Steve whips us through side streets to avoid morning traffic on Wilshire. "Appreciate that, bruh, but our little clique is more than money. Our wins, us turning up in the office with bottles popping, bouncing cases off each other, last-minute decisions like you getting married and starting a family—that's brotherhood type shit with no dollar sign on it, bruh."

"Dude, I'm not moving to Antarctica. For now, I'm only getting married." Just those words, the sound of them out of my mouth, massages my little scars from seven years ago, and then two years after that.

Steve chuckles. "Negro, you know what happens to fools once their ladies hem that ass up. You might as well be at the North gatdamn Pole."

As he parks in the garage of the courthouse, my cell vibrates. I peek at it. Shit.

Dad recorded a voice message:

Hey, son, your secretary says you're out of town now. Not good how we parted ways. I could have handled it better. Let me know when you're back in town. You're one of the smartest people I know, Easton. Sometimes it's a little disheartening how you don't use those smarts to further the family. We could really use you here now. Love you, son.

All that stops me from going to him is Kori's voice.

"I just don't want your father in this process. Let's do this ourselves first. We can make our own rules."

Steve taps his watch, an indicator we should go. "You won't leave your dad hanging forever. Just long enough for him to start loving you as a man and not a boy."

Chapter Seven

ONE DUMB F*CK

Nine Years Prior - Two Weeks After Start of Kori's 2L Year & Easton's 3L Year

University of California at Berkeley is not far from Stanford, only an hour drive or less. But I've deliberately avoided taking my ass to where Kori is. 2L year is the most important for setting a lawyer's GPA in stone concerning future jobs and opportunities, and she just made law review.

Also, since our date, hopefully, she's had something on her mind.

Me to Halo (Kori): What's good, cuteness?

Halo: Hey, how r u?

Me: Not well.

Halo: Oh, no. What's going on?

Me: I was sick all morning.

Halo: U came down with a bug? Did u go to a clinic, or at least take some meds?

Me: Hell nah. No clinic or meds can ease the pain of u not responding to my good morning msg.

Halo: LOL, and here I thought something was seriously wrong. Just u being drama.

Me: U not speaking IS seriously wrong.

Halo: Lol, we had practice this a.m. and I was late. Then class afterward. My day fell behind. I apologize.

Me: Practice for?

Halo: Moot court. I'm one of the finalists so I'm going to state competition.

Me: As a 2L, huh? Look @ u. Congrats.

Halo: Thk u.

Me: Maybe I cn come visit, watch one of ur practices.

Halo: Nope. U can't watch and then take our secrets back 2 ur school. But u cn come visit if u behave.

Me: That's too bad. I like studying my competition.

*Halo: *Scratches head* Ur competition???*

Me: Yeh. My competition.

Halo: Wait. Ur on moot court, too?

Me: Shhh. Don't tell anybody.

Halo: U will b at state?

Me: How else wld that make u my competition?

Halo: U serious?

Me: Check the website roster.

Waiting patiently for those three dots to appear, I sip Gatorade, chuck a few potato chips, and imagine how she sounds when she's arguing a case. I caught a whiff of it this summer at the firm during all-hands meetings. Poised, calm, and purposeful, she's sexy as hell and doesn't have to try.

Damn. I wonder if she'd let me see her. She and I have a jammed-up fall calendar between law review, moot court, and interviews for law firm jobs once I graduate in the spring. But I'd make time.

Halo: Omg. So I have a chance to beat u.

Me: A chance is all u'll get, cuteness.

Halo: Oh, how funny. U think cuz I'm a 2L, u got this locked.

Me: No, I think cuz I'm me I got it locked.

Halo: Care 2 put a wager on it?

More than my funny bone is tickled at her confidence. I can't stop myself from laughing so hard.

Me: Go ahead. We playin for Skittles? What?

Halo: Fun. Winner picks the crazy activity of their choice on ur first visit. Heads-up: mine will be skating.

A small smile tugs at this Negro's heartstrings.

Me: My "first" visit?

Halo: If u behave.

Me: I'll do my best. U don't make it easy. Mine will be skiing.

Halo: There's no skiing around here.

Me: I wld take u to Lake Tahoe, angel. But I'd like to come c u b4 the competition.

No harm in shooting my shot.

I hold my breath for her reaction. Kori and I have never kissed or been alone.

* * *

Nine Years Prior - Berkeley, CA

Kori's & Easton's Second Date, First Weekend Together

"But if you vote for that proposition, it means taxes will increase for small business owners, too." Against the night, Kori's face glows over candlelight as she explains this to me. "I'm sure you know, East, a million dollars does not go far in California. Or," she pauses a moment, "do you know?"

I pause and pretend to be hurt. "Why wouldn't I know how hard the cost of living in Cali is?"

She tilts her head aside in that cute way I like. "Maybe because you grew up in Hollywood Hills, where people don't have to worry about that."

I lean over my steak. "And you had to worry about the cost of living over in Black Beverly Hills?"

She pushes over her food and matches my energy, which absolutely warms my heart. "Living right up the street from what used to be South Central, I was closer to the 'hood than you were, so...yeah."

Laughing, I can't help but keep this going because she brings that out in me. "Cuteness, growing up close to the 'hood is not the same as growing up in the 'hood. As evidenced by how there's nothing about you that's 'hood. I could have grown up in Alaska, and I'd still be more 'hood than you."

"And yet you're not aware of the issues affecting the 'hood, which goes to show that behaving a certain way, Mr. Worthen, has no actual correlation to whether a person truly loves black people or the 'hood."

"Can we also agree then, Ms. Haughton, that proximity to the 'hood also doesn't dictate our degree of blackness, or for that matter, our concern for the 'hood, and therefore, it's unwise to assume that someone's proximity to the "hood is a fair measurement of whether they grew up worrying about the cost of living in California?"

Those eyes shine at me, as she realizes I just tied this argument back to the first incorrect assumption she made in this logic game. I could bask in those eyes all night.

Suppressing her impressed grin, she acquiesces. "Fair enough, Mr. Worthen."

That'll be the last time she assumes that me being a spoiled rich guy makes me a dumb *rich guy.*

Though we're on the water and surrounded by yachts, our second date at a sleepy restaurant in the Berkeley Marina is nothing fancy. When I made that forty-five-minute drive from my campus to hers, I wasn't looking for extravagance. Only the gift I'm receiving now.

Excited and energized, Kori talks with her hands, only stopping to occasionally flick her hair back once it falls in her way. Infused with passion, she definitely cares about the world around her. And I'm learning that's the source of her focus. Baby girl wants to make an impact on society. Most women I know work hard for a status and the bag. Nothing wrong with that, but the difference gives Kori's wine a more distinctive flavor.

"Why do you care?" I ask.

Surprise sprays across her face, and she shrugs. "I suppose it's how I was raised. My parents were always explaining why we had our money, what my grandparents and great-grands had to sacrifice to have it. When they moved to LA in the nineteen twenties, they could only live on Central Avenue despite having successful defense jobs during the war and having good money. My father always says, as a black professional you're only one scandal or bad write-up away from ruin. So we have to pay attention. We can't afford to look away from the struggle or be ignorant. It could always be us."

I've never given a damn about politics, and honestly, only vote in the bigger elections—for president, the governor, and the senators. My family might be cool with a few state senators and congresspeople down the chain, but I'm more of a tech man and I make my personal money off venture capitalism and startups like my friend Kevin Middleton's MoneyCruncher and SocioPath.

But Kori is urging me to start caring about local issues, especially since I'm graduating in the spring and have been toying with the idea of hanging my own shingle with my boys. If we go through with it, I would be one of those small business owners who needs to watch my tax dollars.

At the end of the evening, on our way back to her place, I take a chance, and take the journey across the center console and open my hand. The vibe between us is hitting.

I had no idea a woman's fingers intertwining with mine and me closing my hand around hers would elevate my sexual awareness to a different atmospheric level on Earth, as if I'm graduating from the *troposphere with mountain peaks in Kori's smile and satellites in her eyes, and rising to the stratosphere with hot air balloons that have got a Negro's mind sailing to new heights. Hell, up here, I'm floating with the polar clouds and shit.*

Opening her car door, I walk her to her condo because I'm staying with a friend and not with her. She made that much clear before I got here.

Her "law school" style is simpler than her "law firm" attire. In a puffer jacket for the Northern California autumn, jeans, sweater and LL Bean rain boots, her dressed-down layers are begging me to peel all that off.

"Thanks for letting me come hang with you, cuteness. I still want my good morning text tomorrow, though. And you hit me up when you're finished studying," I tell her inside her door.

Kori's cheeks and mouth kind of twitch, the way one does when they're making a decision. "I have a lot of work. My first law review article is due, but you want to come over and study together? Sounds extra boring, I know, but—"

"And what, miss a chance to see Kori at her cutest? When she's all hard at work and ignoring me? I'd love that. It'll be like old times back at the firm."

There goes her smile that's made of sugar. "I'll make you some stuffed ravioli."

"Oh, shit, watch out now. She's cooking for me, too? Maybe one of these days, she might even let me talk to her in public."

Cracking up, she replies, "Boy, bye. You have *talked to me in public."*

"You always keep that convo to less than sixty seconds, too. I'll see you tomorrow, gorgeous." Already, I'm backing away, and won't kiss her tonight either, because I can sense she's still feeling me out.

The next evening, I've almost forgotten how I'm trying to stuff her ravioli. I actually brought my laptop and a couple of books to town with me, because it's not like I don't have studying of my own to do. Between reading Kori's law review article and giving her my thoughts on it, swapping notes on our professors, the gossip on law firms back in LA, music and our parents, our conversations veer all over the place. We wind up more immersed in our vibe than in our work.

Restraint with Kori has been pretty cool.

I've had two steady girlfriends a couple of times, both in college. The first was Troi, and the second was Reed. The difference between high school and college is how dudes get our own space away from our mothers. When a man has a mama like mine who was a stay-at-home wife, it takes a minute to adjust to the new reality where he comes back to his spot and not a damn thing is cooked. Campus dining halls and local fast food joints get old real quick.

Since girls are still kind of in their starry-eyed stage, they'll cook and take care of a brother in hopes of it becoming something long term. I won't lie: I parlayed that shit.

Then, it was also nice to have consistent pussy, for those nights when I wanted it, but it was cold outside. Plus, in college, I had to balance partying with responsibility, and I didn't always have time or energy for hunting.

So Troi was more caregiver and fuck buddy than a bond that inspired me to commit. But then Reed came along, who is especially gifted with fucking, and we wound up fucking marvelously in different locales while interning at Apple.

Add in dinner, cool scenery, enlightening convo that held my attention, and movies from time to time, and that's how I fell into consistent pussy that kept me semi-committed. Reed is like having a cool-ass friend who also comes with great extra benefits.

But now? A Negro's romantic experience is clearly ascending into a more psychologically stimulating era—of not fucking.

I'm feeling Kori so much I don't want to screw up what's been dope until this point. As a man still in his mid-twenties, I still live a very "active" life, and I don't want to disappoint her, or tell her a lie, or see her smile crack or her beautiful spirit broken.

Plus, the intrigue of not having been intimate with her heightens my senses, attracts my attention to her every move, and fills in the gaps of my imagination.

The equation shifts, though, once she backs into me, not knowing I'm right behind her, to hand over my plate. Her booty brushes my dick.

"My bad, little mama."

Too late. In a chain of events we can't stop, my hand already reacts instantaneously, cupping her ass cheek through her sweatpants and tugging her to me. Her mouth is already wet, her hand moving to caress my jaw. Shit, fuck this plate.

Licking the curve of her lip slowly, tasting the marinara sauce and tea, I nibble and tug on its edges. Her soft fingers feather my jawline and my neck, with the sensations elevating her gentle tugs at my lips. With perfect rhythm, her tongue clicks and dances on mine. Tasting each other, I'm damn near intoxicated with her hand lightly clawing my back.

I want Kori. The hardest move I've ever made concerning a woman is pull away from her.

The disappointed whine escaping her throat informs me she feels the same.

But I kiss her temple. "I want to do this right, cuteness. Let's give it more time."

I'm not seeing Reed anymore. I shut it down this summer. In anticipation of asking Kori out, I started clearing the field.

I knew I couldn't come at her any kind of way.

Now that I've caught feelings—real feelings, and not just convenience—when I make love to Kori, there can't be any background noise.

In a few weeks, we'll head home to LA for the holidays, and I suspect Reed will hit me up and will want answers. As well as a couple of other honeys who have rocked with my shenanigans over the years. I'd rather shield Korienne from turbulence.

Tonight is the first night in this Negro's life that he's lain next to a woman and not hit. Instead, we fall asleep on her sofa, with her buttery caramel scent wafting up my nose, succulent arms circled around me, soft curls tickling my cheek, and hypnotic kisses fucking me up.

Either a brother is growing up, or he is one dumb fuck.

* * *

KORIENNE

Nine Years Prior - California Moot Court Statewide Competition, October After Easton & Kori's Summer Clerkship Together

"Congratulations, East."

"All right then, East! I see you, bruh. Good job this time. Just watch your back once we pass the bar and meet up in court, dude. Imma wear that ass out in front of a jury!"

"Good job, East!"

"Hey, Kori! Congrats on second place, girl. You did an amazing job for it to be your first year, and you put a lot of 3L's to shame!" One of my competitors squeezes my shoulders. "But it's hard holding up against East the Beast."

He and I sit next to one another at Shaky's Pizza Parlor, where a lot of law students have gathered to hang out before getting back on rented vans and busses and returning to school with our teams. So he and I have zero privacy.

"What's up, Kori? Good performance, baby girl. You'll kill it next year!" someone calls to me.

"Thank you," I reply and roll my eyes at East, whose gloating grin is longer than the Mississippi River.

"You did do a good job, though, cuteness. I got a little run for my money. Your hard practices went a long way." He holds up another slice of pizza. "Just not long enough." With a wink, he takes a big bite.

I can't even be mad at his cockiness that amplifies his flirty eyes and smooth lips.

But I will not give him the satisfaction of worshiping him. "Would you please move that thing?"

Mockingly, he raises an eyebrow and pretends to be confused. "What thing? This?" He points at the huge state champion trophy he's placed squarely between us. "Oh, my bad, girl." Then, he makes a big show of trying to lift it, grunting and straining, like he's hurting himself to lift Thor's hammer. "Shit, this thing is so heavy I can hardly handle it." Eying me, he picks it up. "Oh, would you look at that? I suppose only one Negro in here is worthy to carry the hammer, huh?"

Apparently, girls from other schools don't appreciate the attention I'm getting. They attempt to squeeze in, flirtatiously shoving him, sliding their hands over his shoulders and down his back, clearly communicating that I shouldn't think I'm special.

"Easton! Boy, you so crazy," one of them cackles and runs her hand over his chest, as if they're familiar and she's hoping to be familiar again soon.

Why did I even allow myself to think this could go somewhere? Why have I been entertaining silly fantasies, letting him come and see me, imagining myself as his...

...it's stupid.

He's still screwing around with these other women, and that's why he's not as attracted to me. Tuh. Telling me, "I want to do this the right way, cuteness." *Bullshit.*

"Ms. Lady." East addresses the other law student, and he motions between him and me. "Can't you see we're having a conversation?"

"Aw, my bad," she says. "That wasn't your energy last time I saw you. But go on 'head and get this new booty. Hit me up when you get free, big daddy."

Zak was right. He probably texts all sixty-five women in his phone "good morning" every day.

"Easton," I begin, "I should go. Congrats on—"

"Kori." His fingers brush the edge of my elbow, but he stops me with

the spotlights of his eyes, intimately, attentively. "I know how that just looked, and I'm pretty sure I know what you've heard about me."

"It's not true?" I challenge him.

Those eyes remain right where they are, baring his inevitable truth. "No lies, some of it probably is."

Beyond frazzled, I need to get back on the van and go. Fighting to maintain my calm, I make myself clear. "I'm not interested in riding your merry-go-round of randoms."

Easton leaning toward me must turn down the noise level several decibels in Shakey's, so he lowers his voice to where only I hear him.

"And I'm not interested in putting you on a merry-go-round, Kori-enne." He laces his fingers through mine, our hands dangling off the table, intertwined. "Do you mind if I prove it to you?"

Confused, I follow up. "Prove it? How?"

"Like this."

He takes my chin in his fingers and claims my lips and my life in front of all black law society. Just like the times we kissed in my apartment, Easton's sensual, heartfelt, slow way of lavishing my mouth with his attention revives me with a different meaning of life.

Chapter Eight

OUR ENERGY IS OFF

KORIENNE

Jennifer: *Ms. AAWPA President, u seeing what's on TV today? Wit the Worthen family? Isn't Easton Worthen ur ex? From yrs ago? They say his daddy cld b implicated in this LaShauna Posey thing.*

Jennifer is one of the public defenders assigned to my courtroom.

My phone won't stop vibrating.

Teneil: *U get a chance to review my draft letter on the Posey shooting?*

Elaine Russell: *We should meet this weekend to discuss Kori Kouture: Style Is Life, and when you'll take it live. I emailed u a draft schedule of events, topics, and goals/strategies for growing ur following. Tell me what u think.*

Vashti: *Madam Pres, I'm asking you to recuse yourself from presiding over the AAWPA election this Thursday. Since u are clearly biased toward ur girl, Mac, it's only fair that somebody else oversee the mtg. Not you.*

Mackenzie: *We need to have a quick call.*

Judge Sharpe: *Now that your AAWPA year is almost over, have you started thinking about being California Women Professionals President for the entire state? A great step for being appointed judge like your dad.*

Dad: *You see what's on TV? Carol Worthen? I'm so glad you don't deal with his son anymore. I always knew that family was a bunch of snakes. He never sat right with me. You want to have lunch this week?*

This last text message is a foghorn blaring across the ocean of Dad's blood that runs through me.

Over the last nearly three years that East and I have been back together, by some miracle, my father's never caught us. Once, I hid East in my closet for three hours. Thank goodness for subterranean parking, and Dad didn't see his car. It's not like my father stops by my house all the time, but there were a couple of close calls.

Another time, at a restaurant run-in with Dad and his friends, fortunately, I saw my father entering before he saw us. I made East go to the bathroom, so I could lie and say I was waiting on Shallon to arrive. She then had to leave her sneaky-link hanging to come and sit with me for our fake girls' night. Not to mention the Christmases, Fourths of July, and Thanksgivings where he and I wanted time alone and had to whip up creative lies about out-of-town trips with friends, or dating "somebody new" who's not ready for the family introduction stage yet.

My father is not manipulative or overbearing the way Easton's is. But Dad's heart will break that I'm stooping as "low" as the Worthens, for whom he has zero respect.

Now I'm torn on including Dad in this moment, but he would frown the entire ceremony, the way he did the first time he took me to Howard University instead of his alma mater of Princeton.

Maybe Easton and I are deciding this too fast. What is our plan for how we *will* tell our fathers? And when? Will this secretive, shotgun wedding force our families closer together or further apart?

My phone vibrates again.

Mackenzie: *?*

Add to these challenges how I will spend the next three days transferring my things to Easton's house, and then oversee a contentious AAWPA election between Mackenzie and Vashti on Wednesday, plus finally work up the nerve to give notice to the D.A. on Thursday, and this week will be no honeymoon.

"Kori!" a defense attorney calls from across the corridor. "Deputy Haughton, what are you doing way over here in Beverly Hills? You're far from downtown, aren't you? Did you get reassigned?" Puzzled, he checks out my wedding suit, hair, and makeup. "Wait. Something special happening today?"

Immediately triggered is my years-long aversion to people knowing my business. "I'm here supporting a friend of mine today. It's good to see you."

In fact, several lawyers recognize me and wonder why I'm not in my regular courthouse.

To avoid the constant questions, this is a perfect time to call Mac. For this small civil ceremony, Shal is my oldest friend, and she'll be the only one here. Mac will be in our actual wedding later this year.

"Mac, what's going on?" I murmur.

"Kori, you need to do something about Vashti. She's out of control. She's trying to milk this shooting situation around LaShauna Posey for her own benefit, since she's from that area of LA. She's talking to news stations and saying professional black women don't do enough for urban South LA women in LaShauna's position who struggle. She's making herself look like a warrior for the people and basically shitting on the rest of us. We're supposed to be colleagues."

As I listen to her, I scan the court corridors for Easton.

"You shouldn't be surprised Vashti is playing dirty. She made it clear this weekend she's not going to just roll over and let you have it. You knew she would put up a fight."

Until two years ago, Mackenzie had zero interest in bar association politics. She only joined AAWPA to help me survive the multiple personalities. I wanted my most trusted people at my side during budget battles and big votes. At our meetings, when another officer like Vashti comes for me, Mac and Shal go on the attack when I cannot. I expected Mac to leave the board once I left, but apparently, she's been touched by the allure of the Iron Throne, or rather, the president's seat.

"You can't just sit this one out," she says to me. "Even if you don't take sides, at least tell the past presidents they shouldn't choose so fast and automatically support her based on time served. They should consider what I bring to the table, too."

I can't abandon Mac, not after she gave me two years and had my back when she could have been doing other things with her life.

"I'll make a few calls, see what's going on, and tell the presidents to keep open minds."

My mom comes around the corner with Zak, carrying flowers and gift boxes.

"Mac, I've got to go. Call you later."

"Congratulations, sis! Send pics when you can."

"Mom!"

Her arms have never felt better than when I'm on the verge of a meltdown and second-guessing everything.

She examines me, turning me around. "Girl, this peplum is to die for. And your hair and makeup are just perfection. You're such a little gem. You always have been a foxy, fashionable thing." But her admiration is mixed with concern, the angst on her face expressing all I don't want to say. "I just wish this didn't have to be so secret is all. You deserve the gown and cake and party and to have your special day. Damn that Carol W—"

"Shh. East will be here any minute. And we're still having a wedding this fall. But we're making it legal now. Just to have some peace."

"Did you see all those people protesting outside their house over this murder thing?" Mom frets harder. "Please don't go to their home, Kori. Stay away from all that. Whatever his damn daddy's problems are, they're not *yours*," she whispers.

"You look beautiful, squirt," Zak says, kissing my cheek. "See how your brother's advice all these years kept him on a leash?" he asks with a smirk.

I roll my eyes. "That, and all the headaches that Negro gave me."

Flashbacks of the turbulence East and I have endured through the years returns me to second-guessing my spur-of-the-moment decision.

Finally rounding the corner in a crisp, tailored suit, with a fresh haircut and clean-shaven chin, he's beautiful. He slows up in his tracks and lays eyes on me. Roberta Flack serenades us all over again. Only we don't need string lights and a *Swan Lake* today.

We are the melody. Our love is the water on which we float, and it will sustain us and transport us through anything.

His eyes bathe me with admiration, and he comes toward me for a kiss. "You're so fucking stunning, Kori."

"Deputy Haughton!" a defense attorney calls out. "Good to see you! What are you doing over here?"

Even now, turning my head from Easton, prying myself from the electricity of us, I resume my facade.

"A good friend of mine is getting married, and I'm maid of honor."

East's hurt lays into me. "That's the last time somebody will ask you, and you deny this."

"I'll gladly scream it from the rooftops, E, when we have a plan for how we'll handle the consequences," I murmur so my words don't echo through the halls. "Don't forget, we're standing here now, because we were quiet this time."

East and I are thrilled to stand here, at the threshold of being man and wife.

But our energy is off.

Turmoil still hides behind his smile, so it's not at its brightest. And his arms that hold me must carry sandbags, the way they drag around me. That's the weight of his father's absence. Today is beautiful but still bittersweet.

In his pocket, his cellphone vibrates, and without looking, he silences it.

"Baby, how are you? How are your folks?" I ask. His father and I may not get along, but I care about East's heart.

Speaking of his mother, Essence rounds the corner with warm greetings, but even her demeanor lacks her normal sassy vibe.

"Kori, we're ready for you." Judge Sharpe stands at a side entrance that leads to the judges' corridor not accessible to the public. Instead of sending her judicial assistant or clerk, she came out herself.

Taking back hallways, we avoid walking through her courtroom so as not to be seen by more attorneys and some of my fellow prosecutors. One of my mother's longest friends, she understands how I want to keep this private.

The moment we're inside the solitude of her chambers, East's hand slides around my waist and spins me right into his arms.

Into the mountainous aroma of his Tom Ford Arabian Wood.

Onto his mouth, where his tongue tastes and licks mine, and reminds me why I haven't gone anywhere. And would say yes to him again and again, asshole father and all, no matter how many times we separate and get back together. Because I *can't* love anybody else other than Easton Jermaine Worthen.

His long fingers clamp around my throat and tilt my head up so he can access my tongue better, before nibbling my lips and easing off.

"Aw."

Shal, his mom, and my mom wipe their eyes.

Everybody's phone cameras snap and record.

With Steven at his side and Shal at mine, we complete the paperwork.

However, East is missing his typical swagger. That cocky grin he wore at his law school graduation, and the first time I told him I was pregnant, or when he scored his first million-dollar real estate deal, fails to light up our group now.

Occasionally, his phone vibrates, and as he silences it, he and Essence swap concerned expressions.

I peer over his shoulder just in time to catch his mother mouthing, *We'll be just fine.* In the valleys of fine lines along her eyes are touches of joy but also melancholy.

Judge Sharpe clears her throat, and she begins, "We have before us today, Easton and Korienne."

"Excuse us a moment," I say to the judge and guide him to a corner. "Easton."

"Kor, what are you doing?" he asks, irritated.

"Go be with your father and brother, baby." As I much as I hate to give him up, as badly as I want him to be my husband, we have unfinished business.

Shaking his head, he forces his frustration through clenched teeth. "Kor, you're tripping. Don't do this to me again. *You're* my family. We've waited long enough. This was *your* idea, Kori."

I push back. "But you're standing here torn up, worried about what's happening to your dad." I wipe tears now. "You're upset and antsy, and if I were in your situation, I would be, too. Go support them."

I would do anything to stop that twitching in his eye, but it's not my move to make.

"But we're finally here. We've spent the past year lining this up. My accounts are separate from Dad's, my stockbrokers are hired and paid by me. I bought the house from him completely and transferred full title to me. And then I'll put it in yours and my name. All my investments are chosen by me. I rely on him for nothing now. So we're secure." He shovels his hands between us. "This is best for the baby."

"No, it isn't, and it's not best for *you*. Your body is here. Your heart and head are not." I pour my support into him with more than just these next words. "Go help your dad. I want your whole heart, E, not pieces of you."

"I've had pieces of you for *years*, Kor." Close enough that his eyeballs almost touch mine, he leans toward me. "And I was okay with that, as long as I could just *have* the preciousness of you."

The broken glass on his face is cutting through every layer of my heart, and I'm almost inclined to go all the way this time.

Shallon lowers her head and covers her face. "Kori, damn, just do it, girl."

I wish I could.

I'd love to be the woman who could just say 'to hell with it' and not think twice about the circumstances that come with marriage, or the kind of family I'm joining myself to, or the toxicity and patriarchy his father will try to push onto me.

"E, we're almost there."

Around us, our mothers moan with sadness. But they don't urge us to continue these hasty vows.

East's forehead falls on mine, his eyes squeezed closed, as if he's trying to absorb from me what he's always called his light. "Come with me then. We'll tell him now."

Holding his face, I remind him, "Now? While your family is in a crisis? And you're not even by his side? How accepting do you think he'll be? When he does find out why you're not there with him, *who* do you think he'll blame?"

"She's right, E," his mother says.

He examines me. "Kori, you sure that's what it is? Whatever

happens with Dad and me, will you ever accept being my wife?" Exasperated, he sputters from far beyond his throat.

"I *am* ready. To marry a man who's not torn, who's not standing here looking like he's betraying his father. I shouldn't be an act of betrayal for you. Resolve this discord first. And let's heal these divides. We've got a baby on the way, and our child needs to know family harmony."

"Fine. I'll go handle it then." He backs away from me and out of the judge's chamber.

"Easton, don't."

His mother follows him out. "East, where are you going? Don't do anything rash. *Easton!*"

Chapter Nine
ON ONE CONDITION

EASTON

To hell with it.

On my way to Worthen Properties, I silence my mother's phone calls.

It's time for Dad to know that Kori and I are together and she'll soon be his family. And since he doesn't have any say in this matter and can't toy with my life, he had better start accepting this.

I didn't have the full financial independence to stand on that five years ago, but I've damn sure got it now.

These last two and a half years, my every moment with Kori has been resplendent.

She was the one to suggest that nobody know this time. That our love, our evolution, our heights remain only within the sanctity of our closest inner circle.

The loudest person in the room is usually the weakest, East. Let's lie low for a while and build us. Being quiet gives us the power.

Silence was the right call. Without the noise of my father's demands, her father's expectations, gossips around town interfering,

89

every time she and I get together now, our union is better than an oceanside Sunday morning.

I'm so fucking ready to put as many kids in her as she'll let me.

So for me to hear the words, *I'm pregnant,* come out of Kori's mouth, seven years after the last time she uttered them—and then ripped out a piece of me, the heart of *us*—brings all our sacrifice and maturation to our point of completion.

Add to that how she's finally leaving her grueling day job as a county prosecutor, and we've come full circle, as grown professionals secure in who we are. With no more need for parents' approval or society's validation. For a good thirty-six hours, we were over the moon.

Now it's irritating as hell that, instead of sailing to outer space, I drive in the opposite direction.

Carol Worthen doesn't run shit in my life anymore. I love and admire my father, and I will do what I can to help figure out this situation, but it's time for him to get on board.

Focused on my independence, Kori's well-being, and our future, I round the corner to my father's building in Century City, to go take this up with him. And damn.

"Put Carol's kids out on the street!"

"LaShauna didn't pull the trigger! Carol Worthen did!"

Protestors scream at the tall high-rise as if their rage alone can bring it down. With me riding into the side garage, they don't notice me.

"Indict Carol Worthen!"

"Send Carol Worthen to stay in the 'hood! Let me stay in Holly-wood Hills!"

Even from inside the building, underneath the garage, I hear my last name bellowed with fury.

"Oh, wow. Good morning, East!" The valet's eyes light up to see me. "I haven't seen you around in a while. We've missed you. Real glad you're here. Big man upstairs could use all the support he can get."

"Wassup, Clay?" I offer him a grip.

"Damn glad to see *you* here, young man. What foxy lady's got you looking so good?"

The personnel and staff see me enter, and their collective jaws drop in shock. That's how rarely I come here anymore, in an effort to divest myself from Dad's control over my life.

"Hey, E!" the front desk clerk calls out. "What a nice surprise. Why don't we see you around anymore?"

I pat my heart. "Appreciate the sentiments. But I'm a big boy with a business of my own now, and I've got bills to pay."

"E!" Dad's long-time secretary greets me. "Thank goodness, you're here. He needs to see your face and feel like his sons are behind him. Please, honey, be on your best behavior." She throws me a side-eye. "He's already at wit's end."

With one goal on my mind, I start to breeze past her. "I can't promise you that today, Cyn."

She stops me by my arm, and her gaze stretches back the twenty-five years she's known me. "Be easy, East. Your mama called me. Whatever you're stewing over, you'll only do more harm than good. He needs someone clear-eyed to start the truth-telling."

"What truth-telling?" I ask her.

She opens her mouth.

"Are my ears hearing right?" Dad calls from the conference room. "You mean Hell really must've frozen over? Is that my son out there?"

Cyn serves up one more warning glare, the kind she used to give me as a kid, when I came to work with Dad and had to stay quiet for his important meetings.

But this needs to happen. "Dad, you and I need to talk," I tell him.

Beyond this fourteenth-floor conference room, the protesters raise Cain out on the street.

Throwing his arms around me, he turns to his vice-presidents. "Look who strolled in and blessed me with his presence. You see this fine young man here. I was wondering if he'd come through. This guy's got his own law firm, secretaries, and clients. He's getting his own multi-million-dollar real estate deals and everything. He was even supposed to be out of town today."

With one arm around my shoulders, squeezing me to his side, Dad reaches up with the other. A gleam in his eyes, he straightens my tie.

"But here he is. Instead of going to see his own clients, my son came to support me. The world could be falling in flames, and just to have my sons standing here...fills up a man's heart."

His team of advisors and consultants clap and pound the table.

Among them sits Reed, who winks from the other side of the conference table and offers me the empty seat next to her.

"He keeps saying he'll never come here and roll up his sleeves, but I'm not losing faith in him."

Just the fact that I'm standing here, rather than in Santa Fe holed up with Kori, pushes me to stay focused. "Dad, um, looks like we've got quite a situation out there, but as soon as we can—"

"If that's not the understatement of the year!" he cracks.

The room bursts out laughing.

Dad continues, "Son, we need to talk with you, too. As you can see, I've got news for you. You remember your ex? That Korienne Haughton girl, from five years ago, the one you almost married? Twice. Thank God, you dodged that bullet."

The hell?

The loudest person in the room is usually the weakest, East. Let's lie low for a while and build us. Being quiet gives us the power.

Kori's words two and a half years ago, when we got back

together, reverberate through my head now. With her words in mind, I go and take the seat Reed offers.

Keeping my tone even, my thoughts in check, I lace my fingers. "What about her, Dad?"

"I've gotten word she's after me. That somebody overheard her at her little event the other day, discussing an indictment against me over the murder of this cop. She suggested to the D.A. that I be charged in connection with this thing going on out there," he says, pointing at the protesters outside, "and that she be the one assigned to the case."

My heart feels like it's being fed through a shredder. Kori told me the D.A. is targeting him for a win, but even if my lady hadn't already shared this with me, I still would never believe Kor was after him. Despite how Dad treated her, and their animosity toward each other, she wouldn't do it to *me*.

No, I'm aching in my chest, because my feelings and respect for her compel me to stand up and make unequivocally clear to him that Korienne is the reason I'm even sitting here, at his side, on the same day I should be at hers. *That's* how much she loves me.

But I think of our unborn child and how she's right. Our baby could be a path to healing between our families if I just take my time with Dad and fix us first.

So he stands there gloating, wagging his finger in my direction, as I bite my tongue.

Dad continues, "You see, I was right about her. Aren't you glad now? You ought to be damn grateful I put my foot down with you marrying into that family. Her and her daddy have an agenda to destroy me. He's always had it out for me, and his persnickety daughter, who thought she was too good to have your kids, is coming for us, because I ruined her plans to marry you and leach off my money! Now she's in the D.A.'s ear."

This is one of the reasons she and I stayed quiet this time—the gossips and our rivals constantly in our business and stirring up mess at every turn.

"Are you sure you've got your facts straight, Dad?"

"Who would lie about that?" He laughs. "You were always gullible when it came to her. But I've got plans of my own."

Thankfully, I took aspirin before I got here, but it does nothing for the ache in my chest.

"Plans like what, Dad?"

His eyes aiming at me, he snickers. "Her daddy's not this upstanding judge he makes himself out to be. He's got baggage, and we'll fight fire with fire. There's no way in hell I'll let the Haughtons torch me! I don't give a damn about his daughter being a D.A. You're a leader in that NAABA group, with all the black attorneys. I want you to do some digging of your own and see what you can find out about this indictment."

Running his words through my head, I wonder what dirt he's got against Kori's father.

Around the table, his employees offer me their sympathy expressions.

But not Dad's COO, Edith Zucker. She eyes me long and hard, the way most people do who hate nepotism babies. She's been working for Dad for around five years, since she came to his company from General Motors. I'm used to the occasional people like her, who resent how I'm here because I'm Dad's son, and not because they feel I've earned a seat at this table. If only she knew how little I cared. We all have our cross to bear.

Now the room awaits my response, or more specifically, *how* I respond.

"Dad, I'm not saying what you've been told is true. But even if it were, do you really think the way to avoid an indictment is by going after the D.A.'s office *and* a sitting judge?" I turn toward the protesters outside. "It'll win you some headlines in the papers. But those people out there are not mad about Korienne." I take a breath and try to maneuver his focus away from her. "What's the company's plan for dealing with all that?"

"Mr. Worthen, he's right, sir." Dad's vice-president of public relations shoots me a grateful glance. "We should get back to the issue of your public relations and casting you as a caring individual in your community."

Next to me, Reed gives me a nod. "Mr. Worthen, in that vein, I think you should do a one-on-one sit-down with a local news station on one of the Worthen properties. This way, you don't have to get into direct confrontations with tenants, but you're also explaining your—"

"That's not happening." Dad jabs his fingers on the table. "This is *my* business. Period. I don't have to explain it, and I don't have to apologize. If they want a comfortable place to live, they've got to pay. I have the right to price my rental units as I wish. Just like Apple's got the right to sell a fifteen-hundred-dollar phone, or Bugatti's got the right to sell a four-million-dollar car. Why don't any of *them* have to apologize for their prices? I'll tell you why. They're not black. If a black person's got it, we're expected to give it away."

Dad's entire body stiffens while he preaches. Caught up in his feelings, he keeps flowing.

"And that damn councilman downtown is hyping this up, using it as an excuse to hold up my licenses. He's trying to stop me from breaking ground and making *history*. These news stations are only instigating a fight. I don't trust them."

Now I address Dad's team. "Would you all please excuse us for a moment so we can talk with Worthen's lawyers?"

Surprising me, Reed leans on me before getting up and squeezes my leg. "It's good to have you here, bringing calm to the situation. He needs your personable touch."

Her chest pushes on me, and instant as fuck, I shift to the table. "Appreciate how you came to help Dad out."

It's not lost on me why he called her.

Once everybody is gone, I turn to one of the outside counsel for Worthen. Clearly, this must be the truth-telling part Cyn was talking about. Dad's employees want to keep their paychecks and are too scared to stand up and tell him what to do.

"Dad, what's really going on here? Why are those people outside screaming for legal action against Worthen?"

"They were evicted, and they're mad," Dad huffs. "We need to clear out this riffraff before the Angels Rise groundbreaking in a couple of months. We're lining up a public relations blitz, and you need to lead it."

The days are over when he could distract me by giving me something "special" to do.

"Charles, what are you and him not saying? Why is Worthen open to a potential criminal investigation?" I ask my brother.

He throws up his hands. "Dad's right. What can we do? Worthen put those people out, so they're pissed. Now with this LaShauna mess, they've got a controversy they can use to pile on."

Worthen's lead outside attorney, Sly, stacks the papers in front of him. I'm guessing he's got the actual answer.

"This LaShauna Posey woman who shot the cop...her neighbors are divided. Some of them say she was a menace and they were glad police stayed at Paradise. But other neighbors support her. They complain that sometimes cops go to Paradise even before the eviction process is complete. Neighbors say they're being intimidated—"

"Not intimidated," Dad interrupts. "Their activities are watched closely so they're not destroying the property, and some of those tenants are on probation or parole and subject to unannounced home checks from their parole officers."

I motion for Sly to continue.

"LaShauna Posey's neighbors say the police pressure them to leave the premises without time to exercise their full tenants' rights. It's been happening more often this past year, and it blew up with LaShauna the night Officer Brighton went to her apartment."

Piecing this together in my head, and rubbing it through the knots in my neck, I go to the window.

Protesters scream at me from the street as I push out my next question. "What about LaShauna's eviction? Was it lawful or not, Sly?"

Dad scoffs behind me. "What the hell kind of question is that? Easton Jermaine Gatdamn Worthen, you think I'm some criminal? That I got to be where I am—and got you where the hell you are—by breaking laws?"

What gets said in these next few moments is critical.

My law firm represents some of Worthen Properties' interests. Worthen Properties is a separate legal entity from Carol Worthen, the man. I am not Dad's lawyer in his *individual* capacity.

So what he says to me, or admits to me, may not be privileged. Therefore, it can be admissible in any court.

Not only that, but since I am a board member of Worthen Properties (even though I don't come around very often and cast my votes by proxy), my fiduciary duty is to protect the company, not Dad.

So if the *company* ever chooses to sue the *man* for committing an act that is not in the best interests of the company, I could be called to testify against Dad in court.

My response is careful and cautious, so as not to solicit a reaction from him that could trip him up. "No, Dad. I don't think you break laws. But I'm not asking you. I'm asking the attorney for Worthen Properties. Sly, what's the real story?"

Dad may not break laws, but he does find creative ways to tiptoe around them.

Sly squirms, and his worry lines jump rope on his face. "The eviction wasn't complete yet. She still had the right to respond."

Charles and I exchange nervous vibes.

"But it's strange, East." Sly continues reviewing his investigator's notes. "Police have been going to LaShauna's spot for a while now. For the past couple of years at least."

Charles moves forward. "You mean, they go to LaShauna's more than any of the other units?"

Sly nods. "Yeah. Those cops have been getting free rein around Paradise Gardens, and the neighbors say it was harassment."

"Bullshit," Dad snaps. "Police show up and do their jobs when *tenants* break laws."

I withhold my next question out of fear. If Dad bribed an officer high up in the police department—to go to Worthen complexes and push people out so Dad can build luxury high-rises—I don't want to know.

"But, Dad, the tenants will start giving news interviews, and they will spill what they know, in every direction. But the D.A. hasn't given you anything yet. For now, your attention should be on a niceness offensive. Not on attacking people."

Dad pushes his entire body in my direction. "I know that. That's what I'm asking *you* to do."

Staring down at the street, and all the people ready to devour us, I scrub my hand down my face. "I have a firm to run, and a NAABA presidential campaign this summer, in case you forgot."

"Run it all together," Dad says, his eyes lighting up. "You and Reed. The future of the Worthen brand, since your brother's stingy ass won't settle down and give me grandkids. She was showing me some of your old Harvard pictures the other day. You and her are the perfect power couple, and she looks damn good at your side."

I hold up my hand to stop him. "Reed and I are not together, nor will—"

"And that was one of the biggest mistakes you ever made. That, and going to law school when you should have gone to b-school like me and your brother. But you can still fix one of them. You leaving somebody as smart and charismatic as Reed, for the likes of that uppity Haughton girl, I'll never understand it."

Enough of this shit. "Dad, did you know the real reason I'm—"

Resolve this discord first. And let's heal these divides. We've got a baby on the way, and our child needs to know family harmony.

Kori's words, her face, her fingers around my jaws, shut me up.

He throws his back into that point. "The real reason you what?"

The real reason I came here, the truth, hangs on the tip of my tongue, and I'm ready to scream that shit louder than all those people on the street combined.

He continues without waiting for me to answer, "What is it they called her at Howard? 'Country Club Kori'? I hear that's the nickname she had for spending more time on tea parties and brunches and boutiques than on actual school."

Kori hates that slur her enemies call her behind her back. It implies she doesn't work as hard as she does, that she's only successful because of her connections and pedigree.

"Dad, can we just get back on topic."

With that trademark squint, he points out the window. "Then help us get rid of those folks out there, so we can go on and break ground on Angels Rise, and the name Worthen will go down in history. You can make up for all those years you haven't been around here pulling your weight. So are you with us this time?"

This could be bigger than a cop's murder. If Dad went too far this time, it will wind up at the D.A.'s office. I feel fortunate as hell my baby's leaving, so she won't be part of a mess.

And then, she can come help me with this. Kori is the perfect person to spearhead a goodwill campaign in the community.

Being quiet gives us the power.

Damn, Kori's so fucking cold. I'm in the stronger position precisely because I've kept my mouth shut.

Staring at my father, I nod. "Yeah, Dad, I'll roll up my sleeves and help you out. On one condition."

Chapter Ten

GO WARM HER UP

Eight and a Half Years Prior - Easton & Kori's First Trip, Lake Tahoe

"Where you going, cuteness?"

I scream between puffs, running fast as I can. The weekend before Christmas, the twenty-five-degree brittle air on these slopes freezes my lungs every time I inhale it. That I crack up and laugh constantly doesn't help, my every breath speeding up the icicles that form in my chest. But Easton keeps chasing me.

"Boy, stop!"

He flicks more snow in my face, and I dodge. But he's quicker, and my legs are heavy from skiing. I'm snatched into the air and swung around, and can't escape his fingers tickling my thighs until my noodle legs give out.

"You stop," he mutters in my ear and proceeds with tickling my thighs through my ski suit.

"I'm not..." Snort-laughing now, I struggle to breathe from the bitter wind that bites my chest. "I'm not doing anything."

Once he plants me back on the ground, before I'm out of his grasp, Easton wraps his arms around me, wraps his gaze around mine, and pulls me to him. His mouth disappears with him moistening his lips, and that move alone moistens my womanhood that squirts in my panties. Easton's eyes are shots of hot espresso, lustful and deliciously liquid brown, as they heat up the blood between the slopes of my breasts.

Despite how he always slow-cooks my erogenous zones with just one glance, his gaze hits me in a different way this time. More than lust, today his energy is possessive, humble, decisive and—dare I think it— committed.

"I love you, Korienne, baby."

Right here on these slopes, I melt.

Since the moot court competition a couple of months ago, we've spent most of our fall weekends together, studying, hitting up new movies during study breaks, and swapping law review articles to look over each other's work. The weekends we couldn't connect, we had family or siblings visiting, homecoming shenanigans with friends, or hard dead- lines that took priority.

He calls himself trying to help me cook gumbo for this chilly Northern California autumn, and I'll let him keep thinking he's help- ful. The real hot stew for me is his fine-ass body, goofy jokes, tender sincerity of his affection, and how he's taken his time with me.

Now his fingers tip up my chin, and his other hand grips the bowl of my ass like he's claiming me. In a deep kiss, my head tips back for him to have full access, and he expresses that sentiment with his tongue swishing around mine. Clasping his shoulders over his ski suit, wishing I could grab something else, I return his intensity.

Bystanders hoot and clap, egging us on.

With one last thrust into my mouth, East slows up and sucks, nibbles my lips... intimate and intentional, just as he has courted me these last few months. Which I've appreciated because I was certain he would try and play me. But, no.

"I love you, too, Easton."

"I know." With him laughing, the pearly whites of his teeth match the glistening hills around us. That cockiness is already coming back. "You ready for me to go warm you up?"

"Yeeeah!" a random white dude standing close by yells out, to which other bystanders crack up and start hooting again. "Go warm her up!"

He said that a little too loud. So embarrassing.

Of course, East eats up the attention, biting his bottom lip, his gaze skiing over me as he leads me toward the ski lift.

The way Easton stares at me...

I never want another man's attention on me again.

"You want to eat here at the lodge or back at the cabin?" he asks.

"Back at the cabin. I just want to relax."

We still haven't done the nasty. From falling asleep on the couch, on the floor, sharing a bed, it's just been chill vibes, snuggling, kissing, and groping. A couple of times, he ate me out for the most glorious orgasms of my life. And then, I was more than a little disappointed when he didn't take it further.

I want to do this right, cuteness. Let's give it more time.

Damn. How much more time are we giving it?

There's been no pressure or awkwardness.

I've been checking for how he acts with his cell phone, and when it vibrates, he answers in front of me. None of that hiding his phone crap or turning it off. He's open about his previous links and the last time he messed with them, and shows me the last time he texted, which was over the summer.

Including this Reed chick, his ex as of a few months ago. She still attempts to reach him on occasion, and her calls are "missed" with no responses to her texts. Though it's obvious from his contacts that he had other links while he was with her, apparently, she was hoping he'd make her the one. But since this summer, let East tell it, and he's been "cleaning house" to see what happens with us.

Now, we spend the entire ski lift ride back down the mountain, through the snow-covered forest, with our lips locked. Back at our rented house situated on the crystal-like Lake Tahoe, we start up the fireplace, and I order up room service. With my fingers so numb and cold they might fall off, it's hard to strip down with these little zippers, buttons, and snaps. I struggle to bend over and grab the laces but I'm too frozen.

"Girl, come here," he says and takes over. Undoing my boots and then his, he shoves them off and reaches for me.

Before unzipping me, he lays a kiss on my forehead, another on my nose, and we're already back to tonguing. My fingers might be too cold to grip his zipper, but not to slide off his sweater.

"Cold-ass fingers."

"But you're warm, so I'm using you to heat them up. You said I co—"

My feet fly from under me when he swoops me up. "Not what I was talking about, halo."

"What did you just call me?" I ask between kisses.

"What I nicknamed you in my phone—my halo, this little light of mine. It comes out of your head, glows from your heart, and shines in those pretty teeth I always want to lick."

Still carrying me, he slides his tongue back and forth across my teeth, and I can't help but laugh, even as I kiss him back.

At the Jacuzzi, he sets me down and turns it on, and while he adjusts the water temperature, I find the strength in my fingers to unzip his suit. Getting it off, he helps me and steps out of it. With him standing erect over me, black and statuesque, I'm already a little intimidated at the forest waiting under his briefs.

Once I ease them down, damn. My heart skips a couple of snow hills.

I've seen his dick print through sweats, have felt it when we were making out, but now I'm staring at enough wood to compete with all the trees we just left in the Sierra Nevada Mountains.

A soft chuckle escapes, and his muscular abs ripple. "Don't worry, baby, I promise not to hurt you while I'm training you."

"Who says I need training?"

"Your scary-ass eyes that almost fell out of your head." He talks shit, but his gaze is gentle as he dusts my lips, ever so barely, and reaches around me to unclasp my bra. And he slides down my panties that I step out of, with him kissing my flesh along the way. Behind my knees, between my thighs, he sucks and bites. Up to my navel, each nipple, and the flesh over my collarbone, until we're back to touching and caressing.

But the thought that's been prevalent in my head, my only reservation about him, now pushes me to speak.

"East," I say before swallowing. "What about Reed? Does she still think you and her will be together?" This is probably a stupid time.

He'll get irritated, as most guys would.

Yes, I'm that chick, the overthinker. Why didn't I ask already? A couple of weeks ago, when I made him show me his STD results?

East takes my chin in his, peers straight into my eyes, and answers, "I addressed Reed over Thanksgiving, before you and I came on this trip, so she could understand, in no uncertain terms, that I'm with somebody else." After he blesses my lips, he adds, "If that somebody will have me."

Giddy, I hope I'm not cheesing too hard. "Are you asking me to be your girl?"

The usual cockiness creeps into him. "No, I'm telling you, you're my girl."

"Oh, really now? You've got it like that?"

"Yeah, I do. Where am I now, compared to six months ago? Patience is a virtue."

Talk about the jets in my pussy oozing at full stream, down my leg. Easton slips his fingers in it, feels my womanhood waiting for him, and squats to lick the trail of my cream that crawled down my leg.

"Now that you're ready," he whispers, "how do you want me?"

Surprising him—hell, surprising myself—I push him into the steaming water and step over him. His eyes light up, a trance seeming to overtake him while he stares up at me.

"I haven't ever seen anything so gorgeous as my halo naked."

The lower I slide into the water, the more my anticipation drives me nuts. I'm still nervous and trying not to show it. He must sense my uneven breaths, though, because he brushes my lips again and positions his manhood at the heart of me.

Fire crackles and dances a few paces away, and Christmas passersby playing and laughing outside, Easton and I start our own fire —his wood to my hearth.

Kissing, we both pause and breathe in.

Long, thick, all man, Easton fills me up.

"Haaa..."

"Breathe, baby," he murmurs between kisses, his mouth dragging my cheek. "Breathe."

Though it hurts, I start to ride, and he holds me tight to him, clasps my hips, and moves with me. The pressure of his fingers squeezing my flesh, his eyes heavy and drunk with sex, and his mouth hanging open, all stoke the fire in my nerves as I get comfortable and bounce higher. Come down harder and ski on his mountain.

"Grrr..." My head falls back as his wood feeds my every fantasy, all over me, little fires everywhere. Titties flopping up and down on his face, buried between them, we ascend higher than the pine trees outside.

Pleasure overpowers the pain, and I twirl my hips for my G-spot. Jumping up and crashing down, I open my eyes, and East is studying me, his eyes glazed like he's hypnotized.

Our rhythm synchronized, Easton redefines me from his dick. His lips curled, strong arms holding me, he guides me, and I bury him as deep in my forest, in my secrets, in my life, as I can get him.

"Your pussy getting hotter."

His tree crests the sky of my pussy where I feel the Aurora spread across me.

The way he clings to my ass and seems about to cry, he must feel it, too. Fire in my pussy burns his wood, deeper, harder. Gasping for air, sailing over the trees, we breathe together and form our union.

Magical and otherworldly, out of control and no longer conscious, our joint explosion is so much more heavenly, more intense than the Northern Lights.

"Mm..." Hot and scorching, I'm back at Lake Tahoe, sailing the skies. I moan out my ecstasy, with East's manhood filling me up. My legs still twinging, we grab and grope each other on our way down from our mountaintop.

Eight and a half years later, in the dark, his dick still in me, my legs wide open and strapped around all seventy-three inches, two hundred and thirty-one pounds of him, we breathe through our sexual avalanche.

"You piss me off," he murmurs in my hair.

I check my watch. Eleven twenty-two.

"You were miserable. And I didn't feel good leaving out Dad either. I notice you didn't show up here hours ago. So you managed to survive more than five minutes?"

He rolls his eyes. I suck his mouth.

"So I was right," I declare.

I knew he was in my home before I heard him. Before the front door to my place opened, my eyes cracked open. My mind and soul can detect his aura approaching, and our synergy is powerful enough to awaken me from sleep.

His thumb at the base of my throat, still clamping my neck, he revels in me, even on the same day I didn't give him all he's waited for.

"You wanted me to babysit him, so I did. All through dinner and drinks with him and his consultants. But your ass is on punishment, Kor. Better be glad you're carrying my baby." He finally pulls out of me and leans down next to my navel. "Your mama is a trip. It's a good thing she got sweet pussy."

Laughing, I slap his shoulder. "Don't be talking to my child like that."

"Girl, my son needs to understand his priorities on being a man."

"And what if it's a girl?"

"She won't have shit to worry about since she'll wear a chastity belt, and only I'll have the key."

I cock my head to the side and check him out. "But *you* can have sex with somebody's daughter? Make that make sense."

He lifts me off the balcony and carries me to my bathtub. "It's not my fault your daddy forgot to lock that up." With a side grin and a wink, he adds, "And this snake slid in."

"Goofy-ass man. So you going to update me or not? What's the deal?" He's got me on edge, making me wait for how things went with his father today. "Did you tell him? Not tell him? What are we doing?"

"I got you a new job."

At the sound of this, I crack up laughing. "A what?"

He shakes off his slacks and clothes that he never removed. He simply came in the door, his suit still on, and lifted me from bed by my ass. Carrying me out to my balcony, I barely got his zipper down before he was plunging into me.

I wonder if he saw somebody while out who had him stiff as concrete.

He steps in with me. "You heard me. A job."

"Do go on planning my life."

"That's the price you pay for standing me up again. But first, let's get this straight. In two days, you're giving the D.A. that letter? You're quitting, and you really aren't shitting me about your lifestyle game. Right?"

Something about his tone is...off.

Or maybe it's just in my head.

"Of course. I said I would, and I'm serious. She'll get the letter, and for the next two weeks, you and I will plan our move and how we'll get our families together. So come on and spit it out. Stop being so damn cryptic. Was I right or was I spectacular?"

Begrudging as hell, he grins. "You had a little something going. So yeah, Dad wants me to head a big PR rollout, which I don't know how with a firm to run, and the NAABA presidency. But I like his idea of me doing all of it together—press conferences, news interviews, journal pieces as a spokesperson for Worthen while also running for president."

"It also drums up business for your firm, a win all around," I add and throw him some of my swagger. "So I was right. Keeping your mouth shut got you further than busting his balls. What did you tell him?"

"I would only do it on the condition that I choose whoever I want as a partner."

My jaw falls, and I go to shake his chin. "Look at my man being all shrewd!"

Flinging my sudsy arms around his neck, more kisses follow.

East continues, "While I'm campaigning, if you're working with me, the press will help you build your lifestyle channel and your business. You and me, we'll integrate our hustles."

That's somewhat bittersweet—promoting his father's business that I'm not too fond of.

He catches my vibe.

"Look, Kor, this was your idea. Harmony among all of us before the baby comes, right? This here is our shot. You told me to go make it happen, and I did." My man's eyes divert, though, and part of him is distracted. "There are a couple of other things, though."

In the middle of loving on him, I freeze. "Wow, your energy just shifted left a little...things like what?"

His laugh is small and dry, not life-sized as it normally is. "Dad thinks you are conspiring with the D.A. to take him down or some shit." East eyes me, as if...

Is he checking me out for whether I would do that?

"Easton, D.A. Gray came to me with that, and I told you. Even though I shouldn't have because it's confidential and that's privileged information. Are you seriously wondering if—"

"Hell, nah. No. I'm just..."

I glare at him now and slide away in the water. "You're just what?"

"You and your boss were over there laughing and talking for a good minute at the luncheon. Then, you say you had the letter but you didn't give it to her. Why not, if you're so ready to go?"

"So you think I'm staying at the county so I can go after your father? You actually have it in your head that I would do that to you?" I start washing as fast as I can so I can get out. "East, who's the person that's trying to help you get along better with your dad in the first place?"

"Kor, calm down. Ko...*Kor.*" He stops me from practically scrubbing my skin off with the loofah, continuing, "Baby, I'm only wondering what the hell is going on. You and her were discussing my *daddy*, however I feel about him. And ethically, I know I'm not supposed to ask what you know, but to hell with that. Tell me you wouldn't have questions if the judge's ass was on the hook," he adds, referencing my father. "Come on, don't be giving me attitude the same day you left me at the damn altar. *Again.*"

He might have a point. Might.

"D.A. Gray didn't go into detail, only saying Worthen could have involvement. And that stays right here between us. Now what else, Easton? You said there were two things."

Another awkward moment passes in the time he's silent. Damn, maybe me sending him to his dad and trying a bid for unity was dumb.

"Dad wants me to do the campaign with Reed."

I just got hit with a hammer. *"Reed?"*

That explains why he came in here needing a sexual release.

Once he lays it out, I conclude I definitely boarded the dummy train. I should have followed my first mind and married East in secret while I had the chance, and there wouldn't have been a damn thing Carol Worthen could do about it. But no, I wanted my man to be "happy" with his father's presence and approval, and not feeling torn.

"So you saw her over the weekend and you didn't mention it?"

"I didn't care since I was busy planning a getaway for what should have been our little bitty honeymoon. Steve and the fellas took me out, and I brought food to you and your friends. All of that took up space in my head. That, and marrying my lady who carries my seed. The same lady I *just* asked to do this campaign with me." East flicks water at me. "She is also the same person I left Reed for— twice. Or did you forget all that?"

Every bit as handsome as that day in the Jackson law firm library, he faces me with those angular jaws, sexy mouth, surrounded by a finely trimmed goatee, and immaculate skin the color of sherry-matured whisky.

I flick water droplets back on him, and we settle it in a mini-water fight.

"All right, fine." Still processing this, I wind my fingers around my temples. "So not only do I have your dad to look forward to, but also your ex checking for where she can fit in. And, Easton, you know I don't like how your father operates. He keeps his complexes nicely, but he wants to evict out tenants and bring in high earners? Not cool. And you want to use me to promote inequality to the LA community that my family helped build."

Easton grew up in LA, but his mama didn't push him out in this city. However, my family has been here for generations, dating back to the late nineteen-twenties when my great-grandparents moved to Central Avenue from South Carolina to start over. So Easton's connection to the roots and struggle and rise of Black Los Angeles isn't as deep as mine, no matter how much he swears he cares.

"Change it then. Go into Worthen and hold Dad accountable. Be the bridge between him and LA. Let the community see you holding his feet to the fire. It builds trust, and that's what Worthen needs. Shit, that's the only way *I'll* feel right about it. What was it you said?

Silence makes us more powerful. You and I are now in the power position. He has no idea why I'm really helping him. He'll be looking so crazy when you're not even at the D.A.'s office anymore."

Stress pains twinge in my chest as my reservations still stir in me. I'm not trying to get lost in Worthen's interests. I'm certainly not leaving one job just so I can go to another and get sucked up in other people's priorities to the detriment of my own.

That's always been my biggest fear—losing my identity and potential in a marriage.

"Halo," East murmurs over the water and holds my face. He knows me so well at this point, he must sense my antenna going up. "If we don't do this, our last three years of secrecy and sneak moves are for nothing. Now this was your idea."

"Yes, but I didn't mean I'd work for him! He will *not* be my boss. I don't have anything to prove to—"

East shuts me up when he lunges at me and bites my lip. His head against mine, our heads sway together a moment. Even once he lets me have my lip back, our noses keep snuggling.

"Halo, this is you and me, and we're partners. You're a CEO, a fucking boss. And the queen of my life. You're using Dad's platform to build *your* empire. While you do it, he will come to see in you what I *know*. Okay?"

Sincere, determined, his eyes don't waver.

"Okay."

Now his gaze drops between us, as if his next words are a more complex equation he must calculate before he speaks them. "But whatever happens among all of us, no matter what goes down, don't leave me hanging again. You see I'm here for you. I support you. But don't burn me anymore, Korienne."

Behind his eyes, and his tensed-up mouth, East seems to harbor his own hesitation and questions. Into my naked eye, he dives for my truth.

"East, we're doing this. We're partners."

Next to my bare breast, he holds up his pinky finger.

"You won't pull my ring off your finger again."

Despite us doing this several times over the years, I laugh at the memory of us on our first date.

But he's not laughing.

I hurt him today.

Linking my pinky around his, I answer, "Baby, today was the last time. I want to be your wife. I'm *going* to be your wife. And nothing will change or interfere with that. I swear it."

Chapter Eleven

NO LONGER MY PROBLEM

KORIENNE - SONG: HATE ON ME BY JILL SCOTT

Between watching news coverage on the LaShauna Posey murder and interviews of her neighbors, I've started packing up my condo.

One of the tenants of Paradise Gardens tells a reporter, "They roughed up my boyfriend and then arrested him for no reason."

He probably had warrants you didn't know about, girl. I talk to the TV as I tag my furniture and decide what I'll sell or give away, and what I'm taking in the move to Easton's house.

Last night, in Easton's tone stood a certain finality, carved in stone, as if it's time for me to decide whether I will be chiseled onto the Mount Rushmore of us forever.

Now the first set of boxes line my wall for transition to his place. Since he doesn't want me carrying them in my pregnant state—he's already started acting precious—he's hired movers to come twice a week. We're doing this piecemeal while also preparing how to roll it out to our fathers. I meant it when I told East this is happening.

On the television, another tenant complains. "Cops come here, even when nobody calls them, just to mess with people. It's like they live here more than we do. That's not right."

You're right, sir, it's not. The pain on that tenant's face comes through the screen to touch me.

More exasperation pours from LaShauna's neighbors. "Even though he's black, I don't think Carol Worthen like black people. So he can let us get together and buy this complex and we'll run it ourselves. I like living here in my community so I'm not going anywhere, but we don't want him as our landlord."

Whichever deputy D.A. gets that case strapped onto their backs will have a hell of a load to carry—between managing the general anger of the black community, doing their job as a prosecutor, and assuaging the police whose investigations can make or break a case.

But I click off the television. The prosecution part won't be my problem since I'm handing the D.A. my letter tomorrow. The very thought of it sends a shudder over me, likely from fear and excitement.

For now, I rush out to oversee one of my final AAWPA meetings. Tonight is the election. My phone's been vibrating all day with text messages from board members and past presidents trying to figure out who I'll support—Mackenzie or Vashti. But I haven't disclosed my position to anyone, not even Mac. On my way out of my condo, I'm hit with a text from Judge Sharpe.

Judge Sharpe: *Vashti is what the organization needs now. With the social troubles across the city, AAWPA needs to be more connected to the people. All the presidents should present a united front at the meeting tonight. Next year will be a doctor or engineer, and then, Mac can have her turn in two or three years.*

Me: *Thanks for the perspective. Can't wait to see you tonight.*

Once I enter Harold & Belle's, one of LA's oldest and most highly respected black-owned restaurants, the place brims with activity. AAWPA's board members hobnob, lining up votes for the position they want, and text their supporters who haven't arrived yet.

"Madam President!" someone calls.

"Outgoing," I joke.

"You're not rid of us yet, woman." Teneil collects money from officers and counts it up for her treasurer's report. "Besides, fearless leader, what plans do you have once you're done with AAWPA? I know you won't be at home on Netflix. You running for public office? Going for a statewide position? How will you level up?"

"Mmm." I make a pretense of wavering. "I'm still figuring it out."

Teneil is a great board member, but she's not in my inner circle with Mac and Shallon.

All of a sudden, her eyelids snap up. "Oh, my God! What is that?" she asks, staring at my finger.

I look down. I've been so busy today I actually forgot I was wearing it.

"Girl, you've got a man? A *fiancé*? Since when?"

With a grin, giddy and bubbly as a woman who won the lottery, I try to play it down. "I'm not ready to share that yet."

"Not ready to share? But you came up in here blinding everybody!" somebody else adds.

Of course, there's a pile-on.

"Look at how Madam President is all glowing! Oooweee, I bet that ring finger isn't the only spot that's all lit up either!"

"Girl, let me rub it for good luck, so I'll find somebody who'll have me glowing like that!"

One member after another stargazes at my ring and rubs my hand for some better fortunes in these streets in the wait for their own standup man.

I want to wait a few weeks before disclosing mine is East. We'll reveal it over summer at the groundbreaking of Angels Rise.

This way, I can settle into his home and navigate our families, schedules, and personal lives. On our first round together, there was so much drama from other women, from my law school classmates, we spent too much energy battling schemes and rumors. It shook the foundations of him and me.

Now, we're all a few years older, and I shouldn't have to expect shenanigans—other women openly sharing what they did with him, catching him off guard at events to leave lipstick on his shirt, speaking to him and attempting to ignore me until he corrected them. In my mid-twenties, to experience menacing behavior from some folks I'd known my whole life, thinking a lot of them were my friends, I was naive. Mentally, I wasn't ready for many women to perform that full one-eighty after seeing another woman with something they don't have.

For now, people can know I'm engaged, but not to whom just yet.

"Hey, Madam President, glad to see you two are still pushing forward." Subtly, Mac peers at my ring.

I murmur for her ears only, "We had a little hiccup, but it's happening."

"Of course it is. I'm not looking at the same Kori as when we were in law school, and you and him first started. You're ready."

"Thanks, sis," I tell her inside a tight hug.

"So in other news, have you made up your mind yet?" Mac asks me, steering the conversation back to AAWPA.

"Yes, but I'm not sharing."

She eyes me for clues, but I've always preferred to hold my cards close to the vest and disclose nothing before I absolutely have to. Maybe it's because I learned in high school and college that the most well-intentioned people can still screw up perfectly laid plans.

I give a nod to Shallon, who stands a few paces away.

"All right, ladies," Shallon begins as the parliamentarian. "Let's hop into some seats, and we'll call this meeting to order."

On my watch, AAWPA has exploded in popularity. We've gone from old-school potlucks in living rooms to the most lit skyscrapers and rooftops in LA. Every political candidate in the city who wants validation in the professional black community comes through us. These days we throw the best parties, at the slickest locations, with the hottest speakers and honorees. It's understandable how Vashti and defense counsel want a stab at leading it.

But Mackenzie works as Associate General Counsel at Chase Bank. Their sponsorship check this past year at my installation was a hundred thousand dollars, and Mac's only the vice-president. What will that bank contribute to our organization if Mac is president?

Elections can get tense and testy. The "winner" is kind of "Queen of the World," invited to the most exclusive professional soirees in LA, invite-only dinners and galas, hailed on local magazines and websites, not to mention speaking engagements, TV interviews, and discussion panels. Though it's local, the presidency is a huge platform. Needless to say, candidates throw their backs into the campaign.

Once we wrap up regular business, speeches for elections begin.

Vashti goes first. "AAWPA has entered it's giving season." Her voice pulls me from my thoughts in the start of the election speeches. She looks incredibly nice tonight.

Teneil: *Somebody must have gotten her together and told her to find a decent suit.*

Vash continues, "This is a moment for us to care. Black LA is hurting right now—rising rents, homelessness, inflation, and the cost of food, crime is back up. Beefing up our bag is good, but if all we do is party, we become disconnected from the community on whose shoulders we stand. You need a president who leads, not just at fine hotels and country clubs, but also to be a light in our darkest, most forgotten places. It's time for us to get back to basics, of where we came from, back to the hearts and minds of those looking to us for help and hope. The person who can do that most authentically, and with substance, not just platitudes, is me."

I'm slightly taken aback by "leads not just at fine hotels and *country clubs*." It's hard not to take that as a missile fired squarely at me.

Mackenzie clears her throat and stands, just as she did for moot court at Berkeley, and puts her back into it, her poof of auburn, naturally curly hair swinging around in a ponytail and emphasizing her points.

"We are the African American Women *Professionals* Association. A place for professionals to gather and fellowship. We are not a justice organization; however, we still serve the community. We just distributed over three million dollars in scholarships several days ago. After our long journey to reach our level of success, we want to be among like minds. If people want to save the world and every broken soul in it, there are organizations for that. Equal Justice Works, The Innocence Project, NAACP National Defense Fund, and the Urban League, to name a few."

Even though she was a damn good debater, one of the best, I've never seen Mac this impassioned about anything. Shallon and I silently swap our amazement.

Mac continues, "As for *this* association of professional women, we have the biggest event of this year coming up—the National African American Bar Association conference—here in this city. Lawyers from all over the country will convene in LA, and AAWPA needs to shine like never before. One of LA's own is running for president—Easton Worthen. AAWPA needs to have the finances and organization to back Mr. Worthen up. Now I respect that Ms. Burns has been here longer than me, but the truth is I'm what you need for our goals in *this* particular year. That's what little girls from the 'hood—like myself, who moved here from Missouri—are dreaming of when they think of us. They work hard so one day they can shine right alongside us. And nothing less than that sparkling example is what I will provide."

In the supporting debate, the past presidents make compelling points, and it appears a few of them have broken ranks from Vashti to Mackenzie. Now they all look to me. As do my board members.

"This is hard." I stand to address everyone. "I respect all that Vash has said and the time she's served. I attended undergrad with Vash and law school with Mac, so I truly have been torn. But I'm endorsing Mackenzie."

Gasps and murmurs sweep through the restaurant.

"Mac had no idea of my decision and is just now learning it with the rest of you. And this is about more than her being my personal friend. AAWPA *does* perform in the community. We *do* give back. And I, too, was born and raised in LA, just like Vashti, and care very much what happens here. But the commitment of the president is to AAWPA, a professional organization. After three years of a pandemic that has curbed our activities, the president's priority is to strengthen our position financially and socially. Or we won't have the resources to assist in the community. In that regard, Mackenzie's position at Chase promises to draw more big sponsors and increase our corporate exposure nationwide. We'll spend a lot of money to make a showing at the NAABA conference this summer, and we need to build up our reserves to afford that."

The vote is taken.

In the fall, Mackenzie will be installed as president-elect, and next year, as president.

Vash is selected to replace Mac as vice-president.

"Vash," I say to her after the meeting, while Mac is bubbling over with the women who supported her. "I stayed out of it as long as I could so I wouldn't put my finger on the scales. But you didn't have to give resentful energy by saying I lead from fine hotels. It was petty and unnecessary."

"It's the truth." There is no conciliatory anything on her face. "Why else do you think they call you Country Club Kori?"

My irritation throbs in the nerve along my neck. "Watch it."

"Or you'll do what?" Vash's side-eye is a challenge. "Call your daddy? Huh, Miss Malibu I Wanna Be White Barbie? It was my turn. You only threw your weight behind her because of favoritism. To hell with all your lies about this group's best interests. You look out for you and your uppity-ass friends. The board and past presidents were going to follow you for your connections."

That's her resentment talking. After we graduated from undergrad at Howard the same year, I headed off to UC-Berkeley for law school. Vash came home to LA and went to Whittier, which was seventy percent black. Unfortunately, it closed down the year after we got our Juris Doctorates. It's clear that she carries a chip.

"Everything straight over here, boo?" Shallon strolls up and asks.

Quickly, I assess how far I want to escalate this.

I'm the president. I don't get to act a fool.

"I'm perfect, Shal. Nothing to see here." My eye is still trained on Vash. "Just losers busy losing."

With Vash's "Fight the Power" bumper stickers on her fifteen-year-old Honda, ornaments she wears on her braids, and those thick-soled go-go boots, I cringe at the thought of her going to meet with the governor or the mayor, or the dogcatcher for that matter, on AAWPA's behalf. But everyone has their part to play.

"Your endorsement isn't worth the tissue your country club friends wipe their asses with."

"And yet you still came to me and asked for it. Which must say something about the value of my country club connections."

"Girl, bye, I don't even know why I bothered. One day, you'll see how the other side lives."

"What's that supposed to mean?" I ask, not that I should care.

"Go back to your house on the Hill and shit on people beneath you. It's what you do best. Your shit *will* come back to you, though." She stomps off to thank those who supported her.

By the Hill, she means the prominent area of South Los Angeles known as "Black Beverly Hills", where I grew up in View Park. She grew up a couple of miles from the bottom of the Hill, on West Adams.

I have no idea how she and Mac will avoid killing each other without me around.

Over the next few months, I'll try to broker some kind of working rapport between them. And I still have duties to carry out. But they are grown women, and these politics are no longer my problem.

For the first time in years, I'm just fine with that. Somebody holds the door open for me, and a tremendous, unexpected wave of relief washes over me as I make my exit. Heavy, wooden beams seem to lift off my back as a big chunk of my life is being returned to me. My time and attention will be my own again, and that weightless freedom as I step into the cool, night air is priceless.

"So you're really not telling us who it is?" Teneil asks me on our way to our cars.

"I'm really not telling." I don't belong to them anymore, and gone are the days when I feel the need to overshare so people will "like" me.

"But you don't ever take anybody to the events with you!" another woman says.

"Chile, when does your busy tail even find the time to be boo'd up?" yet another member wants to know.

"Have a nice night, ladies."

Shallon comes over. "You and the Beast straight?"

"Yeah, we're fine." I wave my left hand. "As you can see."

We exchange a hug and hold it longer than normal.

Placing her mouth right against my ear, she whispers, "All right then, Mrs. Worthen, Mama CEO, Madam Boss, you're outta here," she says in a mock baseball empire voice. "Get to leveling up. Go in there tomorrow and tell the D.A. you've got better things to do."

"Whew-hew-hew." I breathe out a couple of nervous exhales at the thought of all those new responsibilities.

Among them is my chief worry now: Can "Country Club Kori" finally build a business on her own and prove she's more than another nepotism baby?

Chapter Twelve

TRAPPED IN THIS JAR

KORIENNE

"Hey, Kori! Welcome back...whoa, Nelly!" Jason Crowley, my courtroom partner in the mornings, greets me. "Looky here! What in Christ's name is *this*?"

This man's eyeballs almost fall out and hit my hand, but his astonishment doesn't end there.

He continues, "Kori, dayum, you mean Ms. Can't Go Out and Drink Because I'm Working Too Hard had a boyfriend all this time? And you're marrying somebody who can afford that?"

I swallow my earthquake of a comeback.

Two more weeks.

"Hold on just one minute." Jason whips out his cell phone to take a photo of my hand.

Do I hide my hand? I didn't prepare for someone having the gall to take a picture of my ring.

Jason bats his eyes with surprise at how I slide my hand in my pocket.

"Maybe you didn't hear me when I said we should get to work."

By ten in the morning, all of downtown Los Angeles, and some outer reaches of the county, know that Korienne Haughton is not only booed up but engaged.

Judge Sharpe: *I keep hearing about the ring. Glad to see you and him worked it out. LOL, is it fair if I take part in the bet on who he is?*

Teneil: *Girl, I'm still tripping on how you had an entire man on lock this whole time. There will NEVAH be another ninja as serious about her private life as you.*

Larry: *Baby, please tell me this isn't true. You and I were really connecting at the luncheon. I could have sworn I saw a spark still in your eyes.*

Mom: *Judge Sharpe told me you were wearing the ring last night. I'm happy you and him are okay.*

Easton texts me a selfie of him wearing an incredibly deep, proud gleam in his eye.

Easton: *Somebody sent me a pic of the ring and asked me if I know who put it on you. *Side-smile emoji**

By noon, the ring has its own dedicated Instagram page, titled "Who is Kori's Bae?" with the blurry photo Jason managed, and guesses and bets of who my man might be.

The shit will really hit the fan when they find out it's Easton Worthen.

He's getting a kick out of this. Mid-morning, the women are gushing when a bouquet of two dozen roses is delivered to my courtroom, along with the note:

Can't wait to spend eternity with you. ~ Mystery Bae

Me to Easton: *Show-off.*

Easton: *Gotta give the people what they want. *Arrow through heart emoji**

"Where will you and your guy be living?" Jason asks. "In those rich people hills where you and your kind of people live?"

The gavel of my glare comes down on him. "My kind of people?"

"Your family live. I meant your family," he self-corrects after reading my face.

But I'm also irritated at him thinking he has a right to ask about my personal life, as if I owe him an answer.

"You know, Jason, let's focus on finishing the calendar so we can get out of here."

He sticks his chest out proudly. "Oh, I'm wrapping up my calendar now. And got some damn good deals, too. You know that one lady who keeps going in people's houses at night and stealing their food? I just got her for three years."

Puke rolls up my esophagus. "Jason, she's homeless. She has no other way to eat."

"In the eyes of the law, she's a repeat offender. See, that's what's wrong with you, Kori. You prosecute your cases with jelly in that heart, girl."

"She has no choice. She's not doing anybody any harm."

He flicks the stack of files with a pen. "Two priors on her record for assault with a broken metal pipe, and a brick."

"I remember that case. People had been throwing things at her on the street. She was likely scared, humiliated, and defending herself."

Humor crinkles up the laugh lines around his eyes. "She should go to Skid Row with all her other people, and no one will bother her."

"Where she will be unsafe and vulnerable to rape."

He side-sniffs dismissively. "Good thing you weren't here Monday and Tuesday. I was actually productive and moved your cases *and* mine. Defense attorneys weren't running me over either."

My bulldozer revs up. "You settled *my* cases? Who the hell...?"

I meet with D.A. Gray in a couple of hours. First on my request list is that I weigh in on who takes over my cases. A tall ask, but it's precisely because I don't want Jason touching a single one of them.

And then, two weeks.

In the meantime, I've already started recording my YouTube videos as I decorate Easton's—*mine* and Easton's—home, and talk about blending our two households, picking colors and setting our vibe. Over the summer, once we announce our nuptials, my videos will be loaded as the public begins researching me.

One of the public defenders, Jennifer, waddles down to our side of the table. "Okay, so I think I guessed who it is. Larry Johnson. You dated him at Howard, and folks saw you talking to him for a good minute at the scholarship luncheon. Come on, Kori. I'm trying to win this money. It's up to fifty a piece. This ring party is getting wild, girl."

I let out a tiny laugh with Jennifer. "You all are too funny. I guess you'll have to wait and see. It won't be long."

Easton: *What time is your meeting with the D.A. again?*
Me: *One-thirty, right after lunch.*

I type that with trembling fingers.

Easton: *You've got this. I love you and I'm proud AF, halo.*
Me: *Thanks, my love.*

Now I have to keep my phone turned over, so no one sees Easton's name.

I'm counting down the time until my meeting with D.A. Gray—two more precious hours and thirteen minutes to be exact.

Since the letter is sealed in my purse, I've already started checking out of the job mentally. I even skim the internet on my tablet for black-owned interior designers, furniture houses, and fabric shops to include in my videos.

Right before lunch, I wrap up my case calendar for the morning and inform the court clerk I'll be in my office if anything comes up.

Me: *What time will you be home?*
Easton: *Late. But I'll do the best I can. How is E.J.?*
Me: *When he's in there, I'll let u know.*

Easton: *I won't have u talking about my son. Need to ready up for this depo. See u tonight. Love ya.*

Those doors are right in front of me, and I gratefully move toward them. The next time I come back, I will officially be a short-term employee.

"Hey, Kori, wait up," the court clerk calls to me. "You should stick around. There's a new case coming in, a one-seventy-point-six from Department 3A."

A sigh tumbles out of me. It just so happens Jason strolls in.

"What are you doing here? I thought you were finished with your calendar?" I ask him.

"Don't see too many one-seventies around here. If you want, Kori, I can handle it for ya. You can go spend time with your, uh, sugar daddy. Or your husband-to-be."

With no oxygen for him, I put my suit jacket back on. And pick up my pen and notepad.

"Like I just asked, why are you here?"

"You know what? I'm nosey. Let's see what this is."

No sooner than he says it do the double doors bang open.

I can hardly believe my eyes.

A barrage of people enter—first, reporters and their camera crews; second are teary-eyed family members, one side white and the other black; and third are black activists wearing the same color purple t-shirts.

"What in the—? "

"Excuse me."

Within seconds, there's barely walking room with news crews crowding the aisle. They unwind cable lines and set up camera tripods.

Upset, fidgety, and curious, black spectators eye every corner of the courtroom for who's who and what will transpire.

No defendant has been brought up yet. But the transferring D.A. approaches me with the file.

"What's going on?"

"Defense counsel just filed an affidavit of prejudice against Judge Stone down the hall. So it's landing here. Boyle would be perfect for this."

"Perfect as in how?" I ask, opening up the file. "What case is this?"

The elevator doors open.

"Perfect as in he'll convict."

My heart doesn't have enough strings to hold it up once my gaze drops to the Information charging sheet.

"We love you, LaShauna!" someone calls from the gallery.

"Ohhh, Lawd, my baby girl," an older black woman wails from what must be parched earth.

On the other side of the room sits a different kind of family—composed, solemn, tearful. And white. With unspoken pleas for justice, they gaze back at me.

Judge Boyle enters the courtroom and takes the bench. "Calling case BA651328 of People versus LaShauna Posey. For the defense?"

"Your Honor," a private defense attorney begins. "Ms. Posey is requesting a public defender."

"All right then, who will that person be?" the judge asks. "And who will be appearing today for the People?" Judge Boyle eyeballs Jason and me.

Jason licks his lips, eying me as if I don't have the cojones to prosecute a black woman who shot a cop.

East's voice, his face two nights ago, now enter my mind. *Don't burn me anymore, Korienne.*

From the public defender's side of the table, Jennifer answers, "We have somebody who's present for us, Your Honor," Jennifer answers. She peers past me, to the back pews.

Through the same double-door exit where I was just planning my escape, in walks chaos. My jaw slips.

"Good morning, Madam President."

"Vashti. What are you doing here? You're not assigned to Central. You work in Long Beach."

"What's the matter? You look like you just saw the Grim Reaper. I was sent here specially for this case only. I asked for it. I've interviewed my client already, and I'm prepared to go on the record."

"You already interviewed...? You *asked* for this? How did you know this case was coming here?"

Vashti's eyes flare. "You're not the only one with connections. Too bad you don't deal with your own people, or *you* might have known."

Flabbergasted, I try to piece together how Vash knew to come here from Long Beach, and that this woman would need an appointment.

My first bout of nausea hits me. An acute urge to hurl gurgles up suddenly, and I force it back down.

Please, Lord, don't fail me. As coolly and subtly as possible in front of cameras and observers, I lay a hand on the wooden divider to steady myself.

Inside this glass jar now, I am suddenly a bug under the burning gaze of black activists. Not all of them are so hushed.

"She's not a public defender. She's the *prosecutor*," the older woman spits it out as if condemning a criminal.

Another woman's glare cuts me up. "I just know this child ain' gonna send another black woman to prison."

A few paces across the aisle is a journey over a desert land, to the world where police officers sit, stoic and frozen, with fully loaded expectations that I'll pursue justice to the maximum extent the law permits. Seated at the very front of them, a woman and family sit tearful and pain-stricken. I'm flummoxed to realize Officer Brighton's widow is black.

Trapped in this jar, my lungs struggle for air under the tightly sealed lid of my blackness. No matter how high I jump to appease one side or another, that lid is not coming off to free me. I'm suffocating either way.

Vash snickers, seeming to revel in the tension. "So, Country Club Kori, will you be handling this?" She snickers. "Or will you pawn it off to somebody who actually works for a living?"

"We'll now recess for lunch," Judge Boyle says. "I've got to absent myself for a little longer than normal. We'll reconvene at two-thirty."

"Saved by the bell," Vash mutters.

* * *

"I'm not letting her punk me!" My whisper carries too much force for that to be quiet.

Inside one of the attorney rooms, I've snuck away for the lunch hour. The bailiff always closes the courtroom at noon, so all the people have left until two-thirty. Now, in a FaceTime huddle, my life coaches cheer me toward my finish line.

"This is *not* your problem. Do you *hear* me?" Shal asks. "Your meeting with Gloria is in an hour. Stay focused! Turn in your letter and leave that mess to somebody else."

"You *know* what she called me!" I cringe at the words that rain on me the worst moments of my childhood. "Country Club Kori" was started by my cousins. "If I quit now, Vash will think she scared me and that is what she will tell everybody."

"I don't care if she called you Satan!" Shal snaps back. "Leave that damn job and go get your life. The next time that heffa sees you successfully running your own company, with the finest man in Cali on your arm *and* his baby *and* his ring, she'll be calling you 'goals!'"

Mac breathes out a heavy sigh. "I don't know, Kori, this is tough, girl. I feel you on needing to bring the hammer down on Vash's ass one good time on your way out. I wouldn't blame you if you didn't turn in that letter right now."

"Wait," Shallon says. "Didn't this happen at Mr. Worthen's complex, over an eviction notice LaShauna got from Worthen Properties? The owner of Worthen is your future father-in-law now, Kori."

Logically, I connect the ethical dots.

You see I'm here for you. I support you. But don't burn me anymore, Korienne.

Easton.

Shal continues, "Kori, now that you're engaged to East, your interests are personally and financially aligned with Mr. Worthen's. Police were there trying to evict LaShauna from one of your father-in-law's complexes. How will you look like a fair and impartial D.A., when you're so closely aligned with one side? That's a conflict, girl. You *have* to let this go."

"I hate to say I agree, girl," Mac adds. "Maybe this conflict is God finally pushing you out the door."

The air deflates out of me. I would have to disclose *why* I'm declaring a conflict. This isn't the big splashy rollout he and I wanted. "East and I aren't ready to tell."

Shal's reply is swift. "Oh, East *been* ready to scream it. *You're* not ready."

She's right.

Once everybody knows me as Easton's woman again, what happens to *Korienne?*

I'm so ensnared in this back-and-forth war between the life I want and the one I'm stuck with, before I know it, the time arrives to head across the street and meet D.A. Gray before Judge Boyle brings LaShauna's arraignment back into session.

After I hang up with them, I call East three times to give him a heads-up, but he must have taken clients to lunch and doesn't notice his phone ringing. He loves socializing and tends to get caught up when he's in the right crowd.

A few moments later, I brace myself and walk toward D.A. Gray.

"Korienne! Good afternoon. Come on in."

There is no hug today. Rather, a firm handshake. This is not an AAWPA event, but the D.A.'s Office. The surrounding secretaries watch and analyze exactly how much warmth I receive, so they can report it back to the other office heads.

"Come on in. So I hear the Posey murder came to your courtroom this morning."

Her chin high and authoritative, she serves up a stare that tells me she knows something I don't.

Kori, with your reputation, training, and your background, I'd like you to be the one to prosecute it. This will make you a star. Her words at the scholarship luncheon a few days ago return to my mind.

She, or somebody she knows, arranged for that case to land in my court.

Not that she would admit it. The matter of where a one-seventy-point-six affidavit of prejudice should go should be a lottery, totally random. If there was backdoor wheeling and dealing, that would be unethical.

"That's what I wanted to talk with you about, Ms. Gray."

Even-keeled, impenetrable, she nods. "I'm sure all this attention will be a lot in the beginning. It'll come at you fast, so be ready." Her eyes crinkle as she smiles with pride. "But there is no better person to handle it with so much grace and wisdom as you."

We both sit, her reclined casually and me perched on the edge. With the letter.

"Actually, Ms. Gray, I wanted to give you this."

She takes it.

There. I did it. It's done.

"My two weeks' notice."

Confusion creases her brow lines. "I don't understand, Korienne. You didn't give any inclinations of quitting when I saw you at the luncheon."

I hold up my hand. "I'm engaged."

Seemingly stunned, she blinks a few times. "Yes, I think I heard about this 'mystery bae' of yours. Congratulations. It is beautiful, but what does that have to do with you leaving?"

"It's Easton Worthen, D.A. Gray. He's my fiancé. And I'm expecting. That's confidential. Our plans were already in the works before today."

Her hands clasp together in her puzzlement. "Well, you are just full of surprises, aren't you? It was my understanding you dated him a long time ago, but nothing recent."

"He and I kept it under wraps for a while."

"Smart. In this mean-spirited social media age we live in, I can't say I blame you." Whatever thoughts she has send her head to the side. "If you don't do this, you are aware of what people will say, right? That you got scared and ran."

Those words out loud, in a tone so unflinching, stab me in my chest and twist.

"Yes, I know."

"And you would truly be happy with that stain on your reputation once you're gone?" She shakes her head. "After you've worked so hard for people's respect. That's not the Korienne I've known over the years."

Don't burn me anymore, Korienne.

That's East's father, and I made a promise.

"What's important is what *I* know—I'm ready to move on."

She eyes me as if she's not sure she believes me.

"There is also the issue of the conflict of interest with it happening around an eviction from my father-in-law's property. So even if I were staying, I'd have to recuse myself anyway."

Scratching her chin, she continues assessing this in her head. "*Future* father-in-law. But even if he were already, I'm not sure that's an actual conflict. Although I understand how it will look to the public. I do wish you and Easton well."

My curiosity gets the best of me.

"I'm only a seven-year DDA. You really would have let me handle this case? Instead of assigning such a high-profile matter to a twenty-year veteran?"

Gloria shrugs. "Why wouldn't I? You've earned it. In fact, Korienne, the reason I'm so disappointed is I can't think of a more suitable *woman* to try Ms. Posey's case. Sure, you'll catch flack about being a black woman prosecuting another one. But I believe this may be necessary, for so many reasons. You are proof that an educated black woman *can* pursue justice against whomever, and will hold the accused accountable, regardless of race. You can withstand the public pressure."

She gets up and moves around to the front of her desk, sits on it, arms crossing her chest.

"The world ought to see what I see all the time—people of color in this office working their asses off, who sacrifice and don't get the glory. The public can name basketball players and rap stars who don't give a damn about them, but they can't name the prosecutors keeping them safe."

Easton stares at me from the other side of my mind, his pinky finger up as he humiliates himself so I'd trust him.

"D.A. Gray, I wholeheartedly agree, but there are plenty of qualified women here."

"And only one you. No rank-and-file deputy would command all the attention you would. You're the president of one of the largest black groups in LA. Tuh. And now engaged to one of its most eligible bachelors. Highly respected. Good family and pedigree. It is *precisely* who you are that showcases the brilliance of this office."

"Or to humiliate myself."

Her focus on me tightens. "Since when have you ever?"

"So you want to trade on my relationship and family name for this case?"

"Just as *you* traded on the prestige of this office to validate you so Black Los Angeles wouldn't view you as another rich girl." Her eyes hard as nails, she leans forward, within inches of me. "I'm going to give this back to you." She returns my letter. "And when you're certain—truly are solid—with your decision, you can always come back. For now, why don't you show the world *why* you're a force? Aside from your money."

If I take on a case that could lead to East's father.

Chapter Thirteen

ONCE WE'RE FULLY EVOLVED

EASTON - SONG: NEVER FELT THIS WAY BY BRIAN MCKNIGHT

Seven Years Prior - A Year and a Half Into Kori's and East's Relationship (Two Years After The Law Library)

"Eh, bae?" Getting home late from the office, I enter mine and Kori's new spot in LA and set out the food I picked up from Pip's On Labrea, a classy, black-owned Italian spot in the heart of the city. Kor loves that place when she's home from school. But two weeks after her law school graduation, she's already deep into studying for the California bar exam. She doesn't make time for anything but workouts, eating, sleeping, and studying. And if I'm lucky enough to get my timing right, fucking.

"Halo, you eat yet?"

Still no answer. She must have her earplugs in and timing herself for a mock exam, so I'll wait for her to finish and feed her.

Once I set down the briefcase and kick off my shoes, I unbutton this dress shirt on the way upstairs. I'm surprised to pass by the office and she's not in it studying away.

"Kori."

She's not in the bedroom either. Finally, I find her in the bathtub, but she's not luxuriating in bubbles. Instead, curled over, head buried between her knees, she hugs her legs.

I pull out one of her earphones. "Baby."

Water splashes all over me when she jumps. "Easton! Say something before you do that."

"Everything straight? Why are you in here like this?"

Her entire demeanor has changed from when I kissed her goodbye this morning. Instead of her bubbly, rambling, nightly stories about logic games and multiple-choice questions, I'm hit with stoic silence.

"We need to talk, East."

I seem to watch a lost woman rise from the tub and reach past me for the towel without so much as a kiss.

"What's wrong? Something happened?" Not coming out of her robe to throw on fresh sweats or one of my t-shirts, instead, she plunks down on the bed.

Shit, I'm sweating over multiple-choice options of what the hell she's wrangling for in her robe pocket. She finally pulls it out and places it in my hand.

I've seen one of these before. In college. Troi.

Neither of us was ready, so it worked out perfectly.

But this *time? With my angel on Earth?*

"Imma be a daddy?"

Baby is having my baby? Lighthearted as fuck to know my love for Kori is about to be multiplied and perfected, I go to hug her.

And run into the wall of her despair.

"Who's going to raise it?"

Her stony face and flat tone shock me more than the question itself.

I swear I must be circling the drain with that dirty bathwater. "Wha...what do you mean 'who' Korienne, what the hell? The only thing better in this world than waking up to you is waking up to you and our child.*"*

Is she stressing?

"But East, who?" That question shakes out of her hands. "Who will get up all through the night and breastfeed, take off weeks to months from work, and give up their career opportunities and social life to be with a new baby?"

The more I realize what's happening, the further I slide through the sewage pipes before I'm dumped into the gutter. "Nobody's giving up anything. We will work to—"

Her fucking finger flicks through the air and wounds me. "You won't give up anything. I will!"

Since I just learned this three minutes ago, I'm at a loss for specific answers, but, "I'm going to be right here with you. We'll figure it out. This is damn good news. It's all I've wanted since I first m—"

"Wait a minute." Eyes squinted, her hand shuts me up. "You'll be here 'with me.' As if it'll mostly be my responsibility and you will be my supporting cast?"

"Why are you talking about our seed we planted in love like it's some kind of punishment? I thought you said you loved me, Kor."

"And I thought you loved me, East! I thought you wanted my success and for your halo to shine. Tell me, Easton, how much shining will I do if I'm always stuck here at the house? While you're the one racking up law victories and making a name for yourself?"

"Kori, lots of women raise kids and practice law. And you've got a man doing it with you. You are tripping and being paranoid. We will be fine. It'll be hard as hell the first year or—"

"It'll be hardest on me. You'll be fine, because you're Easton Worthen. And a man."

I go for her so I can hold her and calm her down. She must've had a bad study day and it's getting in her head.

Kor flinches from me, from our lovemaking, from all the nights I had her knees next to her ears with my dick so deep in her she could hardly breathe, from the way we just know what the other needs without words.

"Kori, stop acting like we're sixteen-year-old kids. We are two grown adults perfectly capable of doing this. I'll marry you and make you my wife, and we will be a family."

"A family makes you more attractive, East. You can talk about it, show off and brag, without the heavy lifting. A family makes me a liability. Bosses and employers see women with kids as a burden—they can't work late, take on extra work, travel, or attend professional functions."

Rubbing at my eyes, I blow out the torrents of shit I'm too frustrated to feel and couldn't articulate if I tried. "We'll get a babysitter."

"It's not that simple. When I do become a mom, East, I want to do it with my whole heart."

Hell, my eyelids snap open. "Whoa. What do you mean 'when?'"

Fear trembles on Kori's lip. "I want the same shot as you, Easton."

"You'll have it." I'm pleading now, because she can't be suggesting what it sounds like. "We're doing this together."

A shake of her head swats off the thought.

"You're going to work every day, building your company, credibility, and reputation. I'm singing nursery rhymes, tracking doctor appointments, and talking in baby babble."

"No, Kor! You're wrong. I'll take my baby to work with me. I can put a nursery in my office."

She eyes me like my brain is missing screws. "You only just opened your firm six months ago, and you and the guys are nowhere near turning a profit. You don't come home until one in the morning most nights. So when will you have time for a baby's needs? Be real, East. You'll have somebody in your office watch my child while you hold meetings, negotiate contracts, come and go for lunches and walk-throughs around the city. And what about those impromptu drinking nights out you love? Face it. You are not in a family-man frame of mind yet."

That was one long-ass continuous string of emotions from which she now pauses to inhale a breath.

"My mom will help us watch the baby, Kori." The ground quakes

under my feet, and the world falls around me like I'm in one of those apocalyptic movies.

"Your mother's social life is more lit than yours! It's not fair of you to expect that from her. Besides, I want a family with you. But as a fully evolved woman who is satisfied and not resentful, who has come into my own, and is bringing a child into the world on my terms."

"Resent... Resentful? Why would you feel that about us? How could you say that shit about something so precious?" I don't get it. Why the hell is she doing this?

Her tears don't reach me because I'm too confused.

"It's precious to me, too, and it'll hurt like hell but—"

"Then why are you talking so coldhearted? Why are you fucking ripping us apart?"

The apocalypse rocks her whole body from her fists jabbing her chest to the rivers of tears crashing her eyes. "I'm the one who'll have our baby ripped from me! I don't want that. But I'm not ready! And neither are you!"

Her every word erupts from her so hard, the veins in her neck pump so full of fury, cheeks quiver with so much force, a volcano in human form explodes on me.

"I could explain it until I'm blue in the face and you still won't understand! You're a rich boy. Respect has come to you automatically your whole life, and you've never had to sacrifice anything to earn it."

My head in my hand, the bedroom dresser holds me up.

"You're not broke. Your mom is an engineer, your dad is a judge, you're in the Links, and you—"

"Have to work triple hard because people punish me for it! People admire you for your trips to Dubai. I get called 'Country Club Kori' for so much as eating at a high-end restaurant."

I can't take anymore. I've known all of fifteen minutes I'm going to be a father with a woman I worship.

Only for my plane to crash before takeoff.

"What are you saying, Korienne?"

The woman for whom I would throw myself into a burning building with no thought for my life steps to my face.

Fire comes at me in the form of Kori's amped-up energy. "I'm saying if we really are shining together, then try prioritizing both of our careers, not just yours while you assign me to birth your babies. I want people to recognize me as more than 'Country Club Kori,' daughter of Mitchell Haughton, mother of Easton Worthen's child. Let me become a mom once my name commands the same respect as yours."

A giant seawall comes at me as Kori's words start to sink in, and take me under.

* * *

KORIENNE - PRESENT DAY

Hastily, I shoot another text to East. He still hasn't answered by the time I return to the courtroom. As soon as I round the corner, the crowd in the corridor has practically tripled in size. Journalists and cameramen jam the doorway, elbowing to get inside for the best shot of LaShauna Posey and Officer Brighton's family.

"Excuse me, please," I say. "I need to get through."

"Oh, it's her," someone in a LaShauna t-shirt turns and says. "Are you sending my sister to prison? You know it wasn't her fault, right?" the woman asks me.

"The D.A.'s office will follow the evidence wherever it takes us. Excuse me."

She stands directly in my face. "But you'd better not send my sister to prison for something that wasn't her fault. You're black. Why are you on the cops' side anyway?"

Fighting to hold my composure and not display a drop of fear, I reply, "Ma'am, I'm on the side of the truth. That's my job. Whatever color it is."

"Step aside, you all, and let the D.A. in. Thank you," the bailiff bellows.

With cameras aimed at me, I attempt a polite smile at the relatives and community who begrudgingly back up.

"Just remember what you are, sweetheart," an elderly woman mutters with a return smile that's fake and mocking, as if she couldn't care less about my respectability.

It's likely my last time trying to be nice.

Inside, the bailiff calls the court to order, and Judge Boyle resumes the calendar of cases. "Starting with where we left off this morning, we have the People versus LaShauna Posey."

"Your Honor, I'm afraid I'll have to declare a conflict."

Vash snort-laughs loud enough for the people in the back.

Judge Boyle peers over the bench. "On what basis, Counselor?"

"Your Honor." Deep inhale. "I'm engaged to marry Easton Worthen."

All the defense attorneys and Jason gasp and exchange shock before snatching out their cell phones.

"And this concerns me because?" the judge asks.

"I don't know if you're aware this incident occurred on one of the Worthen properties, owned by my future father-in-law. His company was evicting Ms. Posey from her former apartment. I have personal family ties that would make my participation appear biased and improper."

The judge pulls out his ethics and professional responsibility manual and spends the next few minutes studying it.

Meanwhile, Vash studies me.

"Tuh. Easton Worthen. I should have known. You were stuck on stupid for him years ago, even though he was screwing around on you. Making you look like a fool."

"Mind your business."

She throws up her hands in mock surrender. "I surely will. While other women mind *your* business."

I've never wanted to smack anybody so badly. "You mad you're not one of them?"

"How do *you* know I haven't been?" Her gaze is loaded with satisfaction. "He had *so* many he probably don't even remember half of them. Or maybe he does."

This is why I insisted this time around we keep quiet.

I'm fully aware of Easton's lifestyle before me. But there's never been a burning urge to know who.

Until right now.

"Counselor Haughton," Judge Boyle interrupts us. "I'll find you have a potential conflict, but not an actual conflict. You were not present at the scene and have no personal knowledge or direct interest in the controversy. I haven't seen any evidence your fiancé was directly involved, or even that your future father-in-law was directly involved. However, your fiancé does serve as counsel for some of the Worthen business. With your involvement, he should be walled off from handling any part of this case. You can bring him in so I can order him." Judge Boyle stares between Vashti and me. "As it is a potential conflict only, you can keep the appointment, Ms. Haughton, unless the defense objects."

I'm confident that I'm the last person she'd want to be with in trial.

"So are you objecting to me prosecuting this case?" I ask her.

The shake of her head astonishes me.

"No. I have no objections. I'll waive Ms. Haughton's potential conflict so she can remain."

What the hell? Why is she not objecting? I would think she'd *love* for me to be off this case.

Judge Boyle concludes, "There we have it. Let us begin with a pre-trial date to see what motions you have."

With smugness in her smirk, Vash's ploy becomes clear. She's forcing me into a corner—where I'm hit with either public hatred for prosecuting LaShauna Posey, or professional humiliation if I walk away.

"What's wrong, Madam President?" she mutters. "Your fiancé will be upset you're getting a front-row seat to his daddy's fuck-ups?"

"Bitter doesn't look good on you, Vash. Being resentful and petty will not get you to the president's seat."

"Apparently, nor does being honest and nice. So, petty makes me feel better." She leans in on me. "Make your move, Kori. What do you have for me?"

My phone vibrates next to my hand.

Easton: *Saw I missed ur calls. Been in a depo all day. Free to talk? Did Gloria shit in her pants?*

"Don't play with somebody's life, Vash. She could go away for a long time." I flip open the file and eye the plea offer that was filled in by the Filing Deputy D.A. "Right now, the offer is nineteen years."

"That's a joke." Vash sniffs. "LaShauna had a right to be in her own house. The full sixty days were not up for eviction. The officer was wrong for being in her house trying to remove her before her time to appeal. And Worthen Properties was wrong for calling the police. So make that two years house arrest and two years parole."

"You're out of your mind."

The auxiliary door opens, and out comes LaShauna Posey. The wails of her family members and activists erupt and close in on me.

Judge Boyle states, "In the case of *People vs. Posey*, we have Vashti Burns for Ms. Posey, and have the People decided who's taking this?"

"Yeah, Kori." Her chest out, sucking her teeth, Vash rocks back on her heels. "That 'conflict' thing was a nice play. So who are you punting this off to?"

It's not the sneer on her face that boils my blood, but her cavalier air, as if her simply showing up here should put fear in me.

Halo, this is you and me, and we're partners. You're a CEO, a fucking boss. And the queen of my life.

As if I summoned him, my phone lights up with a photo of us. He's calling. I silence the call.

Needing to vomit from more than just nausea, I look Vash in her eye.

"Korienne Haughton, Your Honor. For the People."

Chapter Fourteen

THE BLOW

EASTON - SONG: OCHO RIOS BY DANIEL CAESAR

Will Angels Rise Need Wings to Finally Get Off the Ground?

Is Wealthy Carol Worthen the Black Dream or a Black Nightmare?

Dear Carol Worthen: The Black Community Needs Housing, Not High-Rises

Across my desk in my office lay several newspapers featuring my father or Worthen Properties.

"I want to know everything, good and bad," I say to my longtime friend from Harvard, Kevin Middleton, one of the only black tech moguls in the country. "Who is this LaShauna Posey woman? I want her tenant data ever since LaShauna moved into Paradise Gardens. And Fannie Kilpatrick, that irritating activist lady. Spare no details. Phone calls, email chains, text threads. And these cops who go over there all the time, what's their story?" I run off my wish list of digital information.

If Dad wants my help, he's only getting it if all the cards are on the table. We should be fully prepared for our enemies to attack from every direction—activists, the D.A., rival developers, and hell, even the city council that keeps voting against Angels Rise.

"Bruh, you'll get it. Give my squad twenty-four hours," Kevin replies. "But you know the rules."

"Yeah, I do." The information will be encrypted, available for just a few hours, and I'll only be able to view it once. Then it will be wiped.

Now I take a deep breath for my next ask. "I also need to know what conversations Dad and Charles may have 'forgotten,' that I should know about and be ready for. I want their movements, if you can get them."

"Dude, don't insult my skills," Kevin cracks.

My law firm handles real estate and business transactions, a high-brow practice that revolves mostly around properties and commercial assets worth millions—homes sliding off cliffs, underground excavations, fights over beaches and vineyards, and the like.

When it comes to Worthen Properties' day-to-day affairs, such as evictions and landlord-tenant issues, my brother, Charles, hands that off to property management companies and smaller law firms around town.

Dad doesn't personally oversee these matters either. He probably has no clue what goes on at his apartment complexes now that he's so focused on Angels Rise and other luxury projects.

"You sound all worked up. Calm down. You've got a big deal ahead of you tonight. Focus on you and Kori, and I'll get you what you need." Kevin is a software developer and coder with a talent for hacking data without detection.

But Middleton is more than a tech mogul; I also look up to him. Not only is he the son of a powerful man himself, but dude's made his own money since he was fifteen. He has walked my path of being a black heir who builds his own identity, so when I started my firm, Kevin gave me game.

And he's right. I do have plans for Kori and me now that she's leaving the D.A.'s office—giving her a platform to build her lifestyle brand, having an actual wedding, and our baby...

She's having my baby.

Finally.

"Excellent. And also—"

"Easton," my secretary, Bev, says through my doorway.

"Bev, I'm in the middle of a—"

"You have a visitor at the front who says it's important."

I stare at Bev, and then at my calendar. No appointments are scheduled for the middle of today aside from my deposition and this phone interview. For her to come interrupt me, it must be important.

"Dude, go handle your business," Kevin tells me. "And I'll see you tonight at your folks' house."

Once I'm off the line, Bev steps inside my doorway and closes it behind her, before she mouths to me.

"It's Edith Zucker."

"Edith who?"

Oh, shit. Worthen's CFO?

"Tell her I'm in the middle of a depo, and she'll need to schedule a phone appointment."

Bev dismisses that option. "Already tried it. She says it's imperative that you and her speak. *Now.*"

"Who is she to come to my office giving directives? Fine. In seven minutes, if we're still in here, come get me."

"Say less, boss man," Bev says before going to get her.

Meanwhile, I activate the recording option on my phone because I don't care how good this woman is at her job, her side-eye in Worthen's meetings is lethal. She hates Dad and us. She's likely here to siphon information off me to use against him, and despite mine and his disagreements, I would never. Recording this conversation without telling her is illegal, but fuck that.

"Mr. Worthen, thank you for seeing me in the middle of your busy day."

After we shake hands, she waits for me invite her to sit down, and I don't.

"Unfortunately, I have to keep this tight. My client and opposing counsel are waiting for me in the conference room."

Sharp-eyed, she assesses me for the truth. "Of course. I won't be long. I came to ask about all your proxy votes at Worthen. Of the last thirty-five votes that were taken over three years, you only cast six of them in person. Why is that?"

Tuh. So she came to attack me in person? "Ms. Zucker, how do my votes concern you? Those votes are allowed according to the bylaws, and as you can see, I have a business. Why? What's the problem?"

"If you care so much about your father's company, why do you work elsewhere? Should you be on the board if you're not moved enough to vote in person?"

"Not that it concerns you, but I do care about my family's company, which is why I still come when my father asks me."

"And yet it must not be important enough. You don't hold any office in the company." Throwing her hands behind her back, she seems to micro-analyze me in ways I don't appreciate. "In fact, the only actual employment you've ever had at Worthen was as an intern a couple of years in high school."

She's sniffing out a way to get rid of me, so she can fill my seat on the board with somebody who votes less with Dad and more with her.

"Ms. Zucker, unless there's a point you're getting to, I think we're about done here."

"I reviewed some of your work you did as an intern," she notes, in a clear dismissal of what I just said. "On the conditions in South Los Angeles and how it was 'prime real estate' for redevelopment. In your spreadsheets back then, you identified relatively low-cost properties, a chance to clean up a violence-riddled community, and younger professionals looking for nicer housing without overwhelming costs. You put that together?"

If this woman is on the hunt for a way to destroy Dad with our internal research, she won't find it with me. And I *will* be informing him he's got somebody shady in his ranks.

"It's company research. A report written by Worthen Properties, Ms. Zucker."

She snickers. "Nice non-answer, Mr. Worthen."

"That should be your cue to go, Ms. Zucker."

"And I will. Just a couple more questions. It's clear you have a keen eye for business, maybe even real estate. You've certainly got the education and grades." She swings her hands in front of her, motioning around my corner office. "Got your own successful law practice here, so you're not a lazy nepo baby. You put in the work. And yet, you refuse to lend your talents to your father full-time. Only on a partial basis. Why?"

"That's between my father and me. Besides, I like being my own man." And Dad only listens to me when he gets ready.

She shrugs. "Why not position yourself to one day be Worthen's CEO?"

Shocked is an understatement. Where the hell does she get off, assuming something will happen to my father? Is she *planning* for something to happen to my father? It's a possibility I never want to even fathom.

"Worthen *has* a CEO. And a backup, in case he is harmed for *any* reason. And I would pursue justice to the fullest extent against anybody who ever tries it."

She must think since Dad and I have differences, that I don't love my father, and I'm dispelling that lie quickly.

Picking up her purse, Zucker nods and makes her way out. "Of course you would. Appreciate your time."

The hell?

Before returning to my deposition, I handle a few housekeeping matters.

Me to Dad: *You and I need to talk. You've got snakes in your backyard.*

Dad: *Bet. Come by the house tonight.*

Yes, going by the house is definitely what I plan to do, for more than he thinks.

Kor still hasn't called me back, probably wrapping up her court day.

I squeeze in a few more calls and text a few more people to shore up plans for Kori and me to celebrate this weekend.

Judge Sharpe to me: *You're certain about this, East? Does Kori know?*

Me: *I'm certain. She's unaware, and I'd prefer to keep it that way.*

Speaking of Kori, I check my watch. She and I have been missing each other all afternoon.

"Mr. Boss Man, time for you to get back to your depo," Bev calls to me.

Clearing my head, I start out of my office for the last forty-five minutes of questioning the defense's expert witness.

"Oh, my Lord, that must be so awful," my front desk assistant says as I review my notes on my way to my firm's conference room. Other attorneys are back from break already.

Only half-listening, I review my next questions. "What's awful, Bev?"

She stares up at the television we keep muted in the waiting room. "This woman who shot that policeman. I can't imagine what they're about to do to her. I hope they're treating her all right in jail, and those policemen aren't messing with her."

Still, only half listening, I continue reviewing my notes and research. "Oh, yeah, I heard about that."

"Oh, for heaven's *sake*! And then she's going to be prosecuted by another black person! Good Lord! The prosecutor's office knows what they're doing, sending another black woman to go after her! This here will be almost as big as O.J."

My eyes shift up.

Heart stops.

"Turn that up."

"Ms. Posey faces life in prison if convicted," a news reporter tells me through the camera lens. "Meanwhile, outside, a crowd of protestors is gathering."

The screen changes. A small group of about a hundred people stand on the courthouse steps chanting, "Let LaShauna Go!" and "She had a right!"

In the next shot, a soldier couldn't march better than my wife, head high, chin up, cornered by journalists and relatives of the accused woman.

A reporter hustles alongside her. "Excuse me. Will you be the lead prosecutor on this case? Can you tell us what evidence you have so far that this wasn't self-defense, as Ms. Posey's family claims? Can you tell us if Officer Brighton had a right to be in Ms. Posey's apartment?"

Korienne moves to side-step the woman, but they box her in like an animal. "Ma'am, step back."

"But, Madam Prosecutor—"

"I asked you to step *back* and give me space." Korienne's tone is the bee sting that reporter lady clearly wasn't expecting. "You will have the details at the time it's deemed appropriate by our office."

"You ought to be ashamed of yourself for prosecuting another black woman!" one elderly lady admonishes her.

"Coon!" A younger woman barks at Kori. "You're a damn coon for working with the man to destroy your own people!"

I almost yank at the TV to get those fools off her and then come back to myself.

"Bev, call Steven and ask him to come handle this deposition."

I call Kor's phone, but it keeps ringing. With trembling fingers, I eke out a text.

Me: *File a 170.6 against Boyle. Don't keep it.*

Before I send that text, I remember my situation with Dad. Any of my communications about this matter could be judged as one of Dad's lawyers directing a prosecutor's actions. Damn. Why didn't she declare a conflict? How in the hell did this happen?

Me to Kori: *Baby, did you declare a conflict?*

My phone buzzes with Charles on the other end.

"Are you seeing this? Dad's been right about that chick this whole time! She's after us because you left her ass and this is her—"

"Charles, I've got to go."

Phoebe Haughton buzzes through.

"Hey, Ma," I say to Kori's mom as I head for the exit.

Opposing counsel busts out of my conference room. "Easton, where are you going? We've been waiting weeks for this." He must determine from my pace it's not a good idea to try and block me.

I breeze by him. "My apologies. Got an emergency."

Phoebe half pleads, half wails, "Easton, go get my baby. I don't want her doing this one. Goodness, this is a nightmare. She was supposed to be leaving."

"She is. It'll be okay. Calm down," I try to reassure her, and myself. But I double-time down these stairs like Kor is caught in the zombie apocalypse.

Out in the garage, the valet tries to help me, but I grab the keys and head for my car. Fuck waiting.

My dad calls. "Easton, you see what's on TV? Huh? Just like her daddy. But anyway, I didn't call for that. I heard your radio interview this morning. Phenomenal there, man. Why don't you come on over to the house? I've got some people to introduce you to."

Confused and anxious, I squeeze my steering wheel in late afternoon traffic.

Kori, what are you doing?

"I've had something to come up, Dad. Maybe another time."

I want to be your wife. I'm going to be your wife. And nothing will change or interfere with that. I swear it.

If Kor goes through with this, I'll never have my dad *and* my wife beside me.

Another driver lays on their horn, but that doesn't stop me running a red light. Dodging and swerving, I'm fortunate my office on Wilshire is within sight of downtown LA. In about twenty minutes, I'm riding north and exiting the one-ten freeway in East LA, trying not to lose my shit with these jaywalkers taking their sweet time in the crosswalk.

I'm stumped by this energy of reporters and activists on the street, particularly that one damn activist who shows up every time she sees there'll be cameras—Fannie Kilpatrick.

Riding around to the employee-access garage for county staffers, I see another group of cameras lurking at the back entrance. I've driven here on nights after Kor had a trial and she was scared of violent defendants or their families, so I would come to get her.

Protestors creep to this side of the building and underneath the security gate to go wait at the door.

Shit.

Kor hasn't left yet since her navy Mercedes is visible with her sorority plates, in the garage.

Calling her phone, I breathe a fat sigh to hear her voice.

"East?"

"Kor, baby, bring protection with you."

The sight of protestors motioning for others to join them strikes lightning across my fucking heart valves.

With no keycard to get in the gate, I parallel park illegally, put on the emergency lights, and hop out.

"East? Where are...?"

"Kor, baby, bring some protection with you. These protestors are out here!"

"Hello?"

"Korienne—"

Damn! Spotty reception.

Through the glass doors of the building, stepping off the elevator and oblivious to what's going on, out comes Kori, talking on the phone.

My phone buzzes with her calling me again.

She's only accompanied by one police officer, and they both appear stunned at the growing mass of bodies swarming them at the door.

"Will you be making any statements?" a reporter yells at Kori.

"Get back!" the officer yells, pulling out his radio. "Code seventy-seven."

"There's a special place in Hell for you, sellout!" one of them yells at a paralyzed Kori.

Attempting to maintain her composure, she scans around her for a way out.

"Kori!" I call out from behind a group of about twenty people surrounding her.

"LaShauna better not do no time or this will be personal, bitch! Do you hear me?" a woman screams at her.

"Address her peacefully. Peacefully!" Fannie Kilpatrick arrives and calls out to the others. "Ma'am, will you please drop the charges against LaShauna Hoffman? That's all we're asking."

Seeing nothing but Kori, I jerk bodies out of the way and shove toward the mother of my baby. "Get the hell out of her face!"

"Your wife is a coon for protecting oppressors!"

I lunge for this person's throat. "Shut the hell up!"

"Sellout!"

"She's a whore for them cops!"

"I bet she was just in there sucking their *dicks!*"

Lips spit and a *"psst."* A glob hits my neck.

Instantly, my disgust at their gall flies out of me in a smack of my arm at whomever stands next to me.

The isolated cop doubles down and whips out his baton. "I said get back!"

The slave-whip crack of the cop's voice over all our heads only amps up the group.

Infuriated, they scream at the cop and Kori where she stands frozen, unable to walk away.

"Kori!" Every one of the nine years I've waited for her extends into my fingers that reach through all these damn people and pry them out of my way.

Alarmed, blinking, her hunt for me evident on her face, she scans.

"Easton!"

"I wish you would hit me with that damn thing! Get off me!" somebody snaps at the officer.

More officers bust out of the doors. "Break it up! Now! Get back!"

One of them lunges at me. "I said, get down!"

"Give me my fiancée first!" I don't recognize the voice of whatever creature said that.

Another officer, a beast, a threat, rears his baton.

My instinct to calm the sea of fury swirling around Kori wipes out any thought of fear for my body.

* * *

KORIENNE

The blow of a metal baton across the beautiful, picturesque countenance of the man I love is an atomic bomb annihilating my planet.

From my core, every layer of me erupts. *"Naaaaaaooo!"*

"On your knees, you spoiled daddy's boy piece of shit!"

And yet miraculously, impetuously, forcefully, indestructible, East presses forward.

"Don't touch *haaaiiim!*" In this eruption, my soul lunges toward my forever.

A blast-wave shatters every fiber from my skull to my toes at the sound of that second crack.

Other black bodies push in, and elbows and fists lash out.

"A stick isn't keeping me from my fiancée! *Give* her to me!" East means it. They'll need twenty more cops with those damn sticks. Despite the sticks swinging everywhere, East *still* keeps coming to grip my arm, snatching me from the throng and into him.

"Stop it..." The ceiling appears to touch me as the blow cracks into me and I almost black out.

The steel-reinforced, concrete bomb shelter of Easton gives me strength to keep my eyes open and fling my other arm around him. Inside his arms, there is no more protective fortress, and I cover as much of a raging East with my body as I can.

"He's my fiancé! No, Rex, *please*. He's my *fiancé*!" In a field of screams, we bellow over each other.

The next time I peer over my shoulder, East's one arm is outstretched, firmly clutching the assailant-deputy's baton. Quickly, I remember the "D. Quick" on his badge.

"Let go!" Officer D. Quick bellows.

I can't tell if East will yank the baton and start beating Deputy D. Quick with it.

"East."

One more second, one more glare at the officer who hit him, one more dare to try it again, and East lets go.

"Get off of her!" East yells at protestors getting too close, throwing their weight at us, balling their fists.

"Stop resisting!" an authoritative voice yells somewhere around us.

The officers push through the growing horde. "Clear out! Break it up! Get on the ground!"

"Get down! Get down!" Officers jerk bodies to the ground.

"Take her out of here!" Rex tells East and pushes us forward.

But East's head is somewhere else, where his mind still fixates on D. Quick, and he refuses to move.

"He needs medical attention! Call for a medic!" I can't scream it loud enough.

"No," East mutters.

I'm incensed at the steep hill rising on his temple, from which blood streams through a two-inch battle wound. His jaw the color of almost-ripe strawberry, lip cut at least half an inch into the meat, as blood seeps from my garden that is Easton, the officer's heinousness now bears its swollen mark on East's comeliness.

"And I want to speak to that D. Quick asshole's commanding officer," I insist. "We're filing a complaint."

"They won't do shit," East says, still glaring at the officer who hit him.

"Kori, get *out* of here," Rex, one of the courthouse sheriff's deputies, barks at me. "Or do you want to go back in there?" He points at the horde now scattering, some running away, some shoved onto the ground, others facing off with police. "And I could easily book your guy here for resisting an officer's orders and disturbing the peace."

Disgusted at what I'm hearing, I whip out my phone. "That's not what happened, Rex! East wasn't holding a weapon. He wasn't a threat!"

"He was charging at a deputy in direct violation of a command to hit the ground, and that officer did not know who he was." Rex's steely eyes are batons hitting me. "And *that's* what's going in my report."

Translation: Don't fight this.

"We're even." Rex glares at Easton and me. "Go home."

"Bring his ass to me and gimme five minutes." East's fists lock at his sides. "*Then* we'll be even."

"Rex, if you won't get help, I'm calling paramedics." I start dialing for nine-one-one.

"Kor, don't," East says.

"What do you mean?"

East glares at Rex. "I don't trust these fucking people. We'll get our own doctors. And our own lawyers."

I push East back. Hell will freeze over before I drop this violation against *him*.

"Baby, I'll drive," I offer.

"I'm fine."

"Kori, I'll get a patrol car escort to make sure nobody follows you," Rex says, his eyes still insisting we forget this.

I have to pull away when East tries to open the passenger door but stumbles on those stalwart legs that have always walked undeterred. Shoving my shoulder in the crook of his arm, I rush to steady him.

Whatever God-like trance allowed him to absorb those blows and stay on his feet seems to now evaporate. And it crystalizes into human pain. Grabbing his keys, I shepherd him into the passenger seat and plow through the arsenal of cameras hoisted in the air and aiming at the car windows. They film and aim at us like we're animals on *National Geographic*.

"East, I'm taking you to emergency."

"No. I want to go home to my folks and figure this out."

"You may have a concussion. That head wound looks—"

At a stoplight, I reach out to touch my angel.

A radioactive Easton's fist flies off a spring and shoots at his enemy.

Damn near out of my bones, I leap in the seat.

"East..."

Wild-eyed, he continues to defend against his assailant. Slowly, his metal expression cracks to realize it's me he's about to hit.

"I'm sor...I'm sorry."

I can't stop staring at my king, and in my quiet sobs leaking from the river of us that runs through me, I hurt to mend him and make him whole again.

A battered East insists, "I said I'm going home, Kor. To my parents' house."

Cars behind us honk.

But as I drive the car forward, he and I remain stopped.

Going to his parents—his *father*—changes the calculus of everything.

With Carol Worthen present, judging, demanding, we are no longer in control. No longer secure.

"Why didn't you call me and tell me you were on the way?" I need to keep him alert and talking in case he has a concussion.

"I was on the phone with your mom, and then my dad. Calling you wouldn't have stopped this." His voice strives to hold up the pieces of his fortress. Not to crumble into rubble.

Riding through LA with a patrol car following us, I still swing through my consciousness.

Sellout!

For the next few minutes, our only conversation is the terror of our breaths, my hand over his that doesn't grip me back, the infuriated jerk of our bodies as we still squab in our minds.

Each time my phone or his vibrates, or his car speakers blare the ringtone through the Bluetooth, he silences the calls of our family members. He seems to be decompressing.

One glance at him, and my heart ruptures, releasing more tears.

On the backroads of Hollywood Hills, we're almost at his parents', where I haven't visited in five years.

"Kori."

"Baby, tell me how you're feeling. How many fingers am I holding up?" I'm only halfway joking as I hold up three.

"Four," he answers.

A quick glimpse of his bloody grin and it's clear he's kidding. East's humor is intact, even in this atrocious situation, but still, that deputy *will* answer.

He slides his hand over my leg. "You give...your boss the letter?"

In the corner of my eye, he waits.

"Kor."

"Yes, I gave it to her."

His hand squeezes my leg, eyes come back to life, in one of the few signs of vitality remaining in him.

"She gave it back to me, East." Telling him flatlines my heart monitor. "She's asking me to do it."

Turning into his parents' driveway, running out of time to have him to myself before his father gets a hold of him, I track down words to explain, to bridge the brokenness on his face—both physically and emotionally.

"I thought you said...how did she ask...if you quit then..." His thoughts are becoming more scattered, with the effects of that deputy's baton kicking in.

Seeing him this way assaults me at my core. Even if he uses his energy to express his upset, I want him whole.

"East, I tried to conflict off and I gave the D.A. the letter. But it's *Vashti*, Easton. She came to LA from Long Beach just to... Do you hear me? East, stay awake."

The gate opens.

Out runs his harried mother toward us. "Oh, my Lord! Thank *God!* I was praying from the minute I saw it on TV. Are y'all all right?"

Behind her stands an appalled Carol Worthen.

Now he knows.

Chapter Fifteen

HOW YOU RULE YOUR HOUSE

EASTON - SONG: EVERYTHING I MISS AT HOME BY CHERRELLE & ALEXANDER O'NEAL

Five Years Prior - Easton & Korienne's Engagement Dinner

"You all catch us from this angle?" I ask the photographer and flick my tongue toward Kori's mouth.

She's all embarrassed and grips my chin in a funny shot. "Goofy, will you stop?"

Our friends crack up and photo-bomb the pics.

"No. Shit, you made me wait four years for this." My fingers linked around her hips, I slide them over her ass and squeeze my fiancée to my dick.

"Easton Jermaine!" my mother admonishes me from the other side of the restaurant.

"Mama, look somewhere else!"

That won't cut it, and she cuts across the hardwood floor real fast. The photographer's next shot is Moms coming at me with her fist.

"Son." Dad follows her over here with an envelope. He places it against my chest. "Remember what we talked about?"

Damn, what did we talk about? I've been busy as hell these past few weeks, between a couple of big trials my boy, Steven, and I had, closing on the house in Hancock Park I just bought for Kori and me, and then helping my boy, Kevin Middleton, get his new business venture, MoneyCruncher, off the ground. It's been a whirlwind summer, but I wouldn't change the full life we've got for anything.

"Um."

"The papers, Easton. Your agreement for your assets. You said she was good with this. And she and her father aren't up to anything."

My chest sinks a couple of notches. "Uh, yeah, Dad. Okay. Can we not do this now? Damn."

A few paces away, Kori, Shallon, Mac, and a few of her Jack and Jill girlfriends from childhood are posing for photos. That gigantic smile is a big-ass sun that reflects on her skin, and the glow of that five-carat, Harry Winston sparkler she holds up doesn't even compare.

"When will there be a right time?" Dad snatches me out of my thoughts again. "Go ahead and get it over with and stop putting it off. You don't want that law firm, or your house, or any of your investments —our investments—to ever be jeopardized."

"Kori's not like that, and we're never breaking up."

"You never know what'll happen," Charles warns. "This here is just insurance. Dad's doing the tough job and looking out for you. But other than this necessary business you'll need to man up on, I'm damn happy for ya."

A ten-foot pole weighs less than this damn envelope that's only slightly thick. Shoving it in my back pocket, I go to get my girl.

In the crook of my arm, as naturally as the skin fits over a grape, Kori's body slides into mine, her eyes locking with mine, lips connecting with mine.

"Babe, what's this? It's in the way." Kor points out how the envelope *now sits smack in the middle of our water glasses and salad bowls, once the toasts are over and the starting course is being set down.*

"Oh, this isn't anything. We'll talk about it later." I don't even know what's on those pages. Snatching it up, I roll it and shove the eyesore in the inside of my jacket that hangs over the chair. Going in for a hug with my frat brothers, and enjoying our long-awaited night, I almost completely forget. Again.

A couple hours later, Kori shuffles upstairs, in our bedroom.

"East? What is this?" Kor asks.

Hell, I'm trying to fit some of these leftovers and cake in the fridge for me to take to my office staff tomorrow. "What's what, Kor?"

"This envelope in your jacket. You had it at the dinner tonight."

My eyes shift up the long road that's our stairs. "I'm not really sure. I think that's the prenup I mentioned a while back." With lead feet, I start up the stairs so we can get this over with.

Tucked under her butt, Kori's feet are not wiggling the way they do when she's happy. Instead, she's knotted into a little human pretzel and topped with salt and vinegar.

"Baby, wh-what is this about your daddy being appointed Guardian Ad Litem of my kids if I ever violate these terms and conditions? If I cheat on you, or I'm caught with another man, he can have me removed from our home?" That pretty upper lip curls under. "Which is really your home."

"Halo, I'll get it taken out. I haven't even looked at it yet." I slide off my tie and unbutton my dress shirt. "He just passed it to me tonight."

Her eyeballs nearly springboard out of her head while they absorb the info on the page. "In the event you should predecease me, I am to receive lifetime access to one of the Worthen homes, which will be chosen by the Trustee appointed by Carol Worthen. Only if our natural born children meet the criteria of a certain grade point average, attend speci-fied colleges or universities, pursue qualifying careers, and refrain from morally reprehensible behaviors such as homosexuality or gender trans-

formation, will they be considered for inheritance of the Worthen estates and assets."

That gaze of hers, so spicy and still manages to be sweet, lays into me.

"Considered for an inheritance? Easton, your children would be entitled to inherit from you, regardless of how they live their personal lives! As long as they're decent humans and not murderers, Carol Worthen can't dictate to folks how they live!"

"Baby, we can talk about it." I snatch at the papers, and she yanks them from my grasp.

Stricken, Kor glares at me. "Talk about it? You said we were laying out your family's stuff and my family's." With a few hops, she jumps her cute ass onto the bed where I can't reach her and keeps scanning the pages. "I'm expected to sign papers granting power of attorney whenever I leave the state of California, in case of an accident or act of God, so my children don't have to spend any time in foster care should something happen to me. Are you shitting me?"

"Kori, give it here. Sly and his lawyers got a little heavy-handed is all."

Now comes the mouth-drop. "In the event of divorce, I'm not allowed to write any tell-alls, must submit written pieces about the marriage, television show proposals, any scenario in which I seek to capitalize on the Worthen brand or its likenesses, I must have approved by Worthen's attorneys in advance. Easton!"

I grab at her and climb onto the bed. "Baby, come here."

Kor jerks back. "So this is how our marriage will go? Your father literally holding a gun to our throats, and if we do anything he doesn't approve of, he's cutting us off financially? I've got my own damn money! I don't need his, and I don't have to worry about him. But Easton, what about you? Everything you've got has his name on it."

"Not everything."

"Your law firm."

"My firm makes its own money now."

"You used his money to start it. Your first lucrative clients were mostly his friends. Investments, stocks, land, bonds, hedge funds—mostly you share with him."

"I've started setting aside my own."

"This house was paid for mostly with his money."

We're both bouncing around on the mattress now. "Kor, he's my dad. Just like your parents helped you with your crib. Come on. You're being unreasonable!"

"My parents don't use their help as a form of control. He will not dictate to me through you, East!"

I snatch her ass up from the mattress and throw her over my shoulder as I step off. "He's not doing that. I said we'll work it out. Get your ass off the bed."

But two weeks later, we're wrapped up in negotiations as intense as fuck.

"Dad," I say to him at the Haughtons' home with all of our lawyers after three hours. "Can you please drop some of this? Mom, will you tell him he's not running some asylum for misfit kids? That we are adults."

Mom shakes her head and whispers to me in a corner of their house, out of earshot of everyone else. "He already let go of the power of attorney clause, baby. It's his money. What do you want?"

"Mom, it's your money, too," I remind her.

She blinks a moment like she's remembering. "Yes, I know that. It's just that we work hard, and there's bad blood with Judge Haughton from that ruling thing."

Dad reads from his phone, only halfway paying attention. "She ought to be grateful we're letting her anywhere near our money after that."

"She's my fiancée, and a damn good woman who doesn't care about what I've got. Squash this beef with the judge."

He stares at me. "Don't be a fool, boy. Women care what you've got. Controlling their purse is how you rule your house. If she didn't care, she would have signed those papers by now."

"*Easton,*" *Kor calls me over to her.*

"*Baby, we'll get this done. What difference does it make, though? You're going to be with me. What's more important than that?*" *I ask her.*

Kor's doe eyes examine me. "*I'm not his child. That's what. 'I ought to be grateful'? Like I'm some second-class citizen? He expects me to fall in line and—*"

"*You're not marrying him. You're marrying me.*"

"*And we'll be trapped under his thumb. E, you're my life, but—*"

"*But what?*" *I ask her.* "*Okay. Some of this is slightly inconvenient. Do you have to be She-Ra on literally every damn thing? Can you bend sometimes?*"

Indignation rolls into her lips. "*It's not the prenup I have a problem with. It's how everybody around him only exists for his ends. He's a wannabe Joe Jackson or Matthew Knowles, a baby tyrant who feels like his family members are chess pieces.*"

"*Easton!*" *Dad calls out to me.* "*Your mama and I've got a dinner to be at tonight. Is she signing or not?*"

Misty-eyed, Kori's fragmented stare is an answer. "*I can't believe you thought I would do this.*"

"*I believed you love me.*"

"*I do love you. And I will marry you if you didn't have a penny to your name. We don't need those papers.*"

"*Tah. That's unrealistic. I have business and financial assets tied up with this and they pay our bills. I have to work with him in some form, until my business grows more. I'm just asking you to have patience until then.*" *I'm pleading now.*

"*So you'll let him treat your wife like property for you to keep getting his money?*"

Flummoxed, I think fast. "*I'm not letting him do anything. I'm biding my time for our survival.*"

"*Your survival.*"

I'm totally fucked up at the sight of her sliding my ring off her finger and placing it in my hand.

"Kor, what the hell are you doing?" I whisper. "Put that back on."

She wipes tears I can't stand seeing her cry. "I won't be your mom, E. And be the dutiful little wife who jumps when he says so, while you sit by and say nothing."

A part of me wants to go rip that prenup to pieces in Dad's face, but if I do that, Dad will react. He'll yank his seed money from our firm. That would jeopardize my business partners. He'd yank investments I've placed into my friends' projects. It's not fair to any of them.

"Kor, baby, please..."

I almost flinch as she moves toward my cheek with one of those finality kisses. "I want to marry my man and not Carol Worthen's son."

* * *

KORIENNE - PRESENT DAY

This is the last way East and I wanted to reveal to our families that we've been back together.

"What was he doing there?" Mr. Worthen accuses me more than asks. "Did you tell my son you're going after his daddy before he put his life up for you?"

The three of us rush a disoriented Easton into the house.

"Dad..." He slips in and out of consciousness on the way to a couch.

Essence cries, "My baby boy! Why was he in a riot?"

"Why didn't you take him to a hospital?" Mr. Worthen demands to know, like I've got a secret scheme for his son to suffer.

"I tried and he didn't want to go."

"Kor..." East mumbles.

I hold on to his bloodied face, even more handsome from being so badass. "Baby, I'm here. Don't close your eyes. Look at me. Sit up."

Essence starts dialing on her phone. "Easton, just rest. Don't talk, baby. Dr. Jeffries is on his way. Oh, my goodness."

"You can take your hands off my son now." Mr. Worthen's ire is contained, even while it drips with his clear distrust of me. "Whatever he was doing with you, he can tell me that himself. But for now, I don't want you hearing our family's personal conversations for your daddy and his friends, and you can go."

Startled doesn't even begin to describe why I have no quick clapback. I thought that not even Carol Worthen would have the gall.

"Carol, stop it!" Essence waves him off. "Not now. Apparently, East wants her here or he wouldn't have been at her job in the first place, and he wouldn't have asked her to bring him to us."

His father and one of the groundskeepers take over, and I text my parents and friends about what occurred, where I am, and *who* I'm dealing with, to round up my support.

"What I don't understand is, if you love him the way you say, why would you ask him to go charging into a violent group for you? It doesn't make sense," Mr. Worthen admonishes me. "What woman would even put herself in that situation? This is what you call love? Testing him to see what he'll do for you?"

"I didn't! I came outside and saw he was there." This is the way it's always been. No matter what, I'm the problem.

Over the next few terrifying minutes, my parents and Shallon arrive so I don't have to grapple with Mr. Worthen on my own.

"How much does he know?" Shal whispers.

"Nothing."

Dr. Jeffries comes out to address us. "Damn lucky chomp, so far, he looks fine. A couple of bumps and bruises and a slight concussion, with some cuts I've stitched up at his forehead and lip. I don't see any signs of brain swelling in the head, but I still want him brought in for CT scans first thing in the morning so I can confirm that. I gave him a sleep aid for the pain. He'll have a bad headache for the next couple of days, but somebody must have been praying while he was being so careless."

The doctor comes over to my parents and me on his way out.

"Mitch, man, what are you doing here? Phoebe, you still putting up with this old goat?"

My mom rolls her eyes, and I'm too distraught to pay attention, but I could almost swear she doesn't smile at the joke about her and Dad.

"Kori, a word?" Dad asks me and goes to wait in a corner, outside Carol Worthen's hearing.

"Dad, I know?" I don't have to ask.

Though he speaks in a hushed tone, the age lines between his eyebrows deliver an entire diatribe. "Why are you here dealing with these people? That damn man is not fit to shine your shoes. What do you see in that boy? You mean you were with him all this time, while you told your mama and me you were taking these girl trips and lawyer retreats?"

Disappointed and hurt, he awaits my answer.

"Dad, I understand you're upset with the lengths I went to so he and I wouldn't have interference. But aside from his father, Easton literally just charged into a violent crowd to make sure I was safe, if that says anything about why I still love him, okay?"

My father's eyes flare, partly with pain and partly with fury. "This is the same man who profits from tearing down the communities where my family was raised."

The loathing on his face, I feel in my stomach, because I played with my cousins there.

"I haven't forgotten. Trust me."

But right now, I simply don't have the headspace for family infighting.

Most important to me is that East doesn't feel like I betrayed him or burned him in the LaShauna Posey case. Now I'm second-guessing myself and whether I should have pushed harder to quit.

You see I'm here for you. I support you. But don't burn me anymore, Korienne.

"Girl, calm down," Shal tells me under her breath. "East knows you're not up to foul shit and his daddy is a trip."

"But he just got injured when he thought I was rejecting an investigation of his father. I told him I would never." That I fell for Vash's provocation and went back on my word grates my conscience to shreds.

While he sleeps, I'm unconscious along with him. So racked with worry, I almost miss the doorbell ringing.

"Maggie, what are you doing here?" Dad asks Judge Sharpe when she walks through the door.

I'm surprised to see her myself. "Judge, hey."

"Easton and I spoke earlier today. He said he wanted me here. But I also saw the news. You and him all right?" she asks me.

"Yes, but I don't get what he wanted with you." Now I'm really confused.

With a polite smile, she shrugs and gives up nothing. "I suppose we'll find out soon enough when he wakes up."

The confusion only gets worse.

Carol Worthen throw his arms open to greet someone else in a way he's never done for me.

"Hey, woman, get on in here," Mr. Worthen says to whomever is entering in the foyer. "I'm losing my damn mind. He'll need his smartest and best in here with him when he wakes up."

"Carol, I was on my way here before you even called, and I brought my things so we could start handling his media and press right away. We need to talk strategy. The moment he wakes up, we should get him up on social media so everyone sees what he's been through. It makes your family relatable. Also, we should get one of the local news stations over here for a one-on-one."

I'm too numb to be livid.

In her made-for-fucking pencil skirt, Reed turns to me. "Oh, Korienne, it's been a while. Glad you're all right after all that tussling on your job. Have you ever considered another line of work? Instead of hooligans fighting in the streets, maybe a role more conducive?"

Shallon steps in. "Um, Reed, save your fake concern. As one of the top prosecutors in the county, Kori doesn't need career counseling from a professional ass-kisser."

"Shal, never mind," I tell her. "Look, Reed, I'm sure you mean well, but I don't think it's a good idea to put East on social right now. He owns a law firm, and he works hard to brand himself as a tough, no-nonsense dealmaker. He wouldn't want to be plastered everywhere in a bed all beaten up. It might rattle his clients' confidence in his health and send them scattering to other firms. He would want to be fully dressed and sitting up, so the public can see him strong and persevering."

Reed tips her head aside inquisitively. "That's odd. East used to post pictures of himself in bed all the time."

"Yes, *years* ago. Before his law firm took off and he realized he needed to present as aggressive if he wanted to be taken seriously. How many law firm partners do you know who post themselves in bed? Oh, that's right. You don't know any, do you?"

"Thirteen of my clients are law firm heads, and none of them have ever been in a riot. You're right. I don't know any of those."

"Reed," Mr. Worthen stretches his arm toward East's old bedroom, I remember. "Easton is through here. This all happened behind that LaShauna Posey mess we've been talking about."

I start to follow her, so I can watch, but his father stops me.

"You can stay here."

"He would not want you taking his pictures in that condition!" I say louder than I intend.

Mr. Worthen leans toward me. "You're not his wife. It's not your call. He shouldn't have even been with you, or he wouldn't be in there right now. You're the *last* person to say what's best for my boy."

"Now hold on just one damn minute," my father says. "Your son is damn fortunate—"

Essence intervenes. "Carol, East would want Kori in there."

"And where has Easton's judgment gotten him?"

As I watch Reed strut toward an unconscious East, all I can think of is how he'll wake up and the first thing he'll know is I betrayed him.

Chapter Sixteen

I CHOOSE

"Where's...?" The train crash on the left side of my face throbs through my skull, and I can barely form words. But in the fog, I need to fucking feel her.

Soft fingers slide through mine.

Her voice in my ear is...unsettling. "East, I'm here. We're taking good care of you. You're going to be just fine."

I can't fully recall what she said to ratchet up my blood flow in my ears as I stumbled in here.

All I can attest to is how the balm of Kori soothes a Negro's soul so good he'll die a thousand deaths just to open these eyes and feel her sweetness all over again.

"Praise God." My mother crowds over me, kissing me, her tears smearing my skin, fingers tugging my chin. "You're just fine, sweetheart. You haven't been sleeping long. Just an hour."

"Let the boy breathe, Essence," my father admonishes. "Son, we'll get the motherfucker who did this. I'll see to it. Our lawyers are already going after the sheriff. He won't ever see another day of work.

You only need to tell us what you were doing out there. What on earth possessed you to charge at officers in the middle of a damn riot? And why is Judge Sharpe sitting in our living room?"

Through my right eye, I can make out a sea of faces in the room. But none of them is the one I'm searching for.

Instead, I almost jump from my damn skin. The person holding my hand is not Kor. Grateful I can move, I slip my hand out of Reed's.

"Ko..."

I clear my throat, but my mouth is dry, so my mother holds a straw to my lips for me to sip water.

"Thanks, Ma. Where's Kor?"

"She's downstairs, baby. Your father wouldn't let her up."

She gave it back to me, Easton. She's asking me to do it.

Now the last moments I was awake lie in pieces on the floor of my mind, as broken glass. Among them is the image of an imperiled Kori who barely manages eye contact while gripping my steering wheel.

"Easton." My name out of my father's mouth is always a demand. "What the hell is going on? This is what you take us through, Easton Jermaine?" Dad asks. "Not only do you hide and go behind my back with the same people gunning for our family, but your mama and I have to look at our child, *our* flesh and blood, all beaten up. Why would you be this selfish? Not once but twice."

I'm saying if we really are shining together, then try prioritizing both of our careers, not just yours while you assign me to birth your babies.

With Kori's voice in the back of my mind, I sit up.

"Could everybody clear out and give Dad and me a minute? I'll be downstairs in a minute."

My mother scoffs. "You need to rest."

"I'm not staying in here. I didn't fall from a building, everybody." I've got too much to do. "My law firm won't make money with me lying here."

I use work as an excuse, but that's not the real reason I need to push out.

"Easton, you sneaking around with the Haughton girl was low-down." Once the door closes, he starts in. "You don't always like how I try to get you to be a man, instead of some pussy for a woman, but I've only ever looked out for you. You owe us better than lies."

My face is raw with pain, but I focus in order to think. "Dad, for the last three years, I've been happy."

"You were out of line for carrying on with our enemies. That's how you thank your mama and me?"

"Mmm..." Pressing through the ache, I throw my legs over the bed. "They're not enemies, Dad. They're lawyers doing their jobs. Kori is a..." The room spins some, and I give my head a moment to clear. "Good woman. You don't like how she stands up to you. But you need her."

"Like hell I do! I don't want them here anymore. I allowed it tonight because of the circumstances. Apparently, you feel something for her, so I didn't run her out of here. But not only does she persuade you to lie to us, she damn near got you killed. Would Reed have done that to you? No. And Reed would never help somebody prosecute your family. Why haven't you ever given her the respect she deserves?"

I stare at him and strain to keep my focus. "Dad, do you know why I came to see you at your meeting the other day?"

"You're finally coming to your senses and miss your family. You belong at Worthen with your brother and me."

"Kori sent me."

Dad examines me. "If that's true, it's a shame you didn't have the good sense to come on your own. What was her motive? What does she get out of it? You'd better not be helping her and—"

"The two of us were getting married."

I give him a moment to process.

"I was ready, and we c...we could have. She's the one with a big enough heart to stop when she saw me in my feelings. I was anxious about y...you and Charles. She could have married me anyway." My face is a damn furnace.

"You shouldn't be up. You should be resting," he insists.

"I'm fine. Kor didn't have to concern herself with...mmph...you and me. But Kori wants me happy when she and I get together, which involves you. Reed would not be so selfless."

From the edge of the bed, I check myself in the mirror. Shit.

"I never said the girl was dumb. She's—"

"'The girl' has a name. Korienne, Dad."

His voice becomes a rumble. "*Korienne* is quite smart. Too smart for her own good. Maybe smart enough for politics or law or public work. Not smart enough to build or protect an empire. Not choice wife material. Reed is the woman whose smarts will serve you and this family. That's what a woman should be."

"You like how Reed caters to *you*."

Throwing his weight into his next point, he pushes toward me. "What's so wrong with that? You'd do well to learn from her because a true clever woman knows how to manipulate power. And bend it to her will."

His hand in the air, he curls it into a fist.

"Reed's sharp enough to watch out for my company. I would *never* trust all I've built to your little Joan of Arc in there. Don't ask me to, and if you do marry her, I'll always love you, son. But I'll count it as betrayal. Things will never be right with us."

I let him get that out of his system.

"Hrrph..." My damn face... That cop will feel it, too. "Here's where I see the problem with that, Dad."

"*What* problem?"

"I got a visit from Edith Zucker earlier. When I texted you."

"About what?"

"My participation in Worthen. Why I'm not more active. I sus... suspect she's sniffing around for people..." Taking a moment, I swing through dizziness. "To remove from Worthen's board. Maybe sniffing for...blood. If she came to see your son, I can't be the only person she's met with."

He helps me dress since I refuse to lie back down.

"I already know she's making moves, and I'll take care of her."

I stop him with a hand on his arm. "But that's just it. Anything you do will...bring you more smoke. I'm damn sure Zucker's not the only one sniffing around for ways to take shots. If you fire her now, in all these LaShauna Posey protests, you'll fan the flames. Mmph... The press will jump all over you. Like Worthen's hiding something."

"I don't have shit to hide. It's my damn company. I run it as I—"

"Dad, that kind of thinking won't work here. Your slash-and-burn way of...doing business got you this far, but this situation requires more hand-holding and that's not your forte."

He's so irritated at being told what to do, he's probably dizzier than me.

"Who built my company? You or me? So who are you to tell me what it needs?"

Through my one good eye, I glare at him so he can witness the rage I just endured. "Those protestors out on the street are telling you."

That anchor finally halts his ship. Though he wants to pretend it didn't.

"To hell with them."

"You take that road and Angels Rise will nev...never see the light of day. Don't let your dream die on your pride. You're in trouble. Surrounded by wolves, and you need help."

Turning my back to him, I make my way to the door. I wasn't going to discuss my concerns about the company in front of anybody else, but now I've made clear to him all I need to say.

"Where are you going?" he asks.

"I told you I'd help you. And I will. On one condition."

"Yes, that you choose whoever you—"

"That's right, Dad. Whoever I want."

My face feels like it took more than two licks, and I might be more irate than groggy. But the rest of me works well enough to head out.

"Easton Jermaine," he calls after me. "If you do this, we're finished, son."

Getting down the stairs has never been harder.

There was a time five years ago when my law firm was still in its infancy and had only just started making big deals. My money was tied up in his, and those threats scared me.

"East!" In the living room, Kori jumps up from the couch. "How do you feel? Why aren't you resting? What was so important you had to come down here?" Throwing her arms around me, feeling all over my face, she can barely hold it together. "I wish you wouldn't have."

"We need to talk, Kor."

Instant anxiety strikes her. "I gave Gloria the letter. Boyle didn't find an actual conflict. The only way to get off was to quit. And you know what people will—"

"Can everybody give us a m...a minute?" I ask the others before my mom leads them from the room.

Kori flanks me, worried and nervous, quietly explaining herself with her eyes and trembling hands on my face.

But she doesn't have to explain.

This time around, we've got the benefit of nine years we didn't have before. At this point, Kori's quietest, unspoken dreams are the lifeblood of her, flowing from her arteries into my consciousness. She doesn't have to speak them for me to know.

Searching her, pouring into her, nevertheless, I address what needs to be said. "Kori, did you ignore my calls today when you knew you wanted to do this case and weren't going to discuss it with me?"

"East, Vash was standing there talking shit, trying to embarrass me in front of all those people. I called you first."

"But you had already made up your mind." I bring our foreheads together, partly because I'm having a dizzy spell from the meds and primarily because I need us to connect.

"Are you mad?"

Those soft eyes are still tough and reel me in.

"Not mad, just worried as hell. I hate you'll be anywhere near the courthouse while that LaShauna shit is popping off. But this train is already on the tracks. Are you sure you want to ride it? I know you *can* handle it, but is that what you *want* when you're so close to finally leaving, Kor?"

"What needs to be done is not always what I want. You know this."

"You will definitely get your own security because I don't... mmph..." Damn, this headache. "I don't trust those cops."

"What about your father?"

"I'll handle him. I'm only concerned about your state of mind and your safety because nobody's got more enemies than a black woman, baby."

I've learned this from watching her break her back as a black prosecutor.

I know why she took the case. It wasn't just Vashti. A career-defining conviction at that level will silence Kori's critics and elevate her to another plane.

Her name would command the same level of respect as mine, if not more.

Sliding her fingers around my good jaw, she brings us to what I live for—our oneness. "Thank you for understanding."

"If I didn't understand, I'll never hear the end of it. But now, we'll do what *I* want. Mom!" Yelling just shot a pang down my face. Why did I do that? "Is Judge Sharpe still here?"

"Bae, what *you* want?" Kori stands there, perplexed now.

"Here, East," the judge replies, coming over to hug me. "Glad to see nobody can knock you down."

"You're damn right, they can't."

Kori's parents approach me, and her mother comes in to hug me.

"Thank you so much, son, for going to get her. I wasn't expecting this. Not at all. I'm sure you'll want justice, and we'll do what we can to help you get it. I'm glad you're up and strong."

Just behind her is also Judge Haughton, extending a hand. I'm shocked when he surrounds me for a hug, the same man who asked me if my father took me aside and taught me how to apply Vaseline before screwing the poor. Now he slaps my shoulders hard.

"I appreciate what you did for my daughter. We have our differences, but you love her. That much is clear. I'm grateful, if I couldn't be there, that somebody was. Her mother and I are indebted to you for this."

I return Judge Haughton's hug. "Thank you, sir. But making sure she's safe is *my* job now." Scanning the room, I seek out all the people I texted earlier in the day. "Shallon and Mac here? Kevin and Steven? Everybody else here?"

Steven stood up for me a couple of days ago, when Kevin was out of town. But now that Kev's back, I want him at my side.

Kevin steps forward. "Bruh, you look like you been through it. You straight, man? Glad you're standing."

"Of course I'm standing. There's no way some punk cop is taking me down."

"You ready?" Kevin asks me. "I've got the ring."

"I do, too," Shallon adds.

Confused, Kori stares from them to me. "Easton, what is—"

I take Kori's hand and turn to Judge Sharpe. "We're ready."

"Ready for what?" my father grumbles.

"I choose Kori." Man to man, I face him. Not in anger or rebellion. But with maturity and certainty. "In whatever I do next, including helping Worthen, she... mm...must be part of it."

Dad protests, "Look at the pain you're in. At what you *just* went through."

"The violence wasn't Kori's fault, Dad. It's the fault of people who tried to put fear in her." I wait for the fog to pass through my head. "They tried to intimidate a black woman who they thought was unprotected. All the more reason Kori can't back down. She *must* do this now. And we'll make sure she has the support and protection she needs."

Kori is flabbergasted.

I acknowledge her parents. "If that's acceptable with the two of you."

Judge Haughton is so awestruck he can hardly nod his agreement.

My father practically spews, "She's *investigating* us. She won't go anywhere near my company. It's a conflict of interest!"

Judge Haughton shoots back, "My daughter doesn't *need* to go near your company, unless she's watching it fall down!"

"Gentlemen!" Kori's mother admonishes them both. "This is not the night for all that. You've held them up long enough! Whether you like it or not, they're getting married. You can throw each other off the cliff after the baby comes."

"Baby?" both men say at the same time.

My gaze on my own father remains steady.

"Dad, she would be prosecuting a *murder*, based on law and evidence. She is not investigating you. But if the evidence leads back to you, that speaks to what *you've* done wrong, not her."

"At least tell me you signed a damn prenup."

"Kori offered, and I said 'no.'"

Kori's mother adds, "As she showed you the first time, Carol, our daughter doesn't want or need your money."

"I love you, Dad, but the bottom line is you can't get to Angels Rise alone. You might have built all this...mmph..."

My mother clears her throat and cuts me a lethal side-eye.

"You *and* Mom built this. But the two of you by yourselves can't keep it. It'll take all of us to help you. Which means you need Kori and me now more than we need you."

"Where would you like to do it?" the judge asks us.

"I don't care as long as we finally do it," I tell her.

I lead Kori around Dad. On my parents' balcony, taking both her hands in mine, holding her life in mine, cherishing my angel's heart in mine, we face the vast nightscape of LA.

"This isn't the perfect wedding I know you want. Not yet. But at least everybody's here now. Family harmony and all that..."

"Baby," a wide-eyed Kori whispers, *"now?"*

"Yes. Now. This is what I want. You want your respect, and I want you. If today showed us anything, Kori, it's that we don't have forever to keep putting this off."

"I need to ask you about something Vashti said."

In her eyes, it's clear she has a lot of questions about this and that. Somebody probably got in her head, and she's overthinking as usual. So I hook my gaze into hers as the man who just took blows for her, and lift her chin. With the good half of my lip that can now feel again, I touch hers, and subliminally ask Kori with my energy if she really does think somebody gaslighting her is worth questioning my devotion and holding up our forever.

The submission in her head is loud enough I can almost hear it drip from her pussy.

Then I turn to Judge Sharpe. "We're ready."

Reed stands nearby, in the same state of shock as Dad. I do care about her, and over the years, on occasion, we have connected business-wise, passing each other clients and referrals. But at no point did I invite her to come traipsing back with hopes of reigniting us. She's known me long enough to know that, when I say no, it means no. So Dad must've been filling her head with fantasies, and that's unfortunate.

"Reed," I say to her, "I'm glad you're here, too. This way, we can all be on the same page after tonight." I hold out my camera phone to her. "Do you mind taking the pics?"

It takes several eye-blinks for her to figure out how she'll play this.

"Maybe not, East. I'm happy for you and all, but I should probably go." Reed fights to keep it together on her way out.

Shallon snickers loud enough for Reed to hear. "But I thought you liked putting stuff on social media! My girl is his queen. Run and post that!"

* * *

KORIENNE

The fresh scarring on his visage is every bit as handsome and picturesque as sharp-edged Palm Desert's mountain peaks, defiant as they push up from the earth.

Easton is a Black American epic.

My hands in his, gaze inside his, soul next to his, heart affixed to his, I turn to face the most stately man I've ever laid eyes on.

"Would you two like to share what you've written?" Judge Sharpe asks.

Shal holds out my stationery where I wrote my vows, but I don't need it.

"Easton," my heart whispers through my lips, "my hero, you're the roots that anchor me to Earth, hold me up and keep my tree of life from falling. I had no idea when I was twelve years old, and you were thirteen at the Jack and Jill picnics, that the cocky boy who was yanking on girls' ponytails to see if their weaves were in tight enough would one day be the man I can't breathe without."

Our friends break into chuckles.

"I remember those days," Shal mutters.

"Easton!" his mother, Essence, gasps in horror.

"Mama, look..."

184

"Mama, look *nothin'*," Essence fusses.

I continue, "The girls never told our moms, because most of them liked it. They would tell their beauticians to make sure their tails were nailed in because Easton Worthen was coming. I always went home sad, because you would never pull on mine."

East lowers his head, and it breaks my heart to see him grimacing through the pain. But my man stares back at me determined to see this through. "You were too sweet and innocent. It would've been like pinching the wings on a butterfly. Every time I thought about it, I felt bad. But not to worry." His teeth clamp his bottom lip. "Imma pull on it a lot this weekend."

Shal snaps her fingers, and the men snicker.

Bringing myself back from the haze of how sinfully gorgeous he is, even in his condition, I go on. "I had no idea that day in the Jackson law library we were strapping in for this roller coaster we call love. No matter how bumpy, twisted, or scary the ride has gotten, I can't get off. Every curve, spin, and dip brings me closer to you. To your fearless and strong heart. To your clear-eyed sense of purpose. To your fun-loving, goofy, cavorting soul. I couldn't possibly ride this beast called life on my own and wouldn't dream of doing it with anybody else. So, my love, my ride-or-die, I guess we're riding this into eternity, even if the wheels fall off—and a couple of times, they did."

The room collectively chuckles and sniffs.

"But I'm with you until the end."

Kevin hands him a piece of paper that he takes, because though he's a far better litigator than me, East tends to get emotionally worked up. Which is why it's so hard for him to speak against his father.

"My Halo, my kind, perspicacious, precious, incredibly caring and creative Korienne, from the moment you told me I wasn't getting the law library—"

Chuckles break across our little group.

East suppresses his own laughs. "My attraction wasn't as much to your phenomenal body and physical beauty, as it was to your luminosity. How your mind, heart, and spirit radiate inside you, and the outside world is led by the power of who you are. Whether people want to follow you or not, they're simply attracted to your glow. And this mere human man is in love with your light."

Our mothers bawl.

Unblinking, unflinching, unwavering, Easton lets go of one of my hands to place his right hand over his heart, patting it. "I promise to shield your candle from the wind, from rain and the harsh elements, and to protect the power of your glow from any fool who would seek to snuff it out."

Judge Sharpe passes him a tissue to wipe his nose.

"Kori, your love is my light." He takes a big breath, like he'll need it to power up the rest of his words. "And I'll spend my every waking moment for the rest of my life sheltering your throne on which you reign, ensuring that every man and woman respects the crown that is your mind, and clearing the way for your light to illuminate the world as you illuminate me...and giving you damn good loving in every position you can handle."

Again, the room breaks into raucous laughs. Everybody, but not my parents.

"These things I promise you, baby, my love in times of hate, my candle in the dark, my moon in the night."

His words are a time capsule transporting me back five years, especially the times I walked out, ready to pursue someone "better" for me. Though I found none.

Not a dry eye or nose in the house, Judge Sharpe prompts us to repeat the traditional vows.

"Korienne Haughton, do you take this man, Easton Worthen, to be your lawfully wedded husband, to have and to hold, through sickness and in health, till death do you part?"

"I do."

"Easton Worthen, do you take this woman, Korienne Haughton, to be your lawfully wedded wife, to have and to hold, through sickness and in health, till death do you part?"

"I do."

Tears flood my eyes to the point I can hardly see the ring he slides on me.

"I now declare Korienne and Easton, man and wife."

Our circle of support applauds, along with the blood cells pumping through my arteries.

"Easton, you may now kiss your bride."

Sealing my lips to his, I try to convey the groundswell of my past nine years loving him.

Checking in with him through my eyes a final time, in that nonverbal way we have of connecting, I confirm that he really is with me.

"You sure, East?"

I've never seen him be afraid—not even earlier today—as he is now.

"No, I'm not, Korienne. But I understand how you need to go make Vash and those other opps respect you. And I've got you. On Monday."

Again, he stuns me, the way he always has, as he tugs me out of my thoughts and toward his parents' door.

"East, what are you doing? You need to go upstairs and rest. Besides that, tomorrow is Friday and I have work. I've got thirty-one cases on calendar and need to begin my review of the Posey file. And you need to hold a press conference about what happened to you today. The media and the community will want to hear from you about squaring up with cops. Aren't you mad and—"

"Hell, yeah, I'm mad. But I've been waiting on you nine years, and today could've ended a lot worse than me standing here with you."

The force of those words is akin to gravity pulling me onto his planet.

"I could have lost you, Kori. We'll be busy and trying to make time the rest of our lives. But these next few hours, all the noise can wait."

Outside in the circular driveway sits a chauffeured car. The thought of escaping sends my every little blood cell into slow motion through my veins.

"East, you literally just got stitches!"

"One of my heads might be fuzzy, but it's not the one on my dick. Come on."

Chapter Seventeen

MY HUSBAND & HERO

KORIENNE - SONG: HER WAY BY PARTYNEXTDOOR

He still hasn't told me where we're going.

In the back of the car, he tips over, snuggling into my lap to sleep a while longer on our way to wherever we're going.

My fingers travel along his bruised face as I question my decision to stay at the D.A.'s office for this case, if I'm selfish, or high-minded, or haughty, by keeping a job I don't love and putting us through this, in the name of my respect and status.

I'm at a loss once we arrive at a heliport.

The crew—from our friends to the driver to the security to the heliport operators—have remained tight-lipped.

Slightly groggy and still out of sorts from meds, he rises for us to board a helicopter. Because the Pacific Ocean glimmers on our right side, I realize we're flying south out of LA.

Flying out of the Los Angeles chaos, our hands locked together, we peer out the window, at the tranquility of vast black ocean. A silvery strip of the moon's light stretches down the ocean surface toward us. As if God is reassuring us we still have His light in this darkness.

Stress already rolls out of my neck and off my shoulders.

"East." Even in the dark, I can see them swaying underneath us. As far as my eyes can see, is a massive field of buttercups, from tangerine to primrose to magenta and canary, spanning the colors of spring.

"You knew there was no way I would marry you and not take you *some*-damn-where, even if it was up the street to the park. We'll do a whole lot more once you put the D.A.'s office in your rearview."

Though he and I have helicoptered to lots of places, and we kick back in La Jolla often, it's been years since I've visited the Flower Fields during California's "super bloom."

My astonishment touches down in me as the pilot surprises us, or me anyway, touching down right next to the barn house. Excitement fuels me so much now that I spin toward East and smack right into his sore face. "Ooh, baby, my bad!"

Wincing at the pain, he still laughs. "I'm fine. Glad you like it."

"It's gorgeous and all, but why are we out here at one-thirty in the morning?"

Like it's on cue, the doors to the barn open, and one of the staff struts out. Inside, the squeaky-clean barn that looks more like a new warehouse is decked in candles and a single table.

"Mr. and Mrs. Worthen, finally! You guys are a little late," the farm employee jokes. "I saw the news, wasn't sure you'd make it after all that scuffling. Glad you're here. Literally."

"We appreciate you keeping a candle burning for us."

"Well, with the amount of money you paid to rent this out, we'd keep 'em burning a year if it means you'll send us more of your friends with money like yours. Take a load off and let us serve you."

Only now do I realize I haven't eaten since...yesterday morning, almost practically eighteen hours ago. I was on my way to lunch in the office when LaShauna Posey's case came in and ripped a seam right down my plan to exit at last. Ever since then, all I've eaten is panic.

Now mine and East's seafood dinner-for-breakfast meal of shrimp ceviche, steamed ginger oysters, and for dessert, the server sets down in front of us my favorite from Southern Girl Desserts—chicken-and-waffle-flavored cupcakes. But I hold off and our last entree.

Before leaving us, our server stuns East by taking his hand.

"Sir, I don't mean to interrupt," the young black man murmurs. "I just want to say I recognize who you are. You're everywhere in the news. Some people don't like what you did, calling you a rich 'this and that', but a lot of us do. I know not too many folks will say this, but thank you."

Bent over at the waist, almost seeming to bow with deep respect, the guy peeks over his shoulder as if checking to ensure he's not being watched.

"I have a brother who was roughed up by LA sheriffs not long ago, and nobody ever does anything. People in the streets are on probation or parole and won't talk. Too scared the pigs will throw them back inside. I hate what happened to you, bro, but please know, no matter what you hear on the news, some of us were tipping our bottles to you and glad you stood up to them fools. If you're ever in Inglewood and want some barbecue from Phillip's, my cousin works over there, and he'll take care of you."

The sight of this almost bursts from my heart. I've always thought Easton should do something constructive with his affable "playboy" personality.

"Bet, man, appreciate that." A flabbergasted Easton accepts the handshake but then jumps as if he has a thought. "My dude, look, when you clear out of here, will you make sure we don't have any company?"

East slips the kid three hundred-dollar bills.

With a devious grin, the server instantly understands what East wants. "It's done, bruh. You have yourself a good night." The young man addresses me. "Ma'am."

A few moments later, all the lights shut out.

The only remaining light streams from the headlights of our chauffeured car ahead.

It's clear East is doing his best to stay awake so we can finally make time for our moment that's been a long time coming.

"Baby, you're struggling. This is all really beautiful, our little honeymoon in the middle of all our crazy. But I'm out of line if I don't get you to our hotel room."

East's eyes seem to activate their last shreds of strength. "You're out of line if we go another minute without you wetting me up."

The way his voice dived deeper wets *me* up.

I rise and move around to his side of the table. "You sure you're okay?"

Where he sits, legs wide open, his bulge is thick and ready in his slacks.

Lips parted and wet, like he still hasn't eaten, he eyes me with lust. "If I'm okay, I don't want to be. You and my mama are the only two folks alive with permission to hurt me some more."

"I would never hurt you...much."

Our dinnerware has been cleared out, and I remove the long tablecloth before grabbing his hand.

"Out here?" he asks, pointing toward the flower fields where I'm leading him. "Ohhh, okay."

"You *did* pay for exclusive access out here, right?" This scenario reminds me of our careless pre-lawyer days, before we were professionals and wrapped up in our reputations. Back then, we had nothing to lose.

Tonight, the San Diego night air is just the right amount of cool. Meandering through the sea of ranunculus flowers, I pick a spot on the opposite side of the barn that's out of view for our chauffeur.

After a quick scan of the area for doggy doo, bugs, and cameras on this side of the barn, I lay out the tablecloth.

"Yeah, but I didn't think you'd have me out here in the—"

Among the knee-high ranunculus flowers, I drop to my knees.

He was right about the head of his dick that already swings at me through his pants. I must trigger some urgency in him, and he doesn't give me time to wrangle down the zipper. Horny, excited to be far from the prying eyes of LA, we're damn near fighting as we pull it down together. Easton's manhood springs out, and only an overstressed woman is so overjoyed to see it.

I open my mouth wide, and he's thrusting before I push it in. Our first moments, man and wife, lovers and fighters, colleagues and friends, nine years in, amount to more than me jerking my head on his dick.

"Erghhh, fuuu..."

His high-pitched squeak—that I *can* weaken him—puts me in a zone that waters my mouth. With a deep inhale, I take a breath, gather up spit, and jump back on.

The tiny wheezing sounds from deep in his chest, accompanied by silent deep exhales, urge me on.

My hand wrapped around the base of Easton's shaft, I press harder, suck harder on my husband and hero, with the same vicious energy he gave me in a crowd of cops at the risk of his life. With all nine years he's wanted me, I put him in my throat like it will never belong to another and there's no more point in me saving it. Even once he's fucking my tonsils and I gag, I keep bobbing.

He massages my jaws and my throat. "That's right, baby, relax and let me in there." Raspy ecstasy drips off his low voice, lower with each thrust. "This dick is your dessert."

East's shaft is a pound of purple raw sugar cane sticks, bundled up and stiff. Shining from my spit in the night, sweet on my tongue, his cane fills my head like I didn't have to sign a prenup. Like he defied his father for me.

Flower petals rustle in light wind, the whistle forming our background music as I smack and gnaw on this raw, black sugar cane dessert.

Squealing, unable to control his climax, he squeezes his ass muscles, his thighs tense up. Tortured, he releases an ugly-cry. "Oh, shiyaat!"

East finally tilts his head back, faces the sky, and almost gives up the ghost. His warm seeds slide down my throat. For the few precious seconds that he convulses, I cherish his dick, stare up his torso, cling to him, worship him.

His gaze finally meets me again. "I love you, too, baby."

Shocking me, he joins me on the ground. With a second wind and new energy, he pushes me onto my back.

I never changed clothes, and I'm still in my suit from court yesterday. His focus roves over my shirt and stops. Only now stained do I realize the light smudges of his blood on my blouse.

"I'm sorry, I didn't know—"

He shakes his head and kisses me silent. "No, bae. We came close."

The realization seems to hit him all over again, as if spreading to other corners of his consciousness, switching on more lights inside him.

"You're half of me, and my blood is on you, and in you," he murmurs, sliding a hand underneath, warming the skin along my belly. Right above where his seed rests.

Surprised when he climbs over me and lifts me by my ass cheeks, instinctively, I strap my legs around him. Though I cling to his neck, it's not necessary. He holds me up.

Already, his thick shaft is back to concrete, and our mouths connect again. I'm mindful of how he winces.

He parts the entrance to me, and my body is ready for this drug, all seventy-three inches, two hundred and twenty pounds of him.

Entering my wet womanhood, through my vaginal stem up the roots of me, to where his baby grows, he fills me up, and we are botanic.

We can't kiss deep, so I stress with my fingers and my hips, how I feel his pain, deeper than flesh. To his conscience, where that cop seems to have hit Easton's true self.

Our lovemaking always exceeds superficial sex, but we are especially organic tonight. We wake up these sleeping ranunculus bulbs with the pelvis-clapping ecstasy.

Swerving his hips, he rocks hard and rough, his dick buried deep, not pulling out. Synced with him, I lose myself on his dick, rocking with him, side to side, round and round as I meet every one of his thrusts, my feet dangling in the air.

Chaotic, insistent, and poetic, I meet the demand of his emotions and tug his ass cheeks to bring him deeper into me.

He seems to forget I'm pregnant with how rough he sways.

"Easton!"

But wherever his mind is, he's lost, and he's taken my happy uterus with him.

Teeth clenched, he fists my hair tight in his fingers. "I'm married to this pussy now. I can do to it what*ever* I want."

My need for him splashes out of me and soaks his dick, the mere sound amplifying our nine-year love song.

"Aaaggh..."

He swerves his hips faster, hooking his dick up and into the core of me. "*Give* it to me."

East's sheer ferocity sends me over.

With him rocking in my womanhood, I'm locked on to him, fully strapped and riding his spaceship. Leaving the fuckery of college degrees and expectations and parents and prenups, we're physical and metaphysical on our ascent toward the stars.

Deep in me until his balls slap my cheeks, Easton screams his need into my hair, and I give him back every one of the last nine years of me. With our sacrifices, heartaches, joys, and reunions flaming in the crucible of him and me, I follow his orgasm into the fire.

For a few seconds, we lay spent, before I hold up his face to check where his head is. "Baby, you were on some galactic shit with that one. You're about to fall out. Let's get to a—"

With his fresh scars and bruises scraping off my face, *all* of Easton Jermaine Worthen hovers over me.

"I'll always fight for you, Halo. And if anybody—I mean *anybody*—in that building so much as side-eyes you too hard..."

"East, you should absolutely file a lawsuit against the sheriffs. But, baby, please, leave it there. We've worked too hard. We've got too much to lose."

From his eyes to mine, in these fields of nothing else but us, Easton's muscles ripple over me, and they carry his tension and uneasiness.

"You won't lose. I just hope once you win, the victory—whatever that looks like—is what you really want?"

Chapter Eighteen

THE SAME RESPECT

KORIENNE

"Mr. Worthen, raise your right hand," Judge Boyle says on Monday morning, far from the peace and tranquil magic of the Carlsbad Flower Fields, and back in the crucible of LA.

Now my husband raises his right hand for the clerk of the court to swear him in. "Do you acknowledge that you are hereby sworn, and make these statements, under penalty of perjury, as an attorney and officer of the court?"

Around the courtroom, no fewer than ten cameras snap him from every angle, in one of the rare instances they get to scrutinize and inspect the son of one of America's wealthiest black men in person.

"Yes," Easton answers.

"Very well. Is Deputy District Attorney Korienne Haughton Worthen your wife?"

"Yes."

"Hmph," an observer says from the back of the courtroom gallery. "Why have they been hiding it? Why is she even on this case when it happened on her father-in-law's property?"

On the other side of counsel table, Vashti and her defense colleagues side-eye both of us. Whispers and giggles fly among them as they visibly eye-fuck my husband. From head to toe.

For a long time, I avoided these games women play.

I ponder whether to check them with my stank-eye or ignore them and deny them the satisfaction of knowing they're under my skin.

"Order in the court," Judge Boyle says. "Have you held any conversations about specific facts in the case of *People v. LaShauna Posey* with your wife?"

"No."

Each heavy inhale of his lungs steals a breath from one of mine.

"Have you and your wife exchanged any information involving the case of LaShauna Posey?"

Easton thinks, and then answers. "No specifics. No information or materials have been discussed or exchanged."

"Liar!" a family member yells from the back of the courtroom. "All of y'all be lying!"

"Order in my courtroom. One more outburst, Mrs. Posey, and you will be banned from further proceedings." Judge Boyle continues to question Easton. "Mr. Worthen, you agree that you will not discuss any specifics of this case now that your wife is prosecuting it, and these events may involve your clients, Worthen Properties, Carol Worthen, Worthen Management, and possibly even yourself?"

"Your Honor, I will not."

Cameras circle around us, zooming in and out for closeup angles, so the news and gossip shows can play this scene on repeat and dissect it.

Dissect *us*.

"And, Mrs. Worthen, do you understand that you are also ordered to refrain from discussing this case with your husband?"

"Yes, Your Honor."

"All right. Attorney Easton Worthen is hereby ordered to abide by an ethical wall from this case, due to the potential involvement of him or his family business. Mr. Worthen, thanks for coming in. You are excused. Now, for pretrial and four-zero-twos."

The moment he moves, a chorus of cameras shutter in our ears.

In our first intentional public acknowledgement of us being back together—other than the fracas a couple of days ago—East slides a hand under my chin. His eyes squaring with mine, loving mine, reassuring mine, he bends down and lays a kiss on my forehead.

All the noise falls silent in this fraction of a moment, where Easton and I transport back to our bedroom five years ago making a decision, back to a private hospital with my legs open, to the unborn baby we sacrificed to get here, to the deepest, most sacred realms of me where our love meets at the child I now carry.

"Your name *will* command as much respect as mine, Halo," he whispers.

The swelling has gone down on his face, leaving behind darkened bruises that will take weeks to heal. He's never been more beautiful.

Barely moving my lips, I murmur as low as I can manage to keep people out of our business. "I've never loved you more."

He's hired private security, and an agent meets him at the door. "All right, folks, give him space."

News reporters start in.

"Mr. Worthen, will you be suing the sheriff's department for what happened to you yesterday?"

"Did you or your father order the police be called on LaShauna?"

"Do you believe Worthen should have handled the eviction better, rather than resorting to law enforcement?"

Once the room is quiet again, and the army of news reporters have exited with him, Vash turns to me. "Aren't you two quite the shiny couple?"

"Stay out of my business, Vash. Nineteen years. That's the offer."

She sucks the back of her teeth. "Your Honor, Mrs. Worthen will need four-zero-two's because I'm subpoenaing all of the eviction manuals for Worthen properties, all of the instruction manuals for employee training, call logs for Carol Worthen, Charles Worthen, and Easton Worthen, and that's *after* my fifteen-thirty-eight-point-five motion of which I'm noticing the People and the Court right now."

The war begins.

"Whoa, objection," I respond. "Counsel's got serious relevancy issues, Your Honor."

"Let's take it one matter at a time." Judge Boyle skims his calendar. "First, I'll set the hearing on a motion to suppress police evidence, pursuant to Penal Code section fifteen-thirty-eight-point-five."

Lifting my brain from the bench and back into the game, I address Vashti. "To suppress what? The officers had a right to be there pursuant to a lawful eviction. Any contraband they searched and seized was lawful. All evidence obtained from the property—LaShauna's weed, her son's guns, her phone, her son's phone, and the personal items and effects in her bedroom—come in."

"They still needed her permission and had no business just busting into a private residence."

"They didn't need her permission since at that point, she was squatting."

Judge Boyle hammers us to silence with his gavel. "All right, Counsel, I'll take briefs on the matter, and we'll set this hearing for two Tuesdays from today."

Once he gives us the briefing schedule.

Soon as the hearing is over, I turn to her. "Don't use this case to play politics, Vash. You know damn well Worthen's employee instruction manuals don't have crap to do with this."

"*You* know what, Kori? You put up this pretense like you're such a good person from a good family, trying to do the right thing and all that, but you and him didn't even sniff in LaShauna's family's direction or acknowledge their suffering. You look at them and see criminals already, or you didn't notice them there at all."

"And you always play the angry activist, but you wonder why the AAWPA board didn't want you as president. Some of LaShauna's family tried to attack my husband and me the other day. You didn't release a single statement admonishing the incident or encouraging peace. But now you're expecting me to go hug them? How many times have you looked over at the victim's family, Vash? Whether you like it or not, that cop had a family."

Speaking of the family, I go to Officer Brighton's loved ones and his police colleagues. His wife and mother are stricken with grief.

"Please do all you can to get this over with soon as possible. This is awful," his wife pleads.

"Look at those black coons over there," some Posey family members insult us.

I glare at Vashti, who reminds them to stay respectful.

Donning my daily uniform of poise and calm that are threadbare after years, I turn back to the family. And strive to maintain authority in my conversation with a predominantly white group of the officers, despite my own people talking down to me.

"I'll do all I can."

"We appreciate that very much." Brighton's mother asks, "About how long do we have to go through this?"

That's a damn good question.

"It depends on how long she and her attorney are willing to fight the charges, which is their right. But I'm hoping I can get her to plea to nineteen years."

Mrs. Brighton replies, "That plea deal should honestly be thirty years." Her voice cracks, face cracks, chest crumbles. "Deliver justice for my son, Mrs. Worthen. We'll wait however long that takes. He has no history of harassing or mistreating anybody. She shot him in cold blood."

An older man, apparently Officer Brighton's father, steps toward me like a school principal addresses a child who roams the halls during class. As if he found me in the wrong location. "Ma'am, you sure are mighty young to be in charge of such a serious felony case. May I ask how long you've been a prosecutor?"

The condescension always bites far deeper than flesh.

Nevertheless, my role for the office of the D.A. comes before my feelings. "Long enough to have secured seven hundred and twelve convictions and won fifty-eight of my sixty-one jury trials."

Slowly, he processes that I didn't just fall off the cabbage truck yesterday. I'll take his silence as begrudging acceptance.

Before they depart, I acknowledge Officer Brighton's black wife as the final authority and most important voice in this matter. Not his police colleagues, not his parents, but her.

Mostly, because I understand the burn of being overlooked by officials and officers who search for somebody older, or white, whom they think should be in charge.

"Mrs. Brighton, for any developments that come up, as well as important dates and proceedings, I'll inform you."

My words stop her from dabbing at the tiny red veins lining her wet eyes.

Her face loads up with gratitude, and maybe even a drop of relief. "*Thank* you, *Mrs.* Worthen."

She sees me.

And she understands that I'm seeing her.

In another lifetime, outside my professional capacity, she and I could go for drinks.

I understand why D.A. Gray said this case needs to be handled by me.

A detective steps forward with a packet of discovery materials. "Hi, Deputy Worthen, I'm Detective Holland, and I'll be working with you on this. Here are the eight years of service calls to Posey's house, for one issue or another—fighting with her relatives, loud parties, her kids harassing others, domestic disputes, drugs. I'll be getting you a lot more over the next few days."

Vashti approaches us. "And all of it is irrelevant. Whatever happened before does not concern this issue right here. Whether LaShauna shot Brighton in self-defense when he entered her home and used inexcusable excessive force against her son."

Once we've dismissed the families, I make copies of the records to turn over to Vash, and we're face-to-face again.

"It's fine to be passionate, Vash, but find some civility. The city is watching how you and I treat each other." I can't emphasize enough how, as black women, more than ever, we should be an example in all this. "We don't have to make this messy."

"Agreed. We can avoid mess if you go to your boss and talk to her about probation, before your new *husband's* family gets embarrassed."

"What proof do you have of that?"

"LaShauna's neighbors say Brighton and his partner used to go to that apartment complex all the time, harassing the tenants who stopped paying rent. The neighbors say Worthen Properties had the police on payroll, to run the tenants off. Your man's daddy wants to convert it into luxury apartments. LaShauna saw her other neighbors getting forced out before their eviction process was finished. She didn't have anywhere to go and was scared so she got a gun. When they came to her house to force her out, she refused to leave."

That information sobers me, but I still sift through it for how much to believe. I've never given thought to my father-in-law's businesses, and now I'll have no choice.

A slew of questions forms in my mind.

What did Worthen Properties do to evict LaShauna from the property? Was it legal? Did they engage in the kind of practices that would put fear in somebody so they'd seek to defend themselves? Is there another explanation?

Turning over possible theories, I'm lost in my thoughts as I step outside the courtroom and into a maelstrom.

"Deputy Worthen, over here!"

"Deputy Worthen, are you the appropriate D.A. to prosecute this case since your family's business is involved?"

Microphones push into my face so closely they nearly smack me.

"Are you aware of the rent increases on Worthen Properties and the number of evictions carried out by force when tenants like LaShauna Posey could not pay?"

Megawatts of camera flashes explode in my eyes.

"Is it true your father-in-law is chasing out low-paying tenants to convert his properties to luxury units?"

Blinded, I can barely make out where the cables are to avoid tripping.

"Deputy Worthen, were you assigned to prosecute another black woman because of your race?"

Staring into the faces of devastated family members, furious activists, and headline-hungry reporters, I fight not to freeze, and to see a pathway through the fracas.

Underneath my case file, I slip a hand over my belly to protect what grows in me...in mine and Easton's garden.

Terrified I might fall, or somebody might push me too hard, I hold on to my composure.

"Mrs. Worthen, have you ever even been to a low-wage housing complex?"

"Everybody, fall back and give her room!"

From the sideline, an arm extends over the crowd, and one of the security agents pulls me through. Not one of the sheriff's deputies, but a black woman in a dark blazer flashes me a badge and a piece of paper that bears Easton's signature.

"Private security, Mrs. Worthen, we're with your husband."

Through the chaos, I'm grateful to take her hand and escape the noise, but in the quietude of my office, relief still doesn't find me.

I just hope once you win, the victory—whatever that looks like—is what you really want.

Chapter Nineteen

AGAINST MY NECK

KORIENNE

"You all right there, soldier?" my Head Deputy District Attorney, or the HDDA, asks me. "How's your new husband, Easton, doing? We heard it was rough a few days ago, and it's unfortunate how things went, but we're glad you and him came through it."

I've perfected my fake warmth to a science. "He's the strongest person I know, and the world saw just how strong he is."

The smiles they return to me cover up their curiosity. Through thin veils of camaraderie, they listen carefully for any hints I drop of how Easton will handle his scuffle with the sheriff's deputies.

"Of course he is," the HDDA says. "You are one of the toughest badasses I know. It's only fitting you'd marry another badass. So what does he plan on doing while he recovers? Is he going to work today? How will he handle this?"

She's pumping me for information she will no doubt repeat to the sheriff, to help him defend against any potential moves by Easton.

But Easton is smarter than a lawsuit.

He won't leave footprints.

"Thank you for the concern. I'm not sure what he'll do, and I intend to leave that to him and his advisers. Now that I'm assigned to this Posey case, we won't run afoul of any conflict issues." In every conversation, I'm constantly being tested, so I make sure to use all the right buzz words. "I'm a little shaken up, but you're right." The next words, I say with my chest. "Days like yesterday come with the job."

That gets me their approving applause, fists in the air, and thumbs-up gestures. I'll play this game in which I pretend to take it on the chin like a champ.

But I am no fool.

Their camaraderie and respect are conditioned on my ability to win.

The moment I start losing, I lose credibility.

"Deputy Worthen." A firm voice disrupts my case review.

"Detective Holland, hey." Before I even realize he's there, he towers over my cubicle. "Was there something else you needed?"

"Here's more video for you that we grabbed from the Paradise Gardens apartment complex where LaShauna lives. It displays her arguments and physical confrontations with her neighbors three nights in a row before Officers Brighton and Fitzpatrick were called to her place. They were not responding to an eviction removal. They were responding to noise complaints about her."

His gruff, unflinching face is a police car siren that he uses to drive home several points.

"The eviction didn't play any part here. LaShauna was a problem child, the black sheep of her family. The officers had *no choice* but to go inside and handle business. That's the *only* story here. And I also believe that nineteen years is too light a sentence, and you should increase that to thirty."

Along with the packet of evidence, he also gives me my theory of the case.

Like I'm tiptoeing around a landmine, I frame my response carefully. "Detective Holland, I appreciate your insights, and I'll see what the evidence reveals."

"I just told you what the evidence reveals. What I gave you isn't just insights. They're twenty-four years of experience, kid."

Now wait just a gatdamn minute.

"The person who's prosecuting this case will decide what's insightful and what's not. And my name is still either Deputy or Mrs. Worthen. Enjoy your afternoon, and I'll call you for any further evidence I need."

They always try to sneak in the age, race, and gender toxicity, but I've dealt with it so much over the years, it's more detectable than the stench of sewage.

For a moment, he doesn't budge.

And I don't blink.

"You know, *Mrs. Worthen*, there's a lot you don't know about your father-in-law's company. Your husband also had a lot of fun parties just a decade ago. Too fun. In the unfortunate event you don't get that conviction, or if the *wrong* information gets spilled, I'd hate for the world to accidentally find out about the *real* Worthens. Just do what I tell ya, and you'll be just fine."

My heart is a battering ram knocking through my chest, but I strain to pretend I'm cool. "What wrong information? You officers and deputies are such sterling public servants, I couldn't imagine there being anything wrong. I look forward to working with you to reach justice that is fair and transparent in this matter for *both* parties."

The moment he's gone, gusts of dread blow out of me.

So Holland plans to shove his narrative down my throat and prevent me from doing a thorough investigation of what really happened. Or from finding out if the LAPD committed unreasonable search and seizure and entered LaShauna's home illegally.

And what might be Worthen's involvement?

Vashti's words come back to me. *"The neighbors say Worthen Properties had the police on payroll, to run the tenants off. Your man's daddy wants to convert it into luxury apartments."*

Sticking the disk of video footage in the computer for copying, I start up my personal spreadsheet of evidence, with different columns, and create a timeline based on the witness statements, service call logs, and video footage from body cameras and the apartment surveillance.

"Hey, Kori," another black female D.A., Falise, says to me on her way out for the day. "Oh, I forgot it's Worthen now. I heard that little dust-up with Holland just then. You handled him well, but be careful. We all work here, but we're not in their club. Watch yourself, girl."

"Appreciate that. Have a good night."

So Holland and I were not alone, and someone overheard.

The humiliation lights a flame.

Back to the initial witness statements. Early this morning, I started reviewing the first police interviews taken right on the scene. And I noticed a discrepancy.

One of the witnesses stated she'd seen Officer Brighton at the apartment complex the evening after April first. But the service call logs don't reflect said visit.

In fact, there are several times the apartment complex videos show Officers Brighton and Fitzpatrick going to the property, but there was never a corresponding service call.

Shit.

Were officers going there and harassing residents without anyone calling them? Was Worthen giving police free rein over the residents? Which means Vashti is right.

For the public to learn this would be a nightmare.

I set aside a copy of the police-provided videos and logs for Vashti.

But this is the evidence police have *chosen* to give me. There is no telling what evidence they're still withholding, or erased, or doctored, or "lost."

I want the full story. My next phone call should not be made in this office.

Rounding up my binders and bag, I get ready to leave for the weekend I very much need. Before heading out, I leave Vashti's evidence packet at the front desk and shoot her an email.

The new evidence packet is ready for you to come and pick up. Let me know if you change your mind about settling this.

Once I'm out of the office, I make my call.

"Hey, Kori, what's going on?" Kevin Middleton asks from his Santa Monica office.

Detective Holland must have forgotten. I'm a deputy district attorney with *my own* resources.

"Hi, Kevin. How can I obtain satellite imagery of Paradise Gardens for the past eight years? Or for as long as you can get them?" I'm certain my father-in-law knows every move that is made on his properties. "Specifically, I'm interested in the movements of LAPD patrol car number twelve-eighteen. As well as the movements of the private vehicle owned by Michael Brighton, and the vehicle owned by LaShauna Posey. I'd also like their cell phone records."

I'm getting to the bottom of why Michael Brighton was going to the Paradise Gardens apartments when the neighbors hadn't made any calls for service.

On the other end of the phone, Kevin's squeaky office chair whines. He must be leaning back and thinking. "Is this a private ask or formal discovery?"

"Right now, it's for my eyes only in my private capacity. But based on what I find, it could become public, yes."

"I'll get you what you need. But, Kor…"

"I know." The risks are grave. This evidence could be harmful to my husband's family and could carry implications for the police. "My review will only go as far as necessary."

"That's all I ask." For his reputation of being a tech asshole in Silicon Valley, Kevin is a real one. I see what his wife, Cher, has loved about him since she was a kid.

"I'll be fine."

Based on how contentious this case is, how much is at stake, East is right. We can't trust the police or the sheriffs. Most of them have never been a problem. Most have been classy and upstanding men and women who are exemplary professionals. Most. But the force has its seedy outliers. One of them took a baton to the man I love. I'm still appalled at how Rex refused to even call an ambulance to the scene.

Now, Detective Holland has already started applying pressure for me to prosecute this case the way *he* sees it. As if I'm only here to do his bidding. What happens if I don't?

My knees wobble on my way toward the building exit. The sight astonishes me.

On the other side of that door, across the street, a small island of protestors stands in front of the building, fists in the air.

Somebody with a bullhorn shouts loud enough for me to hear inside. "Free LaShauna! Get Korienne Haughton Worthen off this case!"

"Mrs. Worthen, this way," a private security agent approaches me. "We've already cleared a different route for you."

Relief washes over me, and the black woman security agent from earlier escorts me to a side emergency exit. "Thank you so much."

"No problem. Glad to be here for you."

But even once we reach the outside, the protestors have got a lookout at the side entrance. And there's a courtyard in front of me I must cross before reaching the SUV on the street, so I'm exposed.

"Hey, there she is!" their lookout yells.

Not a policeman is in sight.

Some of the crowd runs toward me.

"Kori Worthen, get off the case! Kori Worthen, get off the case!"

Protestors change their chant to, "Betrayed your race! Get off the case!"

I stand my ground. "Do not come near me."

"Mrs. Worthen, come on! This way." The security agent grabs my hand. With her flipping from one side of us to the other, her hand threateningly on the gun at her hip, she faces oncoming protestors. "Stay back. We don't want problems, so just stay back."

Another security agent in a matching uniform joins her. "Back off," he commands. "Let's not get rowdy, everybody. We'll keep this kosher. Back up!"

"Fuck that sellout!" a protestor yells back. "*She* should be in jail! Not LaShauna!"

My first concern—my *only* concern at this point—is my baby.

Please, Lord, protect and keep our child.

"Keep it peaceful. Everyone, come back," Fannie Kilpatrick, notorious activist, says from across the street. "Mrs. Worthen will have to sleep with her conscience at night, but for now, step back and give her peace. We will not stoop to the level of our oppressors. We will not terrorize her the way her police have done to us."

Forcing my chin up, and praying my inner terror doesn't show, I fight to maintain some measure of grace as we hightail it past the faces.

The black SUV waits on the street, just a few more precious feet to go.

"Deputy Worthen!" A sheriff's deputy finally pulls up in a marked black-and-white. "We're your patrol. Let's get you out of here!"

"She's with me!" the security agent barks and shepherds me to the SUV. "We've got her."

We pass up the sheriffs who don't seem relieved that I'm safe. Wearing ominous expressions, they don't wave or wish me well.

We finally reach the SUV, and one of the agents throws open the door. Inside, I find solace in the protection Easton sent me.

Only now, there is no doubt in my mind. The absence of sheriff's deputies when I first came down was a message. Not just from Detective Holland but from the department.

If Easton files a lawsuit or retaliates for what happened to him, they'll play with my life.

If I handle the murder of Officer Brighton in a way they don't appreciate, they can play with my life.

Though we ride away from the scene, the panic still rides through my veins.

With shaking fingers, I sweep away my silent tears and reassess how safe it is to do my job with a metal baton pressed against my neck.

You won't lose. I just hope once you win, the victory—whatever that looks like—is what you really want.

* * *

EASTON

"On your knees, you spoiled daddy's boy piece of shit!"

For the past several days, D. Quick's hatred has swung on me every time I close my eyes.

Now on my way out of the Criminal Justice Center with my entourage, I'm escorted by Steven, Charles, and my security.

With the entrance a few paces ahead of us, we've almost left the building.

The sheriff's deputies line against the wall, and there he is, still holding his job and receiving his paycheck. The deputy who hit me squares his shoulders unapologetically.

Somewhere in the ether, Steven speaks to me, but louder and clearer is my fury. My hot-ass blood boils the reason out of my head, and Steven is not strong enough to contain it.

"East, no!"

D. Quick is now within striking distance, and I don't give a damn how unreasonable it—

My phone vibrates in my hand.

Kevin: *Check the news.*

The text message from my longtime mentor stops me in my tracks. The news?

The interruption seems to ring an alarm in my mind, yanking me from momentary madness, and the pause gives my entourage of lawyers and security enough time to block me from D. Quick.

"Mr. Worthen, will you take just a couple of questions?" a voice shouts to me from across the lobby area of the criminal court building.

As my right mind returns, only now do I notice the news crews lined up along the opposite wall from the sheriffs. Reporters and the public all observe me carefully.

Now I face the exit in front of me, and on my right, D. Quick.

"Easton," Steven mutters, his hand at my back in a subtle push toward the door. "Keep walking, man. You've got a baby on the way."

Baby, please, leave it there. We've worked too hard. We've got too much to lose.

Korienne.

She works too hard.

So I turn and move toward the media. The other night, I was more concerned about taking Kori away from all this and sharing our first night as man and wife in a special place, not holding the press conference all these people clamor for.

"Yes, I'll be more than happy to take your questions, in the future, once my *wife* has finished prosecuting this case. As I've shown you, protecting Korienne's right to perform her role is the first priority for my family and me. I'm asking you all to show her respect while she does her job, which she does damn well. Thank you."

Translation: Touch her, and I will do more than reach out and touch you.

Now I make my way toward the door and past Deputy D. Quick. With my side-eye, I subliminally communicate that he should not confuse my wealth or education with weakness. Law license be damned, I *will* go to prison for Korienne.

Anything I say—any statements I give about my altercation with police, or concerning my father, or Worthen Properties—they will use to undermine Kori. No matter what leadership roles she acquires or how many trials she wins, people attach more weight to the words of a man. I've witnessed this firsthand for the two and a half years we've dated in secret and nobody knew I was watching.

I won't give space for the disrespect.

"Screw them fools," Steven murmurs, barely moving his lips. "We'll get your lick back. For now, don't screw up your good life."

I didn't enter this building to make this situation about me, but to support what she wants, even if watching her kill herself for this job kills me. I'll never tell her.

Once we hit the street, I anticipate a horde of activists, and I'm surprised to find it empty.

My brother throws his arms around my shoulders. "Dude, I'm proud of how you handled yourself back there. I know it had to be hard as hell."

Now that he's in front of me, an observation hits.

"Charles." With him still in my grasp, I examine him, eye to eye. "What's the deal with this Edith Zucker lady at Worthen? She's been sniffing around and came by my office the other day. Is she making moves on Dad and you? You sleeping at the wheel, not looking out, man?"

His laughter is loud as he blows me off. "No, Negro, Edith

Zucker is sizing *you* up. You don't ever come around, East. She's the CFO and wants to make sure you can be trusted. Especially since you're Dad's son, she's making sure you're not on some entitlement bullshit, that you won't embarrass the company or do anything crazy if you help." He rolls his eyes at me. "Damn, bruh, your situation's got you all worked up. Calm down."

"Right." Even once I let him go and he starts toward his car, there's a weird feeling nagging in me.

Steven grabs me in a bear hug and slaps my back.

"Man, your brother is right. Settle down. All this press is putting eyes on our firm, man. But take it easy," he says. "A truckload of athletes in the NBA and NFL have been calling from other states, asking if we'll handle their real estate deals and some transaction work for their side businesses. If you wanted to parlay all of this noise into helping brothas with money, who don't have anybody around them they can trust, this could turn into payday. Just stay your ass out of jail, though," he jokes.

I'm still nervous, and my mind isn't really here, especially as long as Kori is still in that building with those dudes. "All right man, bet. One thing, though. Whatever you do, don't mention Worthen. My father's company is not to be spoken in our firm *at all*. I want complete separation between his business and mine."

With a long look at me, Steven nods. "You've got doubts."

"I've got questions."

"Cool, bruh, I'll see you back at the office later."

First, I head to my home with one thing on my mind.

A cryptic message from Kevin Middleton, telling me to "check the news," could only mean one thing.

At home, I have two safes, one I share with Kori to store the jewels I buy her, and the other is mine alone.

Not because I don't trust her, but some of my business dealings around the world do push the legal line, and if there's ever trouble, I want her to credibly be able to say she didn't know.

Reaching through the entertainment center, installed at the back of it is the opening to a concrete vault. I slide out my encrypted laptop that not even Korienne knows about.

For non-law firm, non-Worthen activities like offshore accounts and investments, collaborations and projects in other countries, research and conversations I don't want anybody else discovering, I only view this when she's not here.

Eyes wide, I sit back on the couch with the personal data for this Officer Michael Brighton—emails, text messages, social media direct messages, and the movements of his personal cell phone. Shit.

Brighton was using it for both his personal activities *and* his work duties, as most officers do. He'd been assigned to work the area of Paradise Gardens for about three years.

Kevin told me Kori also asked him to provide her with this information. I hope she sees what I'm seeing.

I keep reading as fast as I can because, either in ten minutes or when I close the file, this encrypted data will vanish.

That's not all.

In the next file is the rest of the data, and the next set of names, along with bank transactions.

I'm pretty familiar with most of these companies that Worthen pays—apartment management companies, lawn care, utilities, mechanics and maintenance, but...*military* equipment?

The hell? Hilltop LLC? What is that?

The *Los Angeles Times?*

The blood rushes out of my face and crashes down my veins in a damn torrent.

Signed checks from Hilltop LLC to certain individuals.

Shit.

Hands shaking, I put Kevin on speed dial.

"Watch your mouth." It's a warning for me to speak in code. In the background, his eighteen-month-old toddler babbles.

"Kev, man, nah. This here is a mistake." My lungs are contracting. "You got s-something scrambled."

Dizziness hits me, and I can't see with the room spinning.

"Easton. When was the last time my shit came back incorrect?"

The phone falls from my limp fingers, before I pick it back up and answer, "Never."

Chapter Twenty

THE OTHER WOMAN

EASTON - SONG: HUSBAND BY SHIRLEY MURDOCK

"Carol Worthen, we want answers! Stop hiding in there!" LA activist, Fannie Kilpatrick, yells at the Worthen building through her bullhorn. "You will not scare us out of our homes. If you want to build luxury high-rises, do it with your mansion in those Hollywood Hills! Give up *your* home!"

About two hundred residents and protestors crowd the sidewalk in front of Worthen Properties today. They've been alternating their rallies between the courthouse and Worthen's Century City office building.

The moment I step out of my SUV onto the sidewalk, Ms. Kilpatrick points that bullhorn straight at me.

"Well, if it isn't Baby Worthen rolling up. Why don't you come on over here and tell us what it's like to have a wife prosecuting your daddy's tenants? How much money did you and Miss Korienne withdraw out of that Worthen cash machine this morning?"

I didn't bring an entourage with me this time. Security hangs back. Steven is on standby. No suit and tie. The public only sees me.

Moving toward the crowd, I approach Ms. Fannie in front of news cameras and the reporters.

"Good morning, Ms. Fannie." Hands shoved casually in my pockets, I stare at her and the mass of people. "Rather than insulting my wife and me publicly, couldn't you just pick up the phone and call? So we can talk. Is this public spectacle required?"

Through the mass of protestors shouting, I proceed toward the building.

"Easton," Dad's secretary, Cynthia, jumps up from her desk. "Your father's in a conference call with investors in Miami. If you wait, he shouldn't be too much longer."

"No need. I'm not here to see him anyway." I head toward another office.

Her heels thump the floor in their race to stop me. "East, what is your problem? You can't just storm in there. You know the rules!"

"It's too bad I'm the only one who follows them, Ms. Cyn." These legs don't stop moving until I reach the office of Edith Zucker.

Inside, she's surrounded at her desk by investment and accounting officers.

"Mr. Worthen, you're here. Shockingly enough. And here, you pretend not to have any interest in your father's dealings. What can I do for you?"

"Resign."

I'm addressing her *before* I go to Dad. I don't want her to have a chance to call her lawyers or think up a lie or call up her connection at the *LA Times*. I just want her ass gone.

Since Dad won't get rid of her—he *must* be screwing her and can't see straight—I'll address myself.

Removing her glasses, she eyes her underlings. "Could you all please excuse us?"

"Hey, E, dude. You good?" the Director of Capital Management says on his way out. "We hardly ever see you around here. This sudden energy is, uh, not normally your vibe."

"Don't mean to interrupt your workday. This couldn't wait." I stare at Edith. "We shouldn't be long."

The other company employees slowly rise from their seats, eyes as large as cue balls with curiosity as they close the door behind them.

"So, Mr. Worthen, I suppose you know more now than you did the last time we spoke. Care to share?"

"Whatever game you're running here with my father, you will *not* hurt my mother or my wife. I don't give a damn about what Dad wants, or you and him have some secret love, or what the case might be."

I hold up the letter I'm carrying.

"This is a formal notice of my petition to have you removed from Worthen's Board of Directors. Leave, and I won't file it."

It eats me up that Dad's carried on these affairs over the years, but his marriage to Mom is their business. They do things the way they want, and Mom tolerates what she wants. But now, his mistress threatens the rest of us, and I will *not* abide it.

The only reason I can think of for him not getting rid of this snake when I warned him the first time was that she is his side piece.

She nods and removes an envelope of her own from her drawer.

"Be careful about who you accuse, Mr. Worthen. I don't take threats lightly, and I am in a unique position here. Also, I'm not your enemy."

"The hell you're not. I've got pictures of you and him at hotels, in other countries, You're outing my family's company in the newspaper! *After* you conducted transfers of money to police! You. Nobody else! So if you care about him, why are you going to the paper? Unless you and him fell out and you plan on setting him up to be the perpetrator while you come away as a so-called 'whistleblower.' The shit's about to hit the fan with these protestors and a dead cop, and you're running for the exit before you—"

"Enough, Mr. Worthen. Please don't insult me. I wouldn't touch your daddy with a *twenty*-foot pole. And I don't do your father's bidding. My sister does. You might know her. Her name is Gloria Gray."

"Damn liar! Gloria Gray *hates* Dad! Why would she—"

Shit.

Convulsing is not the word to describe what might be happening in me. Not because I'm shocked he's cheating on Mom, but Dad has a type. Gorgeous, smart, and strong but not "too" strong. The kind of woman like Reed, whose intellect would always serve his.

Edith nods. "Now you're getting it. Gloria loves your father. Has for a long time. But he feeds my sister with a long-handled spoon and uses her for his ends. Placates her to keep her quiet." She spreads her arms around her. "How do you think I got this job? She became D.A. with Carol's money, and in exchange, she gave him access to police, city, and county officials she went to school with here in LA. But she can't accept that he'll never leave your mother, and all Gloria will ever be to him is a pawn."

I rub the ache in the front of my skull and calculate how this burning building will fall down.

"You're lying! Why bother going after Dad when she can get in trouble, too?"

"She assigns other people to do her dirty work so her hands don't get dirty—me, detectives, her deputy prosecutors..."

Korienne.

It felt too good to be true, East! I almost wonder if maybe my dad had a hand in that case landing in my courtroom. Or if my boss made sure I got it, instead of the lottery system leaving the assignment to chance.

Gloria handpicked Kori for that case. If what Edith says is true, and Gloria and my father have been together any significant time, then Gloria would know Dad does not like Korienne or her father.

If Gloria really wanted revenge against Dad, she would know the first person she can contact is Judge Haughton. They probably conspired so the Posey murder would land in front of Judge Boyle, and when Kori tried to conflict off the case, Judge Boyle refused to let her off.

None of this is illegal. But it is shady as hell and highly unethical.

So she's out to punish Dad with the LaShauna Posey murder.

"What do you get out of biting the hand that feeds you? Why would you turn on your own sister? And why now? If anything happens to Dad, you won't be CEO. I'll make sure of it."

"I don't expect to be."

"No matter what happens, I'll deal with Dad myself. But I'm not stabbing him in the back, and I'm never teaming up with you against him. I still want you out. And forget any of your little lackeys around here teeing up for the job. My brother, Charles, will promote."

Edith holds her hands up in a surrender position. "Look, Easton, what I just shared is a lot and I understand you might be hurting. But you're right. The shit will hit the fan soon—for Gloria *and* Carol. The LaShauna Posey murder of that cop has brought the dogs to Carol's door."

She leaves her desk and comes to stand directly next to me where I prop myself against the window.

"I didn't go to the *LA Times*. That investigative journalist came to *me*. They're on Carol's ass. At least if I cooperate, I can steer the narrative—the positives *and* negatives—of Worthen Properties. It is a good company, and Carol is a brilliant man with vision. Your daddy won't go to jail. He hasn't broken any laws outright. He's too smart. He may even survive as CEO."

Her gaze shifts down to the protestors who scream up from the sidewalk.

"But Carol's prideful, bull-headed. A good businessman, and he believes his success insulates him from having to listen. Nobody can tell him anything. Angels Rise will never see the light of day."

"You still haven't answered my question of what happens to you and your sister? Don't expect me to think you're some Good Samaritan after you rolled in the mud with them for years. To be telling me all this, you want something."

Jaw set, fingers anchored to the windowsill as if now she needs support to remain standing, she focuses on me. "I might have taken care of myself some over the years. I'm not 'set' like you and your family. Not too much. Just a bit here. A smidge there."

"I won't protect you."

"All I ask is that you don't report me. If the next CFO catches it, I understand you'll do what you must. Until then, let me move on to another job, in another city, in peace, and have a retirement."

"Tuh." I scratch my chin, because this is a crock of shit if I ever did smell one. "I'm guessing there's a hell of a lot you're not telling me."

"Don't forget, Easton, *I'm* the one who came to *you*. I could have bounced and let the chips fall where they may. But there are a lot of good employees here who deserve to see their hard work pay off with Angels Rise. I came to you on *their* behalf."

Moving to her desk, she slides her manila envelope toward me.

"What's that?"

"Something you should take a look at when you're ready. Sooner, rather than later. And then, you might want to talk some sense into your father."

Not a snowball's chance in hell of that happening. "And tell him what?"

"To step down. The only way Angels Rise *will* rise, and Worthen gets through this storm, is with somebody new at the helm. And I don't mean your brother who'll only be a rubber-stamp for Carol."

With a hitched eyebrow, she stares at me.

"I mean, somebody who hasn't been part of all this, who has a mind of his own, and can reassure the company and the public that he is nobody's boy. A principled leader with a young, vibrant family, a community-oriented wife who knows how to work a room, and who cares about those people down there. I didn't come to your office to try and pick you off. I wanted to see if *you* might be Worthen's next CEO."

My mouth falls. I've never thought of myself as that and never wanted it. Charles aspired to follow Dad, with me supporting him, which was no problem for me. It allowed me freedom to live my life and love Korienne.

"Dad doesn't listen to me."

"But the Board of Directors and shareholders will."

"Did you *hear* me when I told you I will *never* go against my father? Flaws and all, if it wasn't for that man, I wouldn't be where I am."

Undeterred, she sweeps the envelope from the desk and places it in my hand. "Don't be so quick to talk. This should make you reconsider. And hurry. Once the *LA Times* piece releases, and these police and sheriffs get name-checked, Carol will need to beef up his security. Your family will have hell on your hands."

Damn. Korienne. In that downtown court building, cops and deputies surround her on all sides. Fuck!

"My wife...she's on this LaShauna Posey case, where a cop died. Is there a way you can tell the paper to hold off? Kori doesn't have a clue. She's not involved in any of this!"

Edith shakes her head. "The *Times* article is a done deal. They want their exclusive. Nothing will stop it."

"I'm not asking you to stop it. Just to wait until this Posey case is finished, for her safety!"

Her expression is a nine-one-one emergency.

Shit, my phone is my next move. Not to call Kori, but to call her security agent. And Kevin Middleton, so he can pull one of his hi-tech stunts and contain the newspaper's story, or at least delay it.

"Dude, call me back ASAP," I say in my voicemail message. "Shit just got real and—"

"Son. My conference call lasted longer than I expected." Dad comes in, arms outstretched, and hugs me. "Cyn told me you busted in here like you had fire ants in your drawers. What are you doing in Edith's office all worked up? Who needs to call you back? What shit just got real?"

Over his shoulder stands Edith, who warns me in a subtle head shake to keep quiet.

Hell no. I won't screw her over. I do appreciate that she came to one of the Worthen family, especially since her sister and my mother have differing interests. But he's *still* my father.

"Dad, um, one of my boys gave me some intel, and since you were hemmed up, I brought it to Edith first. Now that you're free, we need to go in your office and discuss this."

Technically, it's not a lie.

A few minutes later, he's laughing me off. "This damn newspaper thing won't go anywhere. It'll be a blip, and people will forget about it the next day. We're still two months from breaking ground on Angels Rise. That's plenty of time for us to run an advertising counteroffensive. We'll haul out our biggest guns." Throwing his head back with that life-sized laugh of his, he slaps me on the back. "No pun intended!"

"Dad."

He's already off from his desk and ignoring me. "Charles! Where's Charles? Is he back from that tour yet? What about Ross? Page him in so he can give us one of his attack plans. If the *LA Times* wants to mess with me, I can punch back! Oh, and get Reed on the phone. That girl is a damn genius, and she can clean up *any*thing."

"Dad! *Listen* to me." I point out the window at Fannie Kilpatrick and her protestors. "That crowd is bigger than it was the last time I was here. The newspapers are paying attention to them, especially now that a cop is dead. You already clash with the city council. They're looking for a reason to shut Angels Rise down. What do you think they'll do after these secret donations get out? Your competitors will *love* this. Once they all smell Worthen blood in the water, they'll come for you."

His jaw steely as a bear trap, he comes toward his prey. "You know what your problem is, son? You've got a weak heart. I thought you were a businessman, a tough dealmaker who doesn't take shit. You've been spending too much time with that damn girl, and she's got your balls in her hands. Her and her daddy are making you soft. Reed would never have—"

"Cool it on my wife, all right? Kori's not giving me a problem. She's doing her job!" That came out louder than I intended, but this is as frustrating as talking to a rock. "Kori's not the one sending police to apartment complexes and bullying the tenants into leaving. Among *other* shady things you've done." I won't say Gloria Gray's name specifically and inflame an already heated situation.

Hands on his hips, he presses toward me. In the same space, we stand at the same height, but his energy, determination, and strength, have always stood taller.

"I see that girl's also got you smelling your piss. Boy, you might make your own money *now*, but you'd never have that firm without *my* money to jumpstart you, so watch your damn mouth."

Backing off, he releases the pressure gauge between us, though the dial never stops measuring our low-boiling tension.

He continues, "You knew we were building relationships with the people who could help protect our assets. And you've never given a damn what goes on around here. As long as those dollars kept rolling in and your Porsches were paid for, you've never batted an eye, and never cared how we got it. Now I said I'll handle this, and I will."

It's time to conclude this. "Fine. Worthen is your company. Win, lose, or draw, you run it as you see fit. But my wife is over in that court building, and I have to protect her."

"Nobody told her to take that damn case prosecuting your goddamn family. You call that love? Your mama would never have done some shit like that to me."

My phone vibrates in my hand.

Kevin. Thank God.

"How many times do I have to say it, Dad? Kori is prosecuting LaShauna Posey. She's not going after you. Unless you're feeling guilty about something."

Before I head out, I snatch up Edith's envelope. Finding out what it is will have to wait.

Chapter Twenty-One

GET ME MY SHOT

KORIENNE - SONG: THE FACT IS (I NEED YOU) BY JILL SCOTT

"East and I should probably postpone a big wedding until next year," I say to my girls. "So much is going on, and I don't think this is right. What if I can't get Vashti to take a plea and we're still in trial? What if protestors are still attacking Easton's dad? If we have a big splashy affair, it'll look like I'm showing off while a woman sits behind bars, and—"

"We're not canceling shit!" Shallon snaps. "I don't care if an earthquake comes and swallows up you and Easton, and your baby is an orphan raised by your mama, *some*body is getting married this fall, and I'm elevating my dick selection!"

Mackenzie and my co-worker, Falise, crack up laughing. They've come to the house to support me after these last few intense days. East and I have decided on having a large ceremony for our colleagues, family, and friends before the baby comes, so we're planning it in September. To give me a break from the Posey case and distract me, the girls brought ice cream and Southern Girl cupcakes.

"Heffa, stop!" Mackenzie says, cutting her eyes. "You don't even like Easton's friends. You said their dicks have been in too many communities."

Shallon points back triumphantly. "Not the ones from Harvard and Yale! They are choosey about where they put that Ivy League dick. A lot of 'em still ain't married. And they are coming out of their hoe season!"

Mac sucks her teeth. "But you don't want to get married."

"That was old me," Shallon declares. "Before I discovered Easton had a whole other set of friends in Dubai and Monaco. The best part about being the maid of honor is I got these niggas' addresses, and I see where they're posted up." In true drama queen fashion, she throws an arm over her face like Scarlett O'Hara and slides down her chair. "Quiet freaks who don't tell nobody what they're doing."

"Silly ass." Mac throws a tube of lip gloss at Shal.

But Shallon continues, pretending like she's a pastor giving a sermon on Sunday morning. "We're talking top-shelf Negroes. In Michelin-quality establishments!"

"Wellll!" Falise fans herself with a wedding magazine like she's in church.

"Their socials don't have any photos, only check-ins and blue checkmarks."

"Preach!" Falise shakes her head and closes her eyes.

"Now, Korienne, I knowwww you wanna be Moses and suffer for your people on this side of the mountain...but, girl, Imma go on to the promised land! And when I get there, I'll let you know what it be like. I'm having me a bomb-ass Christmas with at least two of these niggas. Let freedom ring! You will *not* take this away from me! This wedding *will* go on!"

"Halleluuujah!" Falise claps and jumps up and down like she's got the Holy Ghost.

Mac turns to me. "Girl, all she had to say was stop stressing, before you have a miscarriage. At first, I was all for you thumping

Vash. But that was before all hell broke loose." She sips her white wine. "I understand you want your respect, Kori. But Vash is—"

"Don't say it, Mac. I hear it enough from Easton. I have to handle this in the way I think is right. Kindness first, and violence only as a last resort."

Mac waves around her glass. "If you ask me, I think the bitch has *been* choosing violence against you, for a minute. And it hurts us to see you just lie down and take it, Kor."

"When did I say I was lying down, Mac? I simply fight different."

"She's luring you into this game of chicken. She knows you'll stay on the case to prove yourself, where she can have you right in front of her and she can keep humiliating you and East. Stop taking her bait."

Falise fans herself with a wedding magazine. "Girl, the move you *should* make is getting rid of this Posey case as quickly as possible. Go on with your lifestyle brand. Do what you love. Life is too short."

"Yes!" Shal cries out. "Have this wedding and bring these Negroes to me!"

Their warnings resonate. How many times over these last two weeks have I questioned if I should have given D.A. Gray my resignation letter?

Still, in my soul, I know better. "If Michelle Obama had not also graduated from Harvard, people would not have respected her."

Mackenzie presses her full energy toward me. "Girl. A lot of folks still didn't respect Michelle. Despite her intellect."

"Oh, they respected her. They just didn't like that they *had* to respect her. Vash doesn't have to like me, but she *will* respect me." I make that much clear. "*Then*, I'll leave."

Falise reaches out for a fist bump, and Mac brings me in for a hug.

A tipsy Shallon rolls her eyes and holds up her drink. "To fucking some Niggas in Paris."

By nightfall, the girls have left, but Easton still hasn't arrived.

Me to East: *Bae, when will u b home?*

Having my friends around and cutting up has been the medicine I didn't know I needed.

Rubbing my tiny belly, I notice it's coming out a bit. Still not noticeable to the rest of the world, but large enough inside me to now be my world.

Though nausea bothers me, and pregnancy fatigue is kicking in, my worry over East is greater, and I can't sleep a wink until I know where he is. Trying not to worry, I preoccupy myself for a couple more hours with the next-to-last subject I want to think about—the trial of LaShauna Posey.

Vashti's Motion to Suppress Evidence was continued to tomorrow.

Scattered around the office are binders of incident reports, photos, medical reports, and toxicology reports, in a puzzle I've been piecing together.

Vashti's brief argues that LaShauna's Fourth Amendment constitutional right of privacy was violated when cops entered her home without her permission. As a result, police should not have been there, and any evidence they obtained was the result of an illegal search and seizure.

She is essentially attempting to get evidence kicked out and weaken my case.

By challenging how police carried out a search or arrest, defense attorneys use a suppression hearing as a strategic tool to preview what a trial may be like. In a test run, they call two or three key witnesses to testify and see what they might say under oath. It gives the defense a chance to peek at how strong the prosecution's case is.

One of the most important pieces of evidence that Vashti is asking to suppress: LaShauna's cell phone.

A cell phone is a prosecutor's gold mine. They reveal so much that a person will never admit—what they search for on the internet, who they know, which contacts are most important to them, who their true friends and associates are, where they've been, and what they're planning.

The only evidence stronger than a cell phone are photos and DNA.

Vash wants the judge to rule that police officers' presence in LaShauna's home was illegal since her eviction still wasn't complete when the landlord called to have her put out. Therefore, the seizure of LaShauna's cell was illegal. On this basis, Vash argues all the evidence they obtained is "tainted" and should be suppressed. That means I would lose my gold mine—text messages, phone call history, direct messages in her social media apps, her private photos, video recordings, internet search history, and GPS locations.

Without that crucial information, my case becomes so anemic it must be dismissed. Or either the charges and sentence must be reduced.

But those discrepancies in the police officers' service logs have started adding up. Officer Brighton was going to Paradise Gardens when there was no reason. The question is whether he was going to harass residents, or for some other purpose?

That answer will change the trajectory of this case, and all these protests surrounding it. It might even end this case.

This is where Kevin's treasure trove of intel comes in. It helps to know a tech mogul. Confidential data I would normally get from a judge-approved subpoena in months, Kevin provided to me in days. This is mostly info not even the police possess, or either they don't want me to have.

These details of banking records, phone calls and Officer Brighton's request to transfer to a different unit, all shed light on the real story here.

Vashti might also suspect the truth. But instead of acknowledging it, she will go to court and hem and haw about Worthen being in bed with dirty cops. She's overplaying her hand.

And hopefully, my strategy won't fail. It may piss off cops. But justice will be served.

I'll give Easton just a few more minutes to walk through that door before I call his mama and mine, and we hit these streets.

Straightening up before bed, I take the unopened liquor bottles to the walk-in wine cellar.

It's an awkward spot to do so, but the moment of panic that strikes me outweighs my concern for a location. But rather than turn around, I bow my head and linger for a while in this quiet, secret place, of my deepest dreams and unspoken fears. The exact words don't form in my brain that's crowded with worry over so much, and I might have too many prayers in my head to pray just one—for Easton, our baby, the right outcome in this case, our marriage, and our safety. I hope the man upstairs will decipher what I can't articulate and hear the prayer I'm not even sure of.

Before I haul myself off the wine slots, another body covers me.

Cuban cigars, bourbon and tall, familiar contours of his physique confirm it's the right body.

"Easton! You couldn't find the—"

No chance to turn around, I'm hemmed in.

Tired and sluggish, he leans on the back of my head. No words, only ragged, heavy breaths communicate that something is off.

"Babe?"

Stiff as these glass bottles, his erection announces his presence, splitting my butt cheeks through my satin pajamas. My arms rise over my head as he nails our hands to the wine rack.

"Halo," he slurs in my ear.

There's an issue. My anger evaporates, since frustration is clearly not what he needs.

"Baby, where have you been? What's the matter? You had me worried."

With one hand, he fumbles at my pajama bottoms, his other hand cuffing together my wrists. My pants drop and, instinctively, I step out of them. Cocking my leg up, I hook it into an empty wooden wine slot and push my ass out. Whatever he's going through, drunk or not, there'll never be a time I don't want him.

On the wooden racks of this sturdy, built-in wine cellar, East slips his fingers in the fruits of my womanhood. Circling along the folds of my wetness, he whines like a lost man who's found his place of refuge. The pulp of my thick flesh responds to him, and just the thought of his wood releases my juices.

"East, put it in me."

My world that was missing its gravity only moments ago won't be rebalanced until he's inside me.

In anticipation, pussy throbbing, I beg with my ass on him. East accidentally head-butts me in his search for my mouth, like he needs to connect to more parts of me than one.

Craning my neck for his tongue, I give him another entrance to me. Another lifeline.

The stress and desperation of these last days, our volatile love, press our fruits together, and we meet in the vineyard of us. He shoves his manhood toward my ribcage. From root to stem, vine to leaf, Easton completes me.

Impatient and needy, we start the fermentation, his dick stroking more than my womanhood. He aims to penetrate my lungs, and to the left, my heart.

"Halo, open wider."

Still gripping the sturdy wooden panel for leverage, seated on his upper thighs, I lift both my feet, and he hoists me up to get more access. In the deepest parts of me, where his seed grows, he grinds the pussy he waited nine years to impregnate.

No air between my ass cheeks and his balls, I throw my hips and ride his wood, but he jerks my hips harder. Taking one of my titties hostage, he squeezes, and one hand still on my hip, he redefines my nirvana.

Knees flying out, thighs flapping open wide indeed, in a loud clap on his legs, I buck on Easton's tree of life that pounds me.

"East, careful!" But my cries are futile while I give up all my fruit.

Every nerve up and down my womanhood, he smashes, and my head falls back in the ecstasy of our drunkenness. My juices splashing and his oak pressing, our noise is fucking music. Harder, faster, relentless, he tosses me up, and my juices are the fine wine pressed in our nine years.

He doesn't pull out the dick but keeps churning, and I'm the fiend who aches for him to juice the sweetest, meatiest pulp of me.

"Fuck your husband," he mutters, his hands gripping my face.

"Take your wiiii—"

Drunk on me, East fucks the merlot out of my pussy, and in my stupor, I no longer close my legs, too inebriated on his dick strokes in the core of me.

Our fingers clinging against the wood rack, we ride out the climax until I'm juicing down his legs and mine, and he's smashing to get full on me.

In a collapse to the wooden beams, we're spent and satiated. His heavy breaths carry so much more than lust.

"Easton, baby, just tell me."

"Get off the case."

That sobers me and knocks me from our afterglow. "No."

Rising off his dick, I drop and pull up my pants.

"Kori, you don't even like being a D.A. Baby, there'll be other opportunities. I'll make it up to you, but you can't do this."

"Are you telling me what I can't do?"

"Ask me *why* you can't," he threatens back.

I don't want to know whatever information will disqualify me from this shot that I've busted my ass to earn, for seven years.

I'm *so* ready to leave the D.A.'s office, and with the Posey case, I can go out on top.

So, no, I won't ask what's got him so upset, why he came home so late and drunk, or what's so catastrophic he waited to tell me until after we fucked real good.

If I know too much, I'm no longer neutral and I would have to recuse myself from the case. Vashti would win.

Plausible deniability. If anyone asks me, I can still say I don't know.

"That's what I thought." East huffs.

Pushing past him, I march out of the small space of this cellar. "Whatever deal your father is making you, or guilt trip he's laying on you this time, no, Easton. He will not control me or my choices or this house, and he doesn't scare me! Vashti doesn't scare me! I will not be intimidated. You said you would support me."

He tails me up the stairs. "I tried! But shit is happening here I had no clue about a week ago, and if I did, I would have told you then not to take this case! You were supposed to be quitting anyway, and *you're* the one who went back on your word. Now we've got protestors, these cops...this shit is out of control! I'll say what I should have said in the first place—I don't want you on that fucking case."

At the bedroom door, I stop him from coming in. "Then you go fix it! Whatever is wrong, just get me my shot. If you want me to put up with your daddy for the rest of his life and smile for the cameras while you go out there, then get me *my* shot."

I strut to the bed, snatch up a pillow and throw it at a stunned Easton. Catching it, he comes at me.

"I will *always* defend your crown, Kor, but this here was the wrong case. You're carrying my seed, and I'm responsible for both of you. You *have* to wrap this up. Not next year, not next month. Now!" His eyes ring alarms for all he won't say. "You got Kevin's encrypted file? On Michael Brighton."

I nod. It was chock-full of information I wouldn't get for months if I used a subpoena.

"But if any evidence implicates your father, I'm not covering for him! I'm not jeopardizing my job and I'll have to refer it to the—"

"It won't." His tone dips into bleakness, where a shadow hangs on Easton's shoulders. Some part of this is personal for him.

"East."

Staggering underneath what he can't say, and I can't ask, my mountain of a husband teeters onto *my* shoulders.

Hard and tight, I wrap around his broad back and cocoon Easton in my arms. We've shared everything with each other these past few years, except for now, when the suspicion that he needs me most calcifies in my bones.

"We need tighter security around the perimeter of the house." With sluggish energy, he rambles on, his mind playing hopscotch from one worry to the next. "Maybe we'll put up some gates, security bushes, a setup like what my folks have. People can't just roll onto my yard whenever."

"That shouldn't be necessary. Protestors don't come here. They go to your folks' properties." Or I may not be ready to believe this is that serious.

Slow across my forehead, his lips give more than a kiss, but an oath.

"Baby, I'm not taking that risk."

Pillow in hand, he eases off, and I close the door between us. Not because we're mad.

But so I can't hear whatever conversations he's about to go have downstairs, and this way, I maintain plausible deniability.

East will always do what he must for me to get my shot.

Success is such a fucked-up illusion.

Chapter Twenty-Two

THANK YOU, LORD

KORIENNE - SONG: FOR EVERY MOUNTAIN BY
KURT CARR

"Good luck today, baby. I love you." The worry in Easton's voice, hanging at his brow, speaks loud and clear. He's trying to support me, even now, despite whatever is going on behind those eyes.

"Easton." I go for his hand.

Too late.

He shuts me into the security SUV that will transport me to work and walks over to the agents outside. For the last two weeks, he's gotten up every morning and delayed leaving for work, to review my protection plan in detail for today's crowd control, threat management, and transport routes. The air around us might be extra thick today.

Though this vehicle pulls off and takes me further from him, my soul lingers in the driveway. A part of me wants to jump out of the truck, like they do in the movies, and say, 'Okay, okay, I give up. I won't do it.' And the very real and sobering reality is Easton's right. I don't even want this job. But I didn't take it because I wanted it. I longed to build my career and earn the prestige. I ought to be able to leave it when I'm ready. I shouldn't *have* to give in. And I shouldn't have to fear for my life.

A few minutes later, my security agent, Sharon, helps me from the SUV, and I step into turbulence. Arm in arm, with that warm smile I now take comfort in each morning, she escorts me to the courtroom.

I pray I'm prepared enough, and that I've thought this through enough, to direct Vash where I want her.

Wielding my mental armor and emotional shield, I march through the private backdoor for courthouse staff and down the hall-ways sprinkled with photographers. They aim their cameras, shove their microphones at me, and yell questions for which I'd be well within my rights to smack them.

"Mrs. Worthen, why haven't you recused yourself since the killing happened on your father-in-law's property?"

Once I reach the courtroom and Sharon gets me to the double doors, I pour all my gratitude into shaking her hand.

"Thank you *so* much."

"You're welcome, Mrs. Worthen. Just text me when you're ready."

I'm on my own now.

Lined up against the wall is a squad of police officers and sheriff's deputies. Among them stands D. Quick. Occasionally, I've seen him in passing around the courthouse, but I'm not familiar. From the way he mad-dogs me now, one would think I shot his grandma. I'm the only one with a right to be pissed since he hit *my* husband.

But something about how they *all* mad-dog me nearly makes me piss in my pants. Though I hope I don't show it.

"Mrs. Worthen, good morning." Detective Holland comes forward, with eyes that lock me up, back in the holding cells where LaShauna is. His frosty attempt at a smile only makes him more

Freddy Kreuger-like. "The guys and I are wishing you well on the hearing. And I'm curious if you have any questions for me. Don't forget, if there's anything you need, I'll be *right* behind you."

"No, Detective. Appreciate your invaluable help on this. I'm good."

Robotic and stiff, he nods. "Excellent." But he stares at me as if he is, in fact, the executioner. "Just remember, we're counting on you. We know you'll make us proud."

"Hey, Kor." Jason serves up a dose of his goofy arrogance at counsel table. "You doing all right there? From the looks of things on the internet, you've been having some *very* rough nights, huh?"

The stink of my eye is so foul, he backs up in his chair.

"One more word, Jason, and I'll report *every single* disrespectful comment you've made the last three years. And I've documented them all—dates, times, locations *and* witnesses."

His face turns beet red, eyes blinking in shock, that his fellow D.A. would dare break the code of silence that allows him to walk around here like he owns the biggest balls on Earth.

"What did your boss say about the two years?" Vash asks in the moments before we go on the record.

My nausea is a hammer that swings on me from nowhere. Despite my skipping breakfast this morning, the room slightly spins, and I could hurl out my insides. "She said what she said the first time, Vash. Nineteen years. LaShauna shot an officer in cold blood who was there doing his job. Don't screw up LaShauna's life."

"You must be out of your mind. Those officers have been going to that housing complex, harassing them, because your daddy-in-law *paid* them to. She had a right to shoot that dude before they could escalate and kill her."

I've given Vashti all the evidence within the possession of the DA's office. However, I'm not obligated to give her my theory of the case—my *personal* reasons and basis that support why I still believe

LaShauna is guilty. Despite whatever else Easton's father may have been doing.

I'm saving that part.

If Vash wants smoke, she's getting it today.

Judge Boyle brings the courtroom to order. "So, ladies, are we ready for the hearing?"

"Yes, Your Honor," I answer.

"Ms. Burns, you have the burden of showing an illegal search and seizure," Judge Boyle states. "First witness you'd like to call?"

"Officer Franks, who was the partner of Officer Brighton."

"Basis?" Judge Boyle asks.

Vash stands. "LaShauna never gave him permission to enter the home, and he had no warrant, no probable cause, and no emergency."

"Proceed," Judge Boyle orders.

After Officer Franks is sworn, Vashti proceeds and asks preliminary questions to lay the foundation.

"Officer Franks, the night of April first, did you go to the home of LaShauna Posey alone?"

"I did not. My partner, Officer Michael Brighton, and I, responded to a service call."

"Did you meet the woman in this courtroom who is the accused?"

"We did."

"At any point did you ask the accused if you could enter her home?"

"Objection." I'm grappling with the overwhelming urge to curl up under the table and sleep. "Foundation?"

I'll be damned if Vash tries to skip over the entire incident that led to police being there in the first place.

"Sustained." Judge Boyle reads the exchange on his screen.

Vashti backs up her questioning. "Did you respond to a service call for an eviction, Officer?"

"Objection," I call again, as I fight to keep my eyes open. "Leading the witness."

"Ugh!" One of LaShauna's supporters snickers from the gallery.

"Mmph. Sellout," another whispers loud enough for me to hear.

"Order in my courtroom. One more of those, and bailiff, please show them the door." Judge Boyle doesn't look up from his computer. "Counsel, Mrs. Worthen's objection is sustained. This is direct examination, not cross."

Throwing her hand on her hip, Vashti puts on a show for LaShauna's family. "Officer Franks, do you know who put in the service call that you responded to?"

"Yes, one of the residents at Paradise Gardens, a neighbor of LaShauna's."

"Didn't you also receive a call from the apartment manager hired by Worthen Properties?" Vashti insists on knowing.

"Yes."

"Thank you. When you arrived, did anybody in LaShauna's home need your protection?"

"No."

"Did anybody in LaShauna's home ask you or Officer Brighton to come in?"

Officer Franks fumes and sucks his teeth. "No."

"Did you suspect a crime was being committed in LaShauna's home?"

Officer Franks answers, "No."

Vash stares at me. "In fact, Officer Franks, didn't you go to residents' units *many* times when you had not been invited and there was no crime?"

"Objection. Relevance?"

Vashti responds with alternative reasons why the answer might be useful for the judge to decide today's issues. "Pattern or practice. Modus operandi. Defendant's state of mind."

"Overruled, Mrs. Worthen," Judge Boyle finds. "I'm interested in whether police had a pattern or practice of going to residents' homes, which might have caused Ms. Posey to be fearful."

"Hahaaa, bitch," one of the relatives whispers.

"Bailiff!" Judge Boyle bellows. "Please escort that person from my courtroom with a warning."

Officer Franks stares at me, apparently irritated that the line of questioning is now entering uncomfortable territory. "Yes, we entered people's homes to remove their belongings."

"And, Officer," Vash continues, "when you did this, you didn't always have an eviction order, did you?"

Officer Franks rolls his eyes. "No. We did not."

My heart dives.

Vash smirks.

Officer Franks swallows and glares between me and Detective Holland.

Vashti digs in. "About how many times would you say you've gone into residents' homes uninvited over the past year?"

With a shrug, he begrudgingly gives up the answer. "Maybe four or five times."

Extra dramatic, Vash clears her throat. "You sure it wasn't more like fourteen or fifteen, Officer?"

"Argumentative," I object.

"Overruled," Judge Boyle finds. "He can clarify."

"We don't count when we're trying to keep people safe," Officer Franks snaps. "All the calls from the general neighborhood start running together." He side-sniffs his disdain at having to answer. "The number of which locations we went to and how often gets confusing."

Smug, satisfied, Vashti sits. Her point from this short, tight line of questioning was to establish there was no reason for police to go inside the house.

She wants to create the impression that police were busting into people's houses regularly, and these intrusions happened so often,

LaShauna was reasonably scared they would do it to her. Vash is trying to set up a defense that Officer Brighton's killing may have been justified.

Time to rehabilitate my witness. With a quick prayer that I don't faint, I get up.

"Officer Franks, did you say you received calls from *both* the neighbors *and* the apartment manager?"

"Yes."

"Did both of those calls initiate your trip to Paradise Gardens?"

"No, it was the call from the neighbor."

"Who?"

"Mrs. Gunther's niece. She sounded terrified. She said..."

"Objection. Hearsay," Vash objects.

"State of mind," I cite an exception to the general rule not allowing hearsay.

I throw a hand onto the witness stand and ride out my stomach dry heaving on me. The room sways sideways.

Judge Boyle leans forward. "Overruled. He can explain the present sense impressions of the person who called police."

For a quick moment, I press my eyes shut. *Thank you for the strength to stay on my feet, Lord.*

"You all right there, Mrs. Worthen?" Judge Boyle asks.

My stolen moment wasn't quick enough.

"Yes, thank you." I force my focus on Officer Franks. This next hour is crucial. "Officer?"

"Ms. Gunther's niece was breathing heavily, visibly upset. She was distraught to the point she could hardly get out her words. She explained to me that LaShauna had thrown one of her kickback parties. And that her aunt, Ms. Gunther, went over to Shaun's home to complain about the noise and people. As you read in the police report, Ms. Gunther and Shaun exchanged confrontational words. Ms. Gunther tried to leave, but Shaun followed her into the court-yard, cussing the woman out. Ms. Gunther's niece reported that she saw LaShauna hit her aunt and threaten more violence if Ms. Gunther complained again."

"Officer, did you speak with other residents who were present?" I ask.

"Yes, several others reported seeing this. Their statements are in the report, and they can testify to them."

Vash needs to know that if we proceed to trial, I will not hesitate to call every one of those witnesses who saw Ms. Gunther being hit, which is why some neighbors—the silent ones who don't go to the protests—were tired of LaShauna living on that property.

"Now, Officer, you referred to LaShauna as 'Shaun', as if you know her personally. Do you?"

Lacing his fingers in a cavalier manner, Officer Franks answers, "That's just the name we call her."

"How did you come to call LaShauna by a nickname?" I ask.

"Because we see her often."

"Could you explain how?"

His disdain shifts from me to Detective Holland, as if to convey I need to be chastised for my conduct when this is over.

"Officer Brighton and I were familiar with many of the residents at that apartment complex. Sometimes they made us food, to-go plates, called us when a problem came up. We engage in community building, so the relationship between us and residents was somewhat informal. By us having this rapport, we get more information about the streets, potential dangers, who's beefing with whom, and it helps us be better prepared. It's far more effective than simply getting a nine-one-one call and showing up out of the blue, with no prior insights on how to investigate."

"Had you been to Shaun's home before?" I ask.

"Yes. Several times."

I close in on Vashti's previous points. "With Officer Brighton?"

"Yes."

"And each time you entered her home, did she always invite you?"

Officer Franks hesitates, as if he's pressed to answer. "No."

Despite the thorn bush I'm walking into, I push. "Why not?"

The officer now glares at me. I didn't give him my theory of the case either.

But I need Judge Boyle to see the story unfolding in the officer's stiff moves. The judge needs to see the raw embarrassment, and how I didn't prep my witness for what's coming.

On the witness stand, the cop sort of sinks away from the microphone. He bolts an ankle over his knee, thinks about what he'll say.

Judge Boyle finally has to press. "Officer, go ahead and answer."

"LaShauna didn't need to invite Officer Brighton and me into her home. Brighton had a key."

The courtroom erupts.

Cameras snap away. I turn to Vashti, who now sits in her chair as if she's sitting on nails. She read the evidence wrong.

Kevin Middleton provided me with text messages from a burner phone Officer Brighton owned. *I left your key in the top kitchen drawer. Don't call anymore and don't do anything stupid, Shaun.*

"And Officer Franks, how do you know about this key?"

"I've been with him when he used it to enter Shaun's home. He'd stop by her house for breaks. Or to eat. Or to have a breather before going home to his wife."

From the gallery at the back of the courtroom, the gang of police and sheriff's deputies whip me with the lash of their mad-dog stares for tarnishing their dead brother's memory and humiliating their brother on the witness stand. Just three paces away, Detective Holland issues his own silent judgment against me.

Maybe what I've felt all this time hasn't been nausea but terror.

Mrs. Brighton's cry sounds like it claws from the depths of Hell. But I called her last week, once I put the pieces together of the video surveillance from the apartment complex. It shows Officer Brighton going to LaShauna's unit at questionable hours, and without receiving a service call to go there. I prepared his wife for this line of questioning. I couldn't imagine somebody coming to me with that information about Easton.

More noise and murmurs fly around the courtroom.

I continue, "And would you say that Officer Brighton and LaShauna were comfortable with one another?"

"Yes."

"For the two years before he was killed, do you know about how often Officer Brighton was using his key to LaShauna's home?"

"Yes." The officer rubs his chin as he guesstimates. "Maybe once or twice a week. He would tell me when he was going over there, so I could cover for him if anything came up."

"Do you know when he stopped using it?"

"Yes, three weeks before she killed him."

"Objection!" Vashti says, jumping up. "Calls for a legal conclusion."

"Sustained," Judge Boyle finds. "It'll be stricken. Mrs. Worthen, you've made your point. Go ahead and wrap it up."

"Officer Franks, how many times have you gotten into confrontations that turned physical at Paradise Gardens?"

"Twice, with people who had been lawfully evicted and they didn't want to go."

I swallow. "But the night Officer Brighton died, you weren't responding to an eviction call that night, were you?"

"No. Initially, we responded to two calls from tenants—one for assault and another call for disturbance of the peace. But as we were en route to the complex, the apartment manager also called. He asked if we could go ahead and radio in the sheriffs to help put Shaun out. The apartment manager then gave us permission to enter her home for that purpose."

"Before that night, had you ever gotten into a physical confrontation with the woman you comfortably refer to as 'Shaun?'"

"No, not at all. We were on very good terms until three weeks prior to Brighton's death."

"And what happened three weeks before he died?"

Yet again, Officer Franks side-sniffs and cuts his eyes from me. I'm certain he and all his brethren will now come for my job. I've betrayed the "law and order" brotherhood of cops and prosecutors. "Officer Brighton broke off their relationship."

Again, a second sea wave of shock surfs around the courtroom.

"Nothing further, Your Honor," I say with an eye toward Vashti.

She wanted my theory of the case. Now she has it.

Judge Boyle sits up from leaning far back in his leather chair and faces us all. "There's clearly a whole lot more to this story that the jury will definitely be interested to know. This hearing is only the tip of the iceberg. On the night Brighton died, several people called police to quell LaShauna Posey's behavior. First, Mrs. Gunther's niece called them to the property while her aunt was being assaulted. Then, another neighbor called to report it. Finally, the apartment manager called as the officers were arriving to the property. The apartment manager asked the officers to remove LaShauna from her unit since she was already being evicted anyway."

Judge Boyle studies the transcript and his notes.

"I'm ruling that, even though LaShauna did not give permission for the officers to enter her home, since Worthen Properties was effectuating legal process to regain possession of their unit, the landlord had proper authority and standing to give officers permission to enter. Therefore, the officers' presence in LaShauna's apartment fell within the law."

The shouts and fists that rise in these walls damn near breaks out into a civil war, with LaShauna's supporters and community protestors confronting the police.

"Order in my courtroom! Order!"

A few minutes of that, and once the judge regains control of his courtroom, we hang on to every word. How much evidence I've got determines who'll have negotiating power—Vashti or me.

"Once officers were lawfully inside," Judge Boyle continues, "LaShauna should have cooperated and complied with their requests. But she did not. Now it's time to find out the story behind all that, and whether the People can prove beyond a reasonable doubt that LaShauna intentionally killed Officer Brighton in a heat of passion. Therefore, her cell phone and all evidence obtained at the scene was not seized illegally. Ms. Burns's motion to suppress that evidence is denied."

"Oh, my Sweet Lord!" LaShauna's mother cries out behind me.

"Damn them Worthen fools! Y'all the ones who got that cop killed. You shouldn't have sent them into Shaun's house! She was defending what was hers," one of the family yells.

Though the ocean waves swish up and down my esophagus, I plow through the nausea and turn to the defense end of the table. "Vash, once I subpoena Officer Brighton's phone records and admit his burner phone and his cell phone into evidence, I'll have his GPS locations. They will show him going to see LaShauna when he was off duty, as well as his private calls and texting with LaShauna. You're toast, Vash. Tell your client to take the nineteen years. You can try to embarrass Worthen all you want, but it doesn't change how LaShauna and that cop were sneaking."

Vash throws me her side-eye. "Five years."

Last week, she demanded two years. She knows her defense is slipping down the drain.

"She's only thirty-seven. In nineteen years, she'll be fifty-six. Still young enough to go back to school. Get a trade. Build some sort of life."

With a hard neck jerk, Vash throws out her chest.

But before she opens her mouth, Judge Boyle calls us.

"Counsel, in my chambers. Now."

Mission accomplished.

Judges hold in-chambers conferences with attorneys to avoid wasting taxpayers' money on pointless hearings that can go on for days or even months. I knew if I presented a compelling narrative today, Judge Boyle would have zero tolerance for any further shenanigans from Vash. He only wants to preside over a trial where there are legitimate questions of fact.

Now, he opens up a jar of bite-sized Snickers on his desk, pushes it toward us.

I reject the offer. Too afraid of what my nausea might turn up.

The judge begins. "Mrs. Worthen, I'm guessing you're going to tell the jury that Officer Brighton broke off an apparent affair he was having with the accused. She got upset, didn't take it well. Three weeks later, he receives an unfortunate call to go handle her assault on someone. On top of that, the apartment manager asked officers to remove the accused from her home. This must have been salt on an open wound for Ms. Posey, who became enraged and shot him in her anguished state."

This is the reason I didn't file an affidavit of prejudice against Judge Boyle to have the case removed from him. This judge has excellent common sense.

"Not only that, Your Honor," I continue, "but I believe, once I subpoena all cell phone data for Ms. Posey and Officer Brighton, the evidence will support how he was ignoring her and had requested a transfer to a different beat. And Ms. Posey was deliberately escalating fights with her neighbors and causing problems at the complex—"

"She was trying to get him there to see her," the judge finishes.

"Exactly."

"Ms. Burns." The judge reviews his case file. "What evidence can you share that LaShauna Posey was so afraid of law enforcement, who had a key to her house, called her by a nickname, and from the appearance of things, turned a blind eye to some of her behaviors when the neighbors complained?"

Vashti reviews her notes. "Your Honor, I have witnesses that say these officers harassed several tenants. There was a shouting match between Brighton and LaShauna a couple of times before the breakup, and some neighbors even heard glass shatter. Yes, there may have been a sexual liaison here and there, but that doesn't negate how my client could have felt intimidated by these officers who took over her house. I have text messages where he once told her he'd hurt her if she was with somebody else."

The judge crests his hands and peers at her over the rims of his glasses. "But that all flies in the face of him terminating the affair. If Mrs. Worthen produces more proof of her theory, particularly that LaShauna escalated her confrontations to the point Brighton sought a transfer and was making efforts to cut off any further involvement with her, you've got yourself a big motive problem, Ms. Burns."

The judge gets up from his desk and moves to his mini-fridge for water. "Either of you want a water?"

"Thanks," I say. "I'll take one." I need it.

"Ms. Burns, it's not my business to tell lawyers how to run their cases or advise their clients," the judge says. "But no matter how this turns out, this case could get nasty for everybody involved. The police definitely have some inappropriate conduct investigations on their hands. And you, Ms. Burns, will have your judgment questioned for pushing a narrative of inequality and unlawful evictions, and causing civil unrest in the streets, when this mostly comes down to a love affair. If the People get a conviction, your client is looking at life. Are you prepared to play Russian Roulette with this woman's life?"

Vash sucks her teeth and squints. "I'll go talk with my client."

"Smart," the judge says. "I'll set this matter for pre-trial in a week so we can come back for your answer. Nineteen years is damn good for somebody killing an officer of the law."

With my game face strapped on tight, I address her once he's stepped out.

"How did you know, Kori?" Vash asks me. "And don't bullshit me."

It's time for a talk that's long overdue. "You were hoping to use this case to embarrass East and me, with the bad press."

Her quiet, simmering attitude smolders in her twisted lips. "I don't have to explain shit to you. I'm out for myself and my 'hood, just like you and your bougie friends. My concern was only for LA. I go hard for LA, unlike you when you're selling out to the highest bidder with Mackenzie."

Despite being infuriated, I'm careful with my words. Anything that comes out of my mouth, Vash will gladly take all over town to paint herself as a victim, threatened by spoiled, arrogant Korienne.

"Don't ever come for my family or me again, Vash. If you love LA so much, get out of your feelings. Start *acting* like a leader. We can have a discussion about poverty in LA if you don't think AAWPA does enough for the people. But cut this public charade where you use the community's emotions for your personal flex and call it fighting for the streets."

Now I bring my own emotions down as we exit the judge's entrance, just in time for me to catch a final glimpse of LaShauna Posey.

Cameras are pointed straight at her, silent, anguished. All the blood in her body must have rushed into her face that now shines with tears.

I've seen a lot of murderers over the last few years—stony, blank, indifferent.

What I'm seeing now is the complete opposite: shredded.

She hasn't made a single outburst. Not a crass word. No attitude. Only grief. Maybe even regret.

LaShauna's sad gaze sweeps the floor, and it may resemble what I've felt these past few days—guilt and remorse over what I've done to the man I love.

Bailiffs help her rise and start walking. Vashti follows behind her client so they can discuss a plea deal back in the holding cells.

Swinging open is the large metal door that separates prison from personhood, and LaShauna crosses to the other side. The slam of that metal on metal echoes throughout the courtroom.

Even though I prevailed in this hearing, there are no winners.

Thirty minutes later, Vashti comes out again.

"It's a deal."

More than relief blows from me. Elation overwhelms me to the point I can hardly remain standing.

It's over.

A groundswell of fright, anxiety, exhaustion from the past two weeks, and a plethora of other emotions all unleash from my chest.

I'm done. I really am done now, and nobody could *possibly* convince me to stay here and do this one moment longer.

That twenty-five-year-old, bright-eyed law school graduate who would one day be the president hasn't gone anywhere, but she has evolved.

"Deputy Haughton," one of the D.A. secretaries beams to me from across the bench. "D.A. Gray would like to see you in her office and have a word with you. To personally congratulate you."

Gathered behind her, armed with their cell phone cameras to take my picture and waiting to shake my hand, are groups of young women and girls. Law clerks, interns, secretaries, fellow lawyers, mothers, and grandmothers, all with their hands pressed to their chests, stand in awe.

But out in the corridor, infuriated protestors continue to yell, and police officers and deputies take them on.

It's hard to leave the circus for the next few minutes.

"Deputy Worthen, LaShauna should have gotten more than nineteen years," Detective Holland asserts. "And that line of questioning you pursued with Officer Franks—"

"I understand you're not pleased, Detective, and you are more than welcome to take it up with my boss."

The Filing Deputy D.A. in charge of reviewing cases and deciding which to file, probably made the plea offer that low because of Officer Brighton's inappropriate conduct and how embarrassing it is for the department. The D.A.'s office reduces plea offers when there's a problem with the case, particularly if a cop rough-handled a defendant, or if public image concerns are at play, such as the likelihood that cops really were at Paradise Gardens bullying tenants.

I'm confident there is likely more to this I haven't even touched on, which Kevin did not send me.

For now, I turn to the D.A. Office's secretary. "Ailene, I'm not feeling too well and I should probably go home early and lie down. Will you tell D.A. Gray I'll come over first thing in the morning?"

Once I have my updated resignation letter signed and sealed.

"Sure, I'll let her know. Take care, hon, you've earned it."

On my exit out of the courtroom, I'm thrilled to see my security agent, Sharon. Our arms linked, we press through the cameras, news reporters, and protestors. I must have developed tougher armor at some point, because they're not so scary anymore. Riding away from here feels far different now that I have nothing to fear.

"Mrs. Worthen, do you need anything else from us?" Sharon asks, dropping me off in our circular driveway.

"Oh no, ma'am, I'll just spend the rest of the day catching up on some rest. Nothing interesting going on here. If you want to check out, feel free. I'm home now and I'm fine."

"Well, we just got a text from Easton, and he insists we hang around, just to make sure all stays quiet after what you just did. You know how your man is, sis. I'll tell you what. We'll run and grab lunch, and in thirty minutes, we'll be right outside if you need us."

As if she summoned him, East's name pops up in my phone.

"Your ears must have been itching." Answering his call has never felt so promising and hopeful.

"Is it true what I'm hearing? That LaShauna Posey took a plea deal?" He sounds giddier than when he got his first multi-million-dollar deal.

My heels are off before I enter our front door. In bare feet, I haul this tired, barely pregnant body up the staircase. "Maybe."

"Congratulations, Madam President, Counselor, Mrs. Worthen. So what are you planning on doing with the rest of your day?"

I swear he might be smiling hard enough that I hear it through the phone.

"Absolutely *nothing!*"

We both crack up while I light candles throughout the bedroom and then head to start a bubble bath.

His voice lowers, the way it does when his dick is in front of me and he's ready for me to suck. "Maybe I'll come home and do nothing with you."

"Maybe I'll be wearing nothing when you get here."

"Maybe I'm on my way once I wrap up a couple of things here."

"The Jacuzzi will be nice and hot. Hurry," I murmur. "East?" Hopefully, I caught him before he hung up.

"Yeah, bae."

"Thank you."

"Always. See you in a bit."

Chapter Twenty-Three

THROUGH THE FLAMES

EASTON - SONG: GO ON WITHOUT YOU BY SHIRLEY MURDOCK

"Bev! I'm rolling out early today. You need anything before I go?"

"I'm good, Mr. Boss Man! Go on home and kiss that sweet wife of yours. Lord knows, she sho 'nuff deserves it."

"No lies told there, Ms. Bev. Later!"

Rushing off to my baby, one last thing catches my eye before I bounce: Edith Zucker's envelope. I got so wrapped up with Dad, Kevin, Korienne, and this whole security situation, I forgot to even look.

Saying my goodbyes for the afternoon, I make my way out the door. My mind is in a million other places. The "congratulations" keep rolling in from my friends, as if I'm the one who secured the Posey conviction. But shit, I'll bask in the glory right along with Kor. My heart is so full.

"Thanks, man. Have a good night!" I call out to the valet as he pulls my Porsche around.

Whipping out the paper, I'm surprised to see just two sheets. Nothing more.

What the...?

Paternity test results? From the same year I was born.

Natural born mother: Edith Quick

Child: D'Arrius Worthen

"The alleged father, Carol Worthen, cannot be excluded as the father..."

Suffocating, I punch the goddamn window down. With shaky hands, I shift to the next paper, an application for a name-change in the State of Maryland.

D'Arrius Worthen was changed to D'Arrius Quick.

D. Quick.

Oh, shit...

That shit Edith fed me about her sister, Gloria, she was really talking about herself. Dad had his mistress working for him all these years...a whole other family he probably moved out to LA at the same time as us.

As always, Dad likely made her a deal so she wouldn't talk or cause problems. A nice, cushy office job and a comfortable life for their son in exchange for her contentment with being the side piece.

"*That's* why that motherfucker hit me!" And Dad fucking knew it.

Tuh. This would explain the military equipment for police. Dad probably pays that fool to keep him pacified. And the *LA Times* got wind of it. Now Edith is bouncing to leave Dad holding the bag.

"You all right, East?" one of the guys checks in from the valet stand.

"Yeah, man, I'm just—"

Full stop.

Korienne.

She's turned her phone off.

"Sharon, where are you? Is Kori all right?" I ask in a call to her agents.

"We just left her about five minutes ago to get lunch. We'll be headed right back once our order arrives."

"Shit!"

* * *

KORIENNE

"Baby, is that you? That sure was fast." I make my way out of the closet. The last two weeks have been so jammed I haven't had time to unpack from the move to Easton's place. That'll be the first priority these next few days. That and wedding planning.

Of course, I'll also need to get back to my YouTube videos and planning my brand.

"East?"

"No, babe! Wrong Worthen brother, honeyyy," somebody says mockingly behind me, and I'm snatched off the floor.

Feet in the air while I'm whipped around, I kick at any and everything. I beat whoever the hell's face is next to mine. "Get out of my house! Get out! Helpppp!"

"Nobody's here now, D.A. bitch! Your little honey's nowhere around."

This voice sounds faintly familiar, like I might have heard it at some point in my life, a long time ago.

"Get off me! Get off me!" Still kicking and swinging, I can't land a lick as he totes me toward our bedroom door. Throwing up my legs, I press them against the doorframe so we can't get out. "Put me down!"

"Shut up! Shut the fuck up! Move your legs!"

"Nooo—"

He covers my nose and mouth until I can't breathe, but I'm still swinging and kicking. And praying.

Please, Lord, no. Please protect our baby.

Wrangling me until he maneuvers me out, he hoists me in the air. "Shut up and tell me where he keeps his files. Does he have a safe?"

"No!" I lie.

"Bitch, lie to me again, and I will fucking kill you! Every rich guy has a safe! Now where is it? I will *not* ask you again!"

With a hand over my belly, I try to create a buffer. Our baby is all I care about, and I curl up so whatever he does next, I can lessen the impact. He screams in my ear, and I'm checking out. From somewhere in here, smoke swirls around me. Up my nostrils, smoke creeps into my brain.

"The goddamn safe!"

He tries to drop me, but by some miracle, in his panic, he trips on the belt of my robe and falls down first. When I go to the floor, I fall on him, and he breaks my fall.

Oh God.

D. Quick?

He shoves up from the floor and yanks me up by my hair.

"Where is it? Hm? Where's my brother's secret shit?"

Finally, he whips out a gun and presses it against my belly. Then jerks my face to his.

"Bitch, we are not in court anymore. Where is the goddamn safe?"

I point to the wine cellar, to where he yanks me.

A few candles have knocked over now, and fire spreads over furniture. He's more concerned with whatever it is he wants and shoves bottles of alcohol off the shelves to jerk back the false wine rack. Fire follows us and laps up the high-content rum and tequila Easton also keeps in storage.

"What's the code? Hurry up!"

As I tell him, he twists one way and then the other. I pray that, once he's got the jewels, he'll just go.

But he tosses our personal belongings in one direction, and then the other, totally ignoring our most valuable things.

"Where is his laptop?"

"What?"

"Laptop!" D. Quick screams. "Secret intelligence! Accounts in Saudi Arabia and Dubai. This nigga is worth a lot of fucking money and hides it everywhere. Tell me."

He points the gun at my belly and cocks the hammer. I can hardly see through the rising flames that burst out of control once they connect with liquor and the wooden racks.

"Go! I don't know anyth...about..."

Glass breaks somewhere, and I try crawling so I can escape before the fire reaches the door.

The last vision I make out is a pair of hands snatching him off me.

Coughing and gagging, I try to get up but, it's too hard to bre...

Chapter Twenty-Four
THIS SIDE OF THE MOUNTAIN

EASTON

Flames crawl up the walls of my home, and even though I'm not in there yet, I can't breathe. If I even think of Kori stuck inside, life might leave me.

"Kori!" Through one door after the other, I jump over the broken table and shattered glass, and it's hard to see. The place isn't completely up in flames, but in some areas, I've got to move fast and dodge from fiery wall-hangings that crash as they burn. "Kori!"

Across the foyer, on the other side of the dining room, stands a body. Instantly, I bolt toward the wine cellar, and grip his neck, shocking him. In one punch, before he can fully process me behind him, I ax his fucking throat and slam his head against the burning doorframe.

"Where's your goddamn baton now, bitch?"

Bad as I want to wear his punk ass out, the flames are worsening and I've got to get Kor.

From my lungs to my heart, kidneys, and down my stomach, fire eats up every organ and muscle I've got to see Korienne engulfed in flames. "Kori, baby."

Thick wooden beams burn over her. But by some miracle, she's passed out in a dry patch of the floor I use for tasting.

"Sir!" A firefighter appears next to me. "Get out of here!"

Fuck that. "My wife is on the other side. I'm not leaving until she's out!"

Snatching off my suit jacket, I roll it around my arms and jerk at the searing heat of fiery beams. Hell, I've got to hustle if we're getting out of here at all.

But, shit, nothing is keeping me from her. I don't give a damn how part of me will burn.

"Aaah!" Flames eat my flesh, but I got through the scorching wood where she lies unconscious. In one scoop, I snatch her up and cradle her as best I can so we can get back out. "Urrrgh."

Thankfully, the firefighter covers us with his suit to lessen some of my exposure to the blaze.

But still, literal hell is not enough to describe the inferno that eats us, and suffocates my damn lungs. But in leaps and dodges, the same way our perseverance delivered us through nine years, I dive past one obstacle after another.

"Take her!" I say to Sharon and the male agent.

Blood splatter is on the ground. Since nobody else out here bleeds, that fool apparently cut himself on his exit. The fire department is already out and spraying at the fire.

Soon as I see Kori's eyes flutter, I refill my lungs with air and sprint off in the direction of blood, where this punk trailed it along the grass. Heavy boot tracks lead around the back of the house, across the pool and toward the bushes. He's losing more blood because the drops turn to smears and splotches. They paint these high thickets that actually lead down a narrow dirt path to the next residential street. His wound must've slowed him down, and on the sidewalk, his boots were dragging blood. Up ahead, he struggles toward an unmarked old vehicle.

Shit, I run harder and catch him right before he can fling the door closed. He punches me in the jaw and tries to close the door, but I'm not going anywhere. Despite the blow, I grab on tight and look for the wound. Inside the bloody tear on his thigh, I stick my fingers and dig in.

"Aaah!" he screams and tries to elbow me. But I use that forward momentum to jerk his ass from behind the wheel.

"Come back here! On your fucking knees, bitch!" I punch him to the street and then raise him back up to clock his ass again.

"Mr. Worthen!"

All the nights I couldn't get this asshole's voice to leave my thoughts, I now bring to bear on his body. Hell, I might lose another baby to this shit on my shoe.

"You did not come into my goddamn home and put your hands on what's mine, you sorry sack of shit!" I can't stop stomping on his ass.

"Eergh, I'm your bro--"

"You're not shit to me! Stay your ass down there. On your knees!" Hitting and stomping, I separate from my right mind. I probably enter a chasm that petrifies me, where if I'd gotten there later, what might I have lost? What could I still lose?

"Mr. Worthen!" one of the security agents rushes me, and gets in my face. "People are watching and recording with their cellphones, sir. I know you're totally justified, but you are not a monster. Miss Kori needs you. Go be with her. Officers are on their way over. *Go.*"

When we get back to the house, I've missed the ambulance that's already taken off.

So the agents transport me to Cedars Sinai separately, and fuck, I'm distraught that I let my personal vendetta get in the way of being in the emergency vehicle with her. Right now, my unborn baby should be hearing me coach it to stay alive, and push through. I should be in there with my family, but, *God, forgive me for screwing up. If I can't be with them, please protect and keep them both.*

I've never prayed so hard in my life.

Hell, I don't even remember the last time I prayed. But I swear on everything that if Kori and the baby are okay, I'll pray the way my mama tells me to for the rest of my days.

For the next hour, the wait in the hospital corridor may as well be a century.

Dad comes out of the elevators and heads toward me.

"Son—"

"Dad, don't. Not now, okay? Just fucking don't." I don't have the mental or emotional bandwidth.

His indiscretions and affairs, his illegitimate son are the *last* thing I want to think about right now. It pisses me off every time I recall D'Arrius towering over Kori in my home, the one place on Earth she's supposed to be safe.

Right now, I just—

"It'll be fine. She'll be fine," Mom reassures me.

Though I'm nodding my head on the outside, on the inside I need to hear it, see it for myself.

"Here comes the doctor," Judge Haughton says.

Father, please.

I've waited seven years. Since she and I sat in a private clinic and I watched the nurses wheel Kori to the back...

The doctor smiles at us.

God smiles on us.

"Mom is doing just fine. And so is the baby. We can even see a heartbeat, Easton. Would you like to come back and see your baby for the first time?"

Joy sends me to one knee. I can hardly even walk to the room where Kor is more beautiful than ever.

On the monitor, all I see is a blob and can't even making out what I'm looking at, but it's almost as beautiful as its mom.

* * *

D.A. Gray entering the hospital room with flowers is like a vine of thorns that chokes my fucking airway. "Mrs. Worthen, wow, wow, wow."

I wonder when it'll be the right time for me to tell Kor she was used, that this woman misappropriated her position to come after my father. And used my wife in the process.

An alert Kori sits up higher, and is her normally gracious self. "Mrs. Gray, thank you for this. We appreciate you dropping in.

"Well, for all you've been through, deputy, the least we could do is acknowledge your valor and bravery. I heard all the highlights of your amazing performance from your supervisors and colleagues who sat and watched. Congratulations."

"I appreciate that you trusted me with such a sensitive case, Mrs. Gray," Kor says, clueless. "This was pretty scary. Needless to say, you can consider today my official two weeks' notice, and I'll submit it in writing as soon as I'm able."

The D.A. takes a seat. "I wish you'd change your mind, Deputy Worthen. You're one of our best and brightest."

"Is that why you put her life at risk?" As much as I try to respect my wife's autonomy, and that she is perfectly able to speak for herself, the irate Negro in me refuses to let this go down. "You knew your nephew was a hothead, and your sister was unhappy being a side-piece. You probably resented what my father was doing with Edith, and you wanted to see him pay. You knew there was bad blood between the Haughtons, so you assigned Kori to the Posey murder, and hoped Kor would find him doing something illegal."

I won't say this out loud, but I'm almost certain Judge Haughton had a hand in his daughter getting that case. Nobody can convince me otherwise.

Kori's entire mood shifts from gracious to spicy. "Easton. What are you talking about?"

D.A. Gray shifts in the seat. "Mr. Worthen, Edith made her own choices, as did D'Arrius. I genuinely just wanted Korienne to shine. Those are very hefty accusations you're leveling without proof to back it up, so I'd be careful."

Confused, Kori stares between the two of us.

"You'd better hope I don't ever find it," I warn the D.A.

"Easton, baby, what happened?" Kor asks.

It crossed my mind to let Kori stay in the dark and allow her to believe she got that assignment based purely on merit. I want that feeling of pride for her, but I also refuse to let this woman play her for a fool.

"Kor, her sister is Dad's mistress. D. Quick is her nephew, and as far as I know right now, he's also Dad's son. She tried to use the Posey case as cover for her own personal ends."

The D.A. glares back, and stands up. "Again, exercise caution with what you allege, Mr. Worthen. You are a highly respected figure in the LA community. People look up to you. Don't develop a reputation for starting fights you can't win."

"Tah. Bet that."

If she thinks she doesn't like Dad, she hasn't seen shit. Dad is clever, but I'm stealth.

She turns back to my wife. "I should be going. Korienne, I've known you most of your life. If you ever need anything from me—a reference, an endorsement—feel free to let me know. As for the press conference announcing this plea deal, I was going to offer it to you, but since you're leaving the office, I should probably handle it."

Trenches of disappointment line Kori's forehead.

"Figures." I face this woman head on. "That's retaliation for Kori not staying at the job. She *earned* that press conference and, whether she's leaving or not, Korienne should stand on that podium."

"We don't want the media distracted by Kori's departure. The public should focus on us doing the business of justice, not wondering why this deputy is on her way out and spurring rumors."

I step toward the D.A.

Kori sits up from the pillows. "East."

Judge Haughton enters the room with Kori's mom.

"Everything all right in here?" the judge asks.

The way their gazes dance between each other, I feel in my soul that they conspired against Dad. Though Dad might have deserved it, Gloria should have pursued her concerns transparently and ethically, rather than with sleight-of-hand-tricks. And the ploy shouldn't have involved my wife.

"D.A. Gray was just about to inform us whether Kori is handling the press conference on the Posey plea deal. After all Kori went through to prosecute this case, the abuse and disrespect she took, and a rogue cop breaking into our home, what's your answer, D.A. Gray?" I insist on knowing.

Since she likes to blackmail people.

The judge peers at her expectantly. I'm sure when he teamed up with Gloria, he must've expected media exposure and professional advancement for his daughter in exchange.

Gray pastes on a smile. "I'll have to discuss it with my advisors, but barring any objections from them, it should be fine."

"Let's hope they don't object," I add. For her sake. Because Kevin Middleton *will* get me the evidence I need to connect the dots.

D.A. Gray turns toward Kori. "Again, feel better Korienne. Whatever you choose to do, you have a long and promising future ahead of you. You take care."

I can't help myself. "She'll take better care now that she's out of your office."

Once she's gone, now I get the third degree from Judge Haughton.

"Son, what was all that?" he asks.

At some point, our families need a timeout of some kind, so these schemes don't continue. For now, out of respect for Kori, it'll have to just be water under the bridge. My babies' safety is a blessing I won't miss out on again. "What was necessary."

I address the most important person in the room, the woman I would risk my life for a million more times if need be. From the way she scans me, it's clear Kori's confused about this exchange, and still working through it in her head. But she also understands there are some matters concerning Dad that she and I haven't discussed.

"Are you okay?" Kori asks me, holding out her hand.

Tired as hell, I close in on her and lay both my hands on her mattress, so she can see the ash, scratches and light burns still on my flesh. "Do you trust me?"

Without hesitation, Halo answers, "Boy, don't ask me silly questions." Her gaze drops to my bloody knuckles. She's already holding them up and touching them. "Do I want to know how you got these? Mom, will you ask a nurse to bring peroxide and bandages?"

Laying my hand on her pregnant belly that grows more everyday, I chuckle. "No, but I know how you got this."

We smell like the smoke and ash we came through, and as always, we're one another's lifelines.

Chapter Twenty-Five

HALO

EASTON

"And now to our final agenda item for today," the president of the Board of Directors of Worthen Properties moves down his notes. "The issue of whether Carol Worthen shall remain on as the CEO of this great company he founded and built."

Dad and I sit on opposite sides of the table from each other. Of course, Charles sits alongside him. Not surprising. Charles is still in the same position I was in years ago—beholden to Dad, with few options but to support him.

Seated on one side of me is Kori, and on the other side is my mother.

"I'm insisting that you not vote me out of what's mine," Dad declares. "There are a lot of wonderful and talented people here, no doubt. But only I know where we've been, and how to get us where we're going. I've shepherded this group through the hardest times, through two major recessions, when nobody wanted to touch real estate and many development companies folded. Nobody can do what I can."

He stares directly at me.

"Nobody. And though I give a lot of credit to my sons for being incomparable men, they are still lacking in how to weather our toughest storms—licensing and overregulation, market fluctuations, and other developers undercutting us and engaging in anticompetitive practices. Now is not the time to change course. Sure, we've got a few protestors and some meddlesome journalists. We've rode through it all before. I got us this far, and I'll take us all the way, until Angels Rise is a shining city that sits on a hill."

I look to Lionel Middleton, one of Worthen's key investors and the father of Kevin Middleton. Lionel flew out from New York to support Dad, and I fully expect him to take Dad's side now, so I wait for it.

"Carol, you miscalculate our company's position."

I'm damn stunned.

Mom is the one who speaks. Wielding an air that feels thick enough to be her armor, she stands from the table, and over Dad.

"You built Worthen up during the tech era—before women's empowerment movements, black power movements and the 'gig economy.' Twenty-five years ago, you didn't have to care about the people, just the property. But now, companies must be humane to succeed." With the candle burning in her eye, she continues, "Worthen is suffering an identity crisis. It needs a leader to help define its next era, and yesterday's selfish money-grabbing that got us here will not sustain us in this new age of accountability. So I'd like to move that you either tender your resignation, or be voted out."

"I second that." The new CFO that replaced Edith Zucker crests her fingers from several seats away.

Charles shifts forward. "Before we take up the question of voting my father out of his own damn house, maybe we should have a conversation first about who is ready to take his place if that happens. I love Easton, but he's only ever been an intern here. He couldn't run this place for one day if he tried. You need somebody who knows the ropes and can hit the ground running, who'll keep all systems and projects running seamlessly."

"You're a great COO, Charles, but it shouldn't be you," one of the employees replies. "Your mother just said this place needs fresh perspective and direction that's fit for these social movements."

My older brother throws up his hands. "We'll get a diversity director."

"You can't just hire somebody, throw the problem at them, and push it aside," my mother counters. "The public needs to see change at the top, an entirely new vision and mission. Not just to build pretty luxury high-rises, but also to improve society. The two must go hand in hand. Prosperity must serve all, not just a few. You're too tied to your father's way of doing things."

My mother places her hand on my shoulder.

"Easton may not be as experienced as you at running this place, but he is more tied to the community whose buy-in we need. Worthen's got great employees to help him. But you can't deny his personality, accomplishments, status as a former bar association president, all tie him to the city. He can make inroads with public officials and city leaders more effectively than you or Carol. East has better relationships because he hasn't been fighting with them all these years."

One of the other board members chuckles. "Not only that, but he's trending on the internet for being a literal god of war."

The other employees clap and whistle at the reference to how a video of me beating the hell out of "D. Quick" went viral.

Kori slides her hand over my leg under the table and squeezes. She has no idea why I really asked her to accompany me here today.

"I'm declining the nomination," I finally say.

My mother is shocked, as are several others at the table.

"Tah," Dad scoffs. "Figures. We can't even get him in here to lift a finger with me gone."

"I'm nominating my wife, Korienne Worthen."

Next to me, Kor's astonishment paralyzes her.

But I continue, "There is somebody who possesses phenomenal relationships across LA. Whose family has a near hundred-year history of business ownership, leadership, and public engagement." Rising, I stand and face the others. "Her family's ancestral home on Central Avenue was torn down by Worthen Properties."

"It was a dilapidated old house! And rightfully granted to us by the city!" Dad snaps.

Kori hammers a fist on the table. "After you sued for it and had papers served on my older cousins, but not my father! If my daddy had known what you were doing, he would have stepped in."

Now I need to break it up. "That house contained their family's history, Dad, whether the judge owned it or not. Who better to connect with Worthen's tenants in its complexes who now face the same issue of possibly losing what's precious to them—their long-time homes?"

"Baby..." Korienne interrupts. "I mean, Easton, I appreciate your vote of confidence and I know you mean well. But there is no way I would attach mine and my family's good standing in the community to Worthen's displacement of LA residents from their homes. I refuse to be the public face of that."

"Attach your talents and skills to creating solutions. Do what you do best, baby. Bring people together and figure out alternatives that will serve everybody. Just as you did with AAWPA, and many times over the years. You rounded up the unlikeliest group of women—Shallon, Teneil, Mackenzie, *Vash,* that one chick who intentionally gets arrested to bring attention to prison issues—and you took AAWPA from a living room and potluck club to a professional king-maker that's known from coast to coast."

Kori twiddles her thumbs and twists in her seat, but I can tell the idea is twisting in her head. "We may be different women, but we all had the same goal, of raising AAWPA's national profile. Here at Worthen, you've got too many figureheads with different motives and objectives all warring with each other. Whose goal will take priority?"

Dad chuckles and nods, as if being proven right. "See? She can't even take a little heat."

My mother and I exchange quiet frustration.

"Can everybody leave the Worthens alone for about ten minutes?" she says to the other board members.

Dad addresses Mom. "Look, Essence, I know you're upset, baby, but--"

"But nothing, Carol!" Mom roars. It's the first time they've seen each other in weeks, since she moved out of our family's home, and into her own Malibu condo. "There is no justification for placing my goddamn family in danger." Mom swings her index finger every which way but at Dad. "You knew that fool was becoming a loose cannon, and after he hit my son and I was going for my damn gun, you told me you had it under control, that he was leaving town! You will do this. Do you understand me? You will step down, or I'll bury your ass so deep in the divorce, your dead ancestors won't be able to find you in the ground!"

I clear my my throat and address my father. "There was no excuse for this. You stepping back and letting Kori turn this around—the way I know she can—is the only way you and I will ever reconcile. That's the only way *my* family remains as part of your family."

Now I turn to Kor. "Halo, what's wrong? Why are you scared?" Because that's all it is.

"I'm not scared. I just know my limitations, and I have no background or training in real estate or property development. Not only that, East, but you and I broke up over your father's control and domination issues. I didn't want to live in his house, but now I'm going to work in the company he built?"

Frustrated, Charles lets out an exhale across the table. "She's got good points. She might have community service credit, but no corporate skills."

"Watch it, Charles," Kori mutters.

After a swivel of my chair, I steer hers to me. "Baby, you have a background in people, and leadership. You're helping the communities of Los Angeles who you love."

"I won't be able to do that with your dad's fingerprints on every part of this place, and I refuse to be his puppet. Or for him to come in here talking to me any kind of way."

Mom steps forward. "Why don't you try it for one year? Charles can take on the chairman role, if he's willing to humble himself and do that. Carol, you'll maintain an 'of counsel' position only, and advise them as they need it, but under no circumstances will you attempt to interfere. It's Kori's and Charles's ship."

Mom lowers herself to where Kori sits.

"For a long time, I thought Carol was the only one who could run this place. He built it, yes, but mostly because he had *support*." My mom's glare strikes a match off Dad's forehead. "Not because his mind is anymore spectacular than the next nigga's."

She takes Kori's hands in hers.

"Now you'll receive that same support, Korienne. Nobody's going to undercut you or your team. These employees will be yours, at your full disposal. And I've got a feeling these ladies are hungry to see a vibrant, innovative mom at the helm who was badass enough to stand up to Carol in ways they can't. I've got a feeling these people around here secretly admire you."

I sniff at that shit. "So long as these dudes don't admire her too fucking much, that sounds good to me."

Kori suppresses her hint of a grin behind her attitude. "East, why can't you do it?"

"I like running my own firm. Dad is right about one thing: nothing compares to entering my own establishment and knowing it's mine. I built it. Kori, you told me to go be my own man, and that's what I did. Now I enjoy the hell out of it."

"I want the same. My own lifestyle brand and company."

But the wheels of Kori's mind are turning.

She can use the CEO platform and connections, all the media coverage she's getting from the Posey case, plus the glow-up and goodwill from breaking ground on Angels Rise, to later springboard into a lifestyle brand.

Her name now commands the same respect as mine. Her star can go even higher.

"Cuteness, if you want to go straight into your lifestyle and decor hustle, I'm behind you one thousand percent. But baby, are you really telling me this challenge doesn't excite you even a little? Turning around a company and putting your 'fierce and fabulous' stamp on it. Inspiring millions of women around the city, showing them what's possible? The chance to become all you've wanted as long as I've known you."

Kori's eyes meet mine, and in the sacred space of our union, she and I rewind the last nine years, to our first meeting, our first date, first time making love, first heartaches....

"You know I'll never let you fall, Halo."

Confusing the shit out of my family, I hold out my damn pinky finger.

She hooks hers into mine and we cement our past promises and future triumphs with the candle of this kiss.

Kori swivels her chair toward Dad and Charles. "One year. And at that point, we'll see how it goes? Charles, trust me, I don't intend to take anything from you. This is only temporary so Worthen doesn't lose its chance to make history with Angels Rise. I'll go to some of my friends on city council, see what licenses they're holding up, what we can negotiate. You and I can work together."

Mom addresses my brother. "Charleston, I agree with you.

You've been at your father's side a long time, honey. Nobody's denying the CEO spot is yours. Us bringing Kori in isn't a question of your abilities, but Worthen's public image. We need to calm this storm."

Chapter Twenty-Six

A NEW RESPECT

KORIENNE

"Easton, what do you see when Korienne is in front of you?" Our new marriage counselor asks on a cloudless Saturday morning.

Grinning and goofy, he eyes me next to him on the couch. "My sun, who is—"

"Turn to face her, and tell her," our therapist instructs him.

East shifts on the sofa, throws his arm around me. The possessive intensity he's giving in his stare, possesses me.

"The largest star in my universe. A magnificent woman who lights up the world around her, gives warmth with her understanding and patience, and illuminates my life, " East says to me. "I realize my parents have provided a lot of material blessings for me. And I'm not ignorant to that abundance. But none of that means anything now without Kori. Since I laid eyes on her, fell in love with her, all I've ever wanted is to protect the star that shines for me and so many others."

The marriage counselor sniffs and grabs a tissue before we all laugh.

East's words take root in my belly and spread across me. And this Negro's gaze must be dew falling on a field of wild flowers. I am his garden—my heart, mind and soul—awaiting his rain, and I grow under his affection.

"East," the counselor continues, "did your star hurt you?"

Easton withdraws inside himself for a moment, and then opens his eyes.

"Not hurt, but disappoint. I kind of felt like my light abandoned me. You took that case while I was calling you, and you didn't wait so you and I could speak about it. I could have prepared, and we should have fleshed out the particulars at least, to be ready for all that smoke."

He thinks and seems to be envisioning it in his head. His eyes settle back on me. The clouds drifting across his forehead, his eyes and downward turned mouth, cast shadows over me. I'm no longer making decisions that affect me alone.

The counselor continues, "And Easton, what do you expect from your star in the future so you'll never have to worry about losing her again?"

It's hard to believe nine years have passed since those two overly confident law students crossed paths in the law firm, so certain of the heights we aspired to conquer.

We thought we had life all figured out, and the answers were crystal clear. But we had no idea of the fog on the other side of our walls. No clue we were dreaming in a glass house.

"Kori, I understand why you did it. For a few reasons, I agreed. The community needed to see a black woman prosecuted fairly and with grace and care. But I also knew a big part of you needed to take that case for yourself. Not anybody else. But I hope now *you* realize how powerful your light is. You no longer have anything to prove. To anybody. Stop stretching yourself to prove something to everybody else."

East is an interstellar force for me. Like the moon, his presence in my life now changes how the ocean tides rise and fall over me.

The counselor turns to me. "Kori, do you hear what he's saying?"

"Loud and clear, baby. I can't say enough how sorry I am."

A couple of times, he's jumped in his sleep and mumbled. Hearing it is like having a meat tenderizer mash on my lungs.

"Baby, I don't want you to be sorry. Just whole and happy. You're my joy, and if you're in the crucible, I'm there too."

"Kori," the counselor says, "what do you see when you look at Easton?"

Now I lay my entire womanhood into this connection with him. "God."

His thumb comes toward me, and wipes off my tears that tell him before I can. Cupping my face, he pulls me to him, and with my tongue, I embrace love so immense I'm not sure I'll ever be able to process it.

"You are majesty, Easton. Glorious, powerful, brave and mighty, and mine. I thought I automatically understood what being your wife meant since I was your girlfriend such a long time. These few years, we've been a simple couple operating in our bubble, having fun and in love. But we lost our innocence the day I walked out of the D.A.'s office with police. You were in the crowd calling for me, and your face was a desolate land we've never been to."

The horror still grips my mind, imagery of that day as clear as Ultra-High Definition 8K resolution.

The salt of my tears stains my cheeks before seasoning the power of life and death that lie in my tongue.

"And I couldn't bear seeing you hurt. I became every other black woman pleading my king and protector would have no harm brought to him. And I saw just how fragile and precious life—and our love—really is."

Even now, his kisses on my forehead, hand massaging my neck and shoulders, are seconds upon seconds of priceless gifts. I'm praying everybody I love in my life will have the chance to receive what East and I are so blessed to have found.

Suddenly, a heavy knock on the other side of the door interrupts us.

"Are y'all almost done in there?" Shallon calls from the other side.

I especially want that one there to find her love real soon, Lord.

"Do we have a choice?" East calls back to her.

"Not if you're trying to get a ride to Old Town. You can always walk," she calls from the other side.

"Why don't you get your friend?" he asks me.

"And what will I do with her after thirty years?"

Our circle of family and friends decided on a forty-five-minute flight north of Los Angeles for the weekend, to Santa Barbara. Thankfully, our new therapist could join us. Since the cloudless skies were perfection, we took off from the Private Suite at LAX in two copters that delivered us to Montecito in thirty minutes.

After these past couple of months of giving one another space, our families needed a reset before the wedding. And our crew simply wanted to get here and release a long exhale. Now that summer is over and we're headed into the wedding and the holidays, it's time to find a truce among the Haughtons and Worthens.

"You two straight?" Kevin asks out in the foyer. "Or are we mounting horses and riding out to go burn some shit down, or what?"

"Not today, bruh," I tell Kevin with a hug. "We'll save the smoke for your MoneyCruncher opps."

His wife Cher comes in next and she's holding their one-year-old baby girl, Dasia. "Girl, the way East was whooping on that dude all over the internet, I thought LA was starting up the next civil war— black folks versus cops."

Kevin adds, "Either you're keeping this Negro under control, or we're calling S.W.A.T. the next time he gets worked up."

"That won't be necessary," I say, and reach for their daughter, "because once Easton has one of these, his days of fighting are over. He'll be a big ole softie cream puff. Let me hug this sweet, yummy girl." I coo with their daughter, Dasia, a baby doll who is heavenly perfection since she was cooked in an oven from two chefs with immaculate genes.

East snickers. "That's a load of crap. Once our kids gets here, I'll fight harder."

Cher is a show-stopping former Olympic swimmer who now owns an entertainment and sports law firm. I never get tired of hearing her love story of obsessing over Kevin since they were kids.

"Girl, are you ready for this?" she asks, her daughter in one arm and oversized bag in another. "Once they come, there's no putting them back in there. We love this angel to infinity, but she is our boss lady now."

As if the baby knows it, she giggles at her mom and dad, and babbles at the same time.

Easton grins and kisses Dasia's head. "This little mama is staring at Kevin like she's got the keys to his heart."

Kevin rolls his eyes. "She's got the keys to more than that—to Daddy's schedule, his bank account, his sanity. Boy, get your sleep in now. After you see her for the first time, it's a wrap."

East rubs my budding hips and belly, and he and I swap giddy energy. Brave, nervous, excited energy.

Minutes later, we're all taking off from the Four Seasons Resort Biltmore Hotel, where we've rented a four-thousand-square-foot villa overlooking the ocean. On a chauffeured bus that takes us to Old Town Santa Barbara, we tell stories and crack jokes.

A lush Garden of Eden, Santa Barbara has no skyscrapers or massive stadiums, and instead boasts sugar bushes, lemonade berry trees, holly-leaved cherry trees, sprawling magnolias, and snow drop bushes. Even if just for three days, we're nestled between the Santa Ynez Mountains and the Pacific Ocean.

Quiet and subdued, it's home to Oprah Winfrey, Ellen Degeneres, Prince Harry and Meghan, Tom Cruise, Jennifer Lopez, and scores of other upscale people who hide out from the chaotic grind of Los Angeles.

For Saturday lunch, we dine on the patio at Bouchon. I tasted some of everybody's dishes that included the lamb, crab cakes, duck, white fish, and the warm cookie pie dessert almost sent me out on a stretcher.

But next to me also sits my father-in-law, Carol. He and I haven't interacted since the LaShauna Posey case exploded, and brought the kind of attention to his company that forced him to start explaining how he operates. He had to answer to the community, from a vulnerable place he's not used to being in.

"You haven't spoken to me since you took over running my company. I would have thought you'd reached out and asked me how things are done," Carol Worthen says as food is being removed. My father-in-law sucks his teeth. He sits on one side of me and East sits on the other. "Quite frankly, I find it rather disrespectful."

He talks low, so only I hear him. While our other friends and family still laugh and kee-kee on full bellies.

On the other side of Easton sits *my* father. But the two of them are engaged in their own conversation to find common ground since they don't share many interests. East and I thought it was a good idea to shake up the seating, so we could all begin learning how to interact. Our siblings sit further down. On the other side of our circular table, our mothers swap their shopping finds and deals and plan their "moms" trip.

"Mr. Worthen." Measuring my words, I think. "You have an excellent team of people who have supported you over the years. And as you saw at the groundbreaking, they've been awesome in guiding and supporting your vision for Worthen Properties to be strong. In that regard, after you brought embarrassment to your company and your family, I don't believe you're the correct person to school me about disrespect."

We broke ground on Angels Rise in July, a few weeks late, but it happened nonetheless. Out of respect for Mr. Worthen, of course, he was present for the celebrations, ribbon-cutting and photo ops. But we made clear to the city of LA, with whom I negotiated, that he played no substantive role in operations or leadership, and that Worthen is an ethically run company.

"Nothing I did was illegal. I'm a businessman, young lady. Not a priest. Or you wouldn't have a company to run. And Worthen Properties wouldn't be the largest, most successful black-owned—"

"Save it, Mr. Worthen. I'm pregnant with your first grandchild, which means I'm more than some outsider who's invading your household. This is *our* family now. The Worthen brand is *our* brand." I slide the stray braids behind my ear so no barrier exists for him to see the sureness on my face. "And rather than you building out the rest of your legacy on a brittle foundation of 'yes' men surrounding you for their paychecks, maybe you could spend your free time now learning redemption and humility."

It's been nine years, and in his eyes, I'm still a "young lady." As in a girl, one who he probably thinks he can talk down to.

He leans toward me. "And how many successful companies have you built, such that I should take your advice?"

I shake my head. "No companies. But I am a daughter of Los Angeles, with my own authentic community that you need, and which is now saving your company. Perhaps with my passion for people and your knack for business, you and I can help each other. The way I see it, Mr. Worthen, I might be your only hope."

Easton finally checks the vibe between the two of us, and leans over me. "Babe, everything good? You alright?"

Resurrecting my polite smile that I've sharpened on these tense exchanges over the years, I stare at my father-in-law. "I don't know, *Dad*, are we good?"

Carol Worthen studies me, and offers his hand.

Like a new respect is being forged between us, perhaps he's starting to see more than a county lawyer, but someone who'll be strategic for him. *In addition* to being Easton's wife who pops out little Worthen grand babies and packs his son's lunches.

"We just might be."

On the other side of Easton, my father also catches my game face that he recognizes from all his years of training me.

After the meal, my dad whispers in my ear, "From Carol's whipped face, it was obvious he didn't see you coming. I'll never stop hoping you use your skills on the judge's bench."

"Kor!" Mackenzie calls for me. "You said you wanted to hit the design shops while we're here. Santa Barbara Design Center is over on Olive."

On one side of me is my father and his undying hopes for me to be a judge. On the other side of me stands Easton, and his urging to chase my love of decor and fashion.

With a last look at Dad, I call to Mac. "Coming!"

Even though I'm Worthen's CEO now, I still haven't let go of my actual dream. Today I'm also shooting some vids for my Kori Kouture lifestyle brand on Youtube.

What's the first episode titled? The Professional Woman's Refuge from Excellence: How to turn our home into our authentic comfort zone.

Before I jet, I pull down on my father and plant one on his cheek. "Bye, Daddy, I'll see you later.

For now, Easton's admiration kisses me before his lips touch mine. "Ma, you need cash?"

"I don't think so, but have your phone on standby."

"Bet."

While Cher, Mackenzie and I head to some interior design shops and furniture stores, mine and Easton's mothers are doing a leisurely stroll down State Street.

The men are headed to watch the NBA finals at a bar.

Shallon's going with them. Of course.

Chapter Twenty-Seven

HER TRUE SKIN

KORIENNE

"**S**o, you are Worthen's new CEO?" a journalist asks in my very first interview in this position. "Are you going to start putting residents out of their homes, like people have been saying?"

It's almost like the air on this side of life is different.

I face her and other women around the lobby directly. "We will try our best to find alternatives before we let that happen. We're going to start working with community committees to see about housing vouchers, resources, jobs and ways to help you support your families."

"Is this why you left the D. A.'s office?" the young woman reporter inquires. "You were at the top of your game, right? Why leave a successful career when you can still do so much more? Some people say you were scared of all the bad press."

On a sofa in sandals and a low-key summer dress, I face the women residents two weeks before Worthen breaks ground on Angels Rise.

287

It's also two months before Easton and I head down the aisle. Between the fittings where I've needed my gown adjusted for my growing hips, the wedding rehearsals, business planning, and the photo shoots, there hasn't been a lot of time to relax. Life as a new, unproven CEO is certainly testing my big-girl panties.

"It's strange how people say I was scared. I actually stayed at the job longer than I intended."

"What do you mean?" she asks.

"I've wanted to leave and start my own lifestyle brand for years, but what truly scared me was failing to follow my dream."

Murmurs and gasps surround us among the attendees of today's woman's event.

"Wait," the reporter says, amazed. "You were scared you might not make it?"

"Oh, absolutely. Like so many women, I struggled with whether I was good enough and if people would like my content or ideas. Practicing law is a hard job, but it's also pretty insulated. To practice law, you put on a mask and go out to be tough, so you can fight for somebody else. But to drive a business, you must take the mask off and sell yourself and your product. That's scary. What if people don't like *you?*"

The past few years flips through my mind now.

"My entire identity is built around my career. People don't just know me as Korienne. I'm 'Kori the Deputy D.A.' or 'Kori the Lawyer'. My profession is who I am, like my skin. After spending years to grow into that skin, it's daunting to simply pull it off."

"So why *are* you pulling it off?" the journalist asks.

I think of how terrified I was the first time I got pregnant. That law school graduate hadn't even passed the bar yet, was carrying so many expectations from her family, was battling vitriol from people who'd labeled her "Country Club Kori," and who yearned for their respect.

"I'm finally at a place that I don't need the mask anymore. It's time for new skin, my *true* skin."

"Mrs. Worthen, you're my shero, and I'm proud Los Angeles has you. Mr. Easton is really blessed to have you as his wife." Suddenly and unexpectedly, she tears up, which triggers my tears.

Now that I'm no longer required to be the hard-charging Deputy D.A., I have more freedom to discuss life and not be so cryptic or guarded.

The air I breathe isn't different.

It's how I inhale through uninhibited lungs.

Every black woman should breathe that weightless liberty. Of not having to stress or fret or cringe because we choose to wear our real skin.

"So tell me what's going on with you today. Where are we?" the student asks.

"This place is called Paradise Gardens," I explain. "It wasn't appropriate for me to come here while I was actively prosecuting a tragedy here. I needed to be neutral until the case was finished. But concerns came up in the trial that stayed with me and resonated for a lot of women around Los Angeles—the problems leading to eviction, the frustration of having few options, education, or resources."

The day of the hearing revisits my mind, where LaShauna could barely pull *her* mind from a mental cave of despair to see daylight.

I stand from the sofa, and in a sense, rise to assert my purpose, own my voice, and claim my brand of blackness *and* success.

"So we're here at Paradise Gardens, where LaShauna lived. I reached out to LaShauna's attorney, who's also present."

Vashti and several of the public defenders are here with Mackenzie, Shallon, Teneil, our mothers, and other officers of AAWPA.

Vash meets my gaze, and she picks up the presentation. "The African American Women's Professional Association plans to set up an ongoing pipeline for women searching for jobs, professional connections, and looking to learn a trade. We'll have a committee in the organization just for that, and it'll be overseen by me, and funded by the Worthen Family Charitable Trust."

Attendees who've come to support me today are surprised as they applaud.

Mackenzie joins. "We'll also collect gently used business suits from professional women and donate them for job interviews and new professionals. Plus, twice a year, a few kind anonymous donors are providing retreats, spa days, and childcare to hardworking women across apartment complexes in South Los Angeles."

I've worked to bring out engineers who are friends of my mother's, judges who are colleagues of my father's, other lawyers, psychologists, accountants, doctors, and women around the city for a show of support.

"If a woman wants to improve her circumstances, we're trying to give her the push she needs," I explain. "We might not be able to hand you your dream job. Success still takes a lot of elbow grease, no matter who we are. But we're here to inspire you and offer the tips and advice we can."

"This was brilliant, baby girl, Madam CEO," Easton's mother, Essence, whispers to me. "Absolutely brilliant. And it was very classy of you to invite that one chick who needs to get over herself." My mother-in-law cuts her eyes at Vashti. "The next time she comes for my family, we're not keeping it classy. We're jumping past petty and straight to ratchet."

"I know that's right, Mrs. Worthen," Shallon adds with hot sauce on her stank-eye.

Easton voices the same objections, that I shouldn't let the women who try to humiliate me into my personal orbit.

I don't condone or excuse Vash's behavior. But it's also unwise to cut oneself off from powerful dissenting voices that raise legitimate points.

See Martin Luther King and Malcolm X.

Or Frederick Douglass and John M. Langston.

Or W.E.B. Dubois and Booker T. Washington.

Or Hillary Clinton and Elizabeth Warren.

Vash may have gone about getting our attention in a foul way, but her activism can't be ignored or cast aside. She represents an entire swath of people in LA, who feel their plights are being ignored.

Between pictures, I reply, "I'm sure that won't be necessary. She's figuring out that she can go a lot further *with* us than *against* us."

Aside from that, I'm not allowing her into my innermost sacred spaces such as my wedding, bridal shower, or baby shower. These public appearances are where we both have something to gain. Sisterhood is beautiful, but I am mindful to protect my energy.

Over loaded burritos and heavy omelets dripping with chili, sausage, and spinach, black women keep stuffing our faces and swapping notes on outfits.

"Chile," Shallon says between munches, "The Serving Spoon never misses."

"Don't I know it?" I join.

Mackenzie shoves a Hennessy-and-Coke-flavored cupcake in her mouth. "If you really want to save the world, just put a Southern Girl Desserts in every apartment complex. Folks would be too busy working their jaws to fight over a damn thing."

Shallon licks frosting from her nails. "Shiid, these men wouldn't start any more wars. They'll be too busy licking cupcake cream off this kitty cat."

"Ugh, Shal!" This girl keeps my side hurting.

"Chicken waffle, sweet potato, put them in my cupcake cream." This damn woman starts singing the cupcake flavors in a song and rolling her pelvis. "If he wants to get with me, lick my frosting, make me scream."

Essence laughs, and her shoulders shake. "I kind of like it."

"Teach it to me so I can sing it to Easton."

Shallon's silly cupcake song picks up, until the ladies are twerking and gyrating to it. Somebody puts on Kelis's "Milkshake," and it's an impromptu nineties throwback.

Vash approaches me in the throngs of dancing and eating.

"I came to give you your flowers. This is cute. Real special." She sucks her cheeks in until her lips pinch like prunes. "Appreciate you for inviting me." But she scrapes that last bit of icing off the saucer, like she's not done. "Hopefully, you're not just using these women as stage props to score street credibility. Make sure your presence here isn't merely performative, but you really do plan to roll up your sleeves and help people outside your circles."

Tuh. The nerve. But Easton's voice rings through my head. I will not give her the power she seeks.

"Appreciate the well-wishes, sis."

I'll just end the exchange there. Vash showed up today when I reached out, and hopefully, that move facilitates her and Mackenzie leading AAWPA forward. It was definitely a good look for us to show these women here at Paradise Gardens how opposing counsel on a controversial case can still gather and connect, despite our different responsibilities and our different backgrounds.

Chapter Twenty-Eight

NINE YEARS STRONG

EASTON - SONG: THE FIRST TIME EVER I SAW YOUR FACE BY CELINE DION

Until now, I thought the best summer of my life was my first summer with Kori. Not the summer we met, because even then, we weren't really together. But the first summer after she and I cemented our relationship, and I had figured out I was retiring my player card.

It was between her second and third year of law school, and I had just graduated and finished taking the bar exam. For a month before she returned to Berkley, we were so turned up. When our law clerk jobs didn't have us hemmed up, it was restaurants, beach outings, boating trips, the Santa Monica pier, arcades, Long Beach brunches, Disneyland. Private outings with our most trusted friends and family, because we were still "getting to know each other" (her words, not mine), and she wanted to keep her business private.

Back then, the Southern California sun couldn't find a better place to cast its rays than through Kori's glittering pearly whites, and the clear, unblemished windows of her eyes.

But once she graduated law school and accepted that rigorous job with the county, a few of the lights shut off in her castle.

We've still had our fun, but the light was dimmer in my kingdom.

I understood why. There is a no-nonsense mentality required to be a lawyer, especially a female prosecutor.

What fed my faith were the little sparks here and there—Kori wiggling her toes, or her eyes growing wide while advising somebody on their color scheme or patterns—told me she just needed to step into her authentic light.

These past few weeks since she left her job on top of the world, the joy and freedom in her voice are candles dancing in me.

Interviews with high school kids, community service at women's shelters and youth clubs, and shaking hands with new employees at my Dad's properties, it doesn't matter where we are, Kori brings her flair, poise and natural effervescence.

Her wooden exterior has been dismantled. And hell, all the laughs, dancing, jokes and sensuality are different points of light flaring through our prism.

So it's only fitting that she and I seal our love a second time, for all the world, inside the perfect prism—a gorgeous church made of glass.

On the edge of cliffs that overlook the Pacific coastline on a twinkling turquoise ocean, after nine long years, I stand front and center at the Wayfarer's Chapel in Palos Verdes. And wait for my Halo.

Announcement

I'm returning to the practice of law.

For two amazing years, I've published fifteen romance novels and I had no idea how much fun I'd have. I had never written romance.

When I left law, I was unhappy, and once we entered a pandemic, I was losing my love of writing, and I had left behind a six-figure salary.

Now, two years in, no, life is not perfect. My brand of empowered women and the men who love them, is still growing. But the stories I've put into the world, the connections I've made with you, are so incredibly life-giving.

Thank you for making me a better human being, for your encouragement and lifting me up.

That said, an awesome opportunity has fallen into my lap that I wasn't even looking for. Yep, talk about the power of God. This would be utter foolishness for me to pass up.

So, I won't be putting my writing on hold (my head is brimming with so many ideas), but publishing might look different going forward.

Instead of four or five novels a year, it may be two, three if I'm lucky.

Also, you will see more of me on social media. Law is challenging, and I'll need the community and some place to be goofy when I'm stressed and need an outlet! I will also start sharing more of my professional experiences and travel adventures that inspire my stories and the characters I write. If you wondered whether I have actually lived what I create, yes, I mostly have.

I *have* been the president of a bar association, a deputy district attorney, and dealt with overbearing opposing counsel and passive-aggressive people who tried to block my success. I *have* been in the middle of several violent conflicts that erupted in the courtroom. So yes, I've got plenty of source material, and much of it has shaped me as a storyteller.

If you want to hear from me more regularly, come hang out on Patreon. My subscriptions run as low as $2 because what I want most is the community.

Gotta run!

Love y'all. Take care and have fun.

xo,

Lula

Thank you for reading *The Young & Luxurious: Love & Fire*! If you're ever in SoCal, hit me up and say 'hey'!

This is me in Lake Tahoe a few years ago, where Kori and East first made love. I got engaged down at the base of this mountain, on the lake front in the distance. Since this series is based here in Cali, many of the locales and spots you read about, I've actually visited and it's my pleasure to share my love of this gorgeous state with you.

If you enjoyed this "Lula White Experience", please help a sister out (because Lord knows writing books consistently isn't easy) and **leave a review!**

If you want to stay updated on when you'll see more series of class, distinction and growth among the black elite, here's how you can stay connected.

Web site: www.lulawhitebooks.com

Email: lula@lulawhitebooks.com

Join Lula's Luxe Suite Reading Group:
Facebook Reader Group
(https://www.facebook.com/groups/lulawhitelounge)

Read the stories before they go on sale:
Patreon (https://www.patreon.com/lulawhite)

You can find me on my web site where I drop short stories once or twice a month. I will also be making books, videos and content available early as I write the books on my Patreon. Come hang out on my writing journey. Much love! 🤍

The Young & Luxurious
Love & Fire - Korienne & Easton
Love Times Who? - Shallon & Mathaq

Stand-Alone Related to Sag Harbor
A New Life for Christmas - **Tazima & Odell**

The *Sag Harbor Black Romances*
Brown Sugar This Christmas - Maddy & Jerrell

Hot Chocolate This Winter - Chrissy & Sheldon Part 1
Flinging All Spring - Adella & Desmond
Overheated for Summer - Chrissy & Sheldon Part 2
Rouse Family Christmas - All Couples

Books in the spin-off *Explore Men of the Hamptons* series
One Tasty Night FREE Novella - Solomon & Chaitra
Explore You - Kevin & Cher
Christmas Down Under Novella - Keenan & Eugenia - (FREE
Download on website only)
Taste You - Solomon & Chaitra
Drink You - Lion & Kamila
See Through You - Keenan & Eugenia
Find You - Roland & Neeraja

www.lulawhitebooks.com
Email: lula@lulawhitebooks.com
www.blackluxuryromances.com

www.ingramcontent.com/pod-product-compliance
Lightning Source LLC
Chambersburg PA
CBHW051130190726
48290CB00006B/1779